Back

For

Good

Best Wishes
Teresa (Terry) Purkis

Teresa Purkis

ISBN: 9781730859625

Synopsis

Laugh, love and cry with this poignant story of love and life. Back For Good follows Jocelyn's adventures in a heart-warming novel about family and relationships.

After years away, Jocelyn has finally come home. She begins to enjoy the life she has been missing. Jocelyn has made peace with herself and some of her family. She is happy and content with her second chance at family life. Trina and her two children have shown her what she was lacking growing up, and Jocelyn is smitten.

However, a chance meeting sends her world crashing to the ground. Will the love and acceptance she found with Trina survive? Or will the old acquaintance drive a wedge between them? Is she truly back for good?

DEDICATION

For Gill. Thank you for your love and support, allowing me time to indulge in my hobby.

ACKNOWLEDGMENTS

I would like to thank Gill for being the first to read through, and for pointing out any typing errors. Also for her patience, which she showed, as the chapters were drip-fed to her.

I'd also like to thank Dee for your help with some grammar issues. And to my friends who encouraged me to continue with Jocelyn's story.

CONTENTS

Prologue

Tuesday

Trina snuggled against Joy's shoulder feeling at peace for the first time in ages. Trina glanced up at Joy from under her lashes. She ran her index finger lightly over the inside of Joy's wrist and was pleased with the slight tremble her action had invoked.

When their hands linked and their eyes connected, a smile swept over both their faces. It felt like a warm glow spread all over them; like a soft blanket enveloping them both.

Looking at Trina, Jocelyn realised that she wanted her and, for the first time since their teenage days, she felt whole again. For Jocelyn, this feeling was so wonderful that it didn't matter what would or could happen tomorrow, she needed to cherish today. A fresh tingle was ignited in her stomach and, even as she brushed the tears that had escaped from her eyes, she could not help saying, "I think I love you."

The sudden rush of those words left her feeling drained and more emotionally exposed than she had ever felt. Jocelyn dared not look at the beautiful woman in front of her so she dropped her lashes to conceal the vulnerability she felt. She waited with bated breath and then stole a quick glance, as she waited for the response.

With a smile on her face that seemed to be reliving every moment of their past together, Trina said, "I know."

After a moment, Trina took one of Jocelyn's hands in hers and with the other raised Jocelyn's chin and stared intently into her eyes, "I know you think you love me. At this moment in time, you want me and I think you need me. In fact, I know you have love for me, but let us put this all into perspective. For the past few weeks, you have been on an emotional roller coaster. First your beloved Nan died, with you having to come back home to face your family for the first time since the night you left," Trina paused.

Jocelyn had experienced more emotion in one week since coming home than she had in all the years in Sunderland. It was as if she had been emotionally stunted for those years. Every emotion she had ever felt tumbled out with an intensity that scared her.

"I'm fine with all that now," Jocelyn stated.

"Are you?" asked Trina, "I remember your little ways when things are troubling you. Like how you nibble on the skin by your nail on your index finger when you're trying to forget about something." She paused again for a second. "Just like you are doing now."

"For goodness sake Trina, I cannot forget that night all those years ago. The betrayal I felt from everyone. But I am a different person now. I have closure on that night."

"Do you?" Trina asked intently. "You are beginning to have closure when it comes to your parents and what your father tried to do to you."

"You mean tried to rape me," Jocelyn stated. "You can say it you know."

"Yes. Okay," Trina agreed, "When your father tried to rape you. But you now know what was behind why it happened," she paused and then continued, "and I still think you should go to the police."

Jocelyn shook her head, "As I said before, it will be his word against mine. And so many years have gone by. Anyway who would believe that my father, or the person I believed to be my father, would try something like that: to try to rape me. My mother certainly didn't," she sighed, "and she still doesn't."

"She might deep down in her sub-conscious. But if the person you loved was accused of something, wouldn't you try to defend them?"

"I honestly don't know. It would depend on the seriousness of it."

"Exactly. He is her husband. Wouldn't you believe him first and then start to question?"

"I might," Jocelyn conceded, "but it would still be his word against mine."

"You now know that the brain tumour changed his personality," Trina replied. "That would give you credence, surely?"

"Yeah. Right," Jocelyn said, and shook her head.

"And second the bombshell your Mother dropped on you."

Jocelyn was still shaking her head. "I still can't believe my Mother had a fling with a bloke called Richard Hendon so soon after they were married. I now know that's why my father treated me differently to Duncan. That's why he abused me physically and mentally because I wasn't his child and he hated that fact."

Trina squeezed Joy's hands, "You're dealing with that now though, aren't you?"

Jocelyn breathed deeply, "Does anyone truly deal with it? I'm sure it will continue to affect me over the years. And because the issue with Dad, I haven't been able to ask my Mum why she had the fling. Was he hurting her as well as me?"

"You will have to ask her."

"I will, when I'm able." Jocelyn grabbed hold of Trina's other hand, looked intently into her eyes, and said, "I will say it again. I think I love you."

"That's just it. You think you love me, you want me and need me, but you don't love me as you loved Sam. I can see it in your eyes and I can feel it in your soul. You and Sam were like Yin and Yang. Two parts of a whole."

Jocelyn again shook her head. "I must be able to put my past on the back burner and to not let it affect my present or my future."

"Is that what you have done with Sam?" Trina asked. "Put her on the back burner waiting for an opportune moment?"

Jocelyn interrupted and said quietly, "Sam is in the past. She is in a different life."

"But your past life is catching up with you at the moment and you need to work through it."

"No Trina. Sam is definitely in the past; she is a completely different kettle of fish. She betrayed me when I needed her most and I am working through it. Otherwise why am I here?" Jocelyn responded, fiercely.

Trina placed her hands on Jocelyn's shoulders and said, "Sam was beside herself after you left. All she kept saying was that it wasn't her fault. That you had got it all wrong."

Jocelyn pushed Trina's hands from her shoulders and placed her own hands on her hips. "I know what I saw. I saw my lover and my friend from work in a passionate embrace. Leslie's hands were in places her hands should not have been."

Trina tried to reach out to Jocelyn, who was having none of it, and dismissed her with a show of her hand.

Trina wouldn't give up and tried again, "Sometimes you see a moment in time that has no relevance to the preceding or following minutes. Sam told me that when Leslie heard your key turn in the door she had suddenly pounced on her. That when you walked in Sam was desperately trying to push Leslie away."

Jocelyn shook her head again and a hint of annoyance crept into her tone. "You weren't there. I know what I saw and the smirk Leslie gave me when I walked in."

"But you haven't seen or spoken to Sam since. You didn't let her explain," Trina almost sounded desperate.

Harshly, Jocelyn retorted, "Trina, stop talking about Sam, will you? There is no me and Sam. Why are you pushing it? I want to talk about us. Not my father and definitely not Sam. There hasn't been a me and Sam since I moved away. It took me ages to get over her. I don't want you to mention her again."

Jocelyn sat down in the armchair, sighed and started to tap her foot in irritation.

Trina moved over and sat on the arm of the chair saying, "I didn't mean to upset you and annoy you and I think the world of you. And to a certain extent, I love you too."

"Then what is the problem? Do we have a future?" asked Jocelyn.

Trina thought for a while.

Impatiently Jocelyn asked, "Well?"

"As I have just said, to a certain extent I love you but I also know that what I am feeling for you now is nothing like what I felt for Mike. Mike was my dream man. He is the father of my two children."

"Do you still love him?"

"No. And neither do I respect him anymore."

"I should hope you don't respect him. For him to have your respect, he needed to behave so much better than he did. He refused to marry you and then kicked you out of the house with his two children in tow."

"He didn't believe they were his."

"Then he moved his new lover in." Jocelyn took a deep breath in, "If he asked you tomorrow, would you go back to him?" Jocelyn asked abruptly.

"No, I wouldn't."

"Exactly. Tell me: what is the difference between Sam and Mike? Both of them took a new lover. The only real difference is that I walked away whilst you were thrown out."

"I wouldn't put it quite that brutally, but Mike and I have talked it through. We have an understanding. You and Sam haven't."

"An understanding. Hah! You only have an understanding because of your two gorgeous children. If it weren't for them, you wouldn't have any contact with him, would you?"

"Okay. I concede," Trina nodded. "I wouldn't have any contact with him if it wasn't for Peter and Cathy."

Jocelyn allowed a smile to creep over her face.

"Please let's stop arguing and enjoy the next couple of hours." Trina slid down off the arm of the chair and sat on Jocelyn's lap. Putting her arms around her she said, "I'm sorry for upsetting you."

"No problem," Jocelyn replied, leaning into Trina and kissed her on the nose.

"Have you decided whether you are driving up to Sunderland tomorrow or Thursday?" asked Trina.

She laughed, "Now you've spoilt it. Anyone would think you want to get rid of me."

ϖ

Chapter One

Monday, Seven Months Later

Jocelyn keyed the code in and pushed the door open. She climbed the two flights of stairs, instead of taking the lift, pulling the small case after her and shook the five-hour drive from her legs. She entered the flat, which she still classed as her Nan's.

She stood on the threshold and breathed in deeply. The ambient, quiet, peacefulness gently enveloped her in a cosy, warm embrace. As though a snuggle blanket had been carefully wrapped around, drawing her into a sense of undisturbed serenity.

Walking into her bedroom, she dropped the case on the bed and proceeded to divide the items into piles of washing, ironing or hanging. Her eyes rested on the photo frame on the bedside cabinet by the side of the bed and a wave of emotion surfaced. Jocelyn shuddered with the sudden feelings of longing, loss, and emotion that appeared.

Walking over she sat on the bed near the cabinet and kissed her first two fingers and laid them lightly on the cheek of the woman whose face had produced this feeling of grief: The face that was now frozen in the annuls of time. The face that had given her so much love and support: The face she missed with all of her heart.

Jocelyn opened the top drawer of the cabinet and gently took out a delicate piece of paper. Whose creases, from the thousand openings it had endured, were threatening to tear. She lightly opened up the letter and laid it on the cover of the paperback to stop it receiving more damage. She held the letter up to her face. It still had the faint smell of lavender and something deeper, which Jocelyn couldn't place. The letter seemed to warm to her touch and a feeling of love spread through her arms and curled its way through her core. She caught a glimpse of her Nan's face in her mind and felt at peace.

She picked up the frame and the book and re-read the first paragraph again. "My dearest Joy. You really are the Joy of my life. I know you will be on the verge of crying, or you will be, by now, crying your heart out. Just remember how much I love you."

A huge smile spread over her face and, where there were once tears of grief, a steely resolve had taken their place.

Jocelyn, looking into the eyes of her Nan, said aloud, "I've done it. I'm finally home. I've sold my house, said my goodbyes and everything I want to keep is now down here in storage. You always knew I would come home, and so I have." She smiled, "We are almost ready to launch the new company. We have a few firms on board and we are in the final stages of negotiations with others. My young assistant has been working hard getting everything ready, she even persuaded me to hire some more help and I will be meeting them later on. I think you will be impressed by the speed we have got everything to this stage. So that is all going well.

What is not going so well is family life. Yes, I know I still have some issues here. I don't mean Duncan, Sharon and the boys. They are all gorgeous. The twins are becoming quite grown up. They have developed your sense of humour and fun. I can't help but laugh at and with them.

Then there is the big elephant in the room. I mean, Mum and Dad, and trying to make peace with them. But the ball on that is firmly in their court. I have accepted what happened. Dad was ill when he tried to rape me, but Mum should have believed me then and now, especially since the diagnosis of his brain tumour and how bad he has become over the past couple of months."

She paused for a second as if she was receiving some divine guidance, and then continued, "I feel as if I should try to find this Richard, my blood father. Was he a family friend or just some random bloke? I know I can't ask Mum whilst we are still estranged."

Jocelyn placed the book back down on the cabinet and took the frame over to the window. She looked at the beautiful face in front of her, "And then there is Sam. She was my first real love outside of the family. Our Duncan and Sharon, and my lovely Trina, wants me to find her, to chat with her, to clear the air and to listen to her side of the story, but I know what I saw. I can hear you tutting and I know, as you kept on telling me, there are always two sides to every story, but.." she left the end of the sentence hanging, shaking her head.

She looked at the photo again and said, "I am deeply in love with Trina, and the more we've been apart these six months, the more I've relished the times we've had together. Her two kids are gorgeous. Peter is always looking for approval and you can see he wants someone to play football with or go fishing. Cathy is sometimes a little too clingy and I can understand the reasons why. Their father is forever letting them down but I cannot say anything against him, even though I think he is a useless waste of space.

Jocelyn took some time staring out of the window at nothing and no one. After a while, she turned back to the photo and said, "I'm glad to be home and I really, truly feel settled now. I feel as though I'm back for good, back where I belong." Smiling, she breathed deeply, "I love our little chats. Nan, I love you with all my heart." Jocelyn again kissed her fingers, touched them to the photo, and placed it back in its rightful place. She carefully refolded the piece of paper and returned it to the drawer.

Jocelyn moved to the kitchen, made herself a cup of coffee, and sat in her favourite chair by the window and daydreamed, whilst she watched the world go by.

She must have dozed off because she awoke with the key being turned in the door and raucous laughter that accompanied Lucy and her two companions.

Lucy saw Jocelyn sitting in the chair and greeted her enthusiastically, "Hi Joy." She gave her a big hug, "You're home early. I take it there wasn't much traffic on the roads today."

"Yeah, for once there were no hold-ups and the traffic moved smoothly and steadily all the way down." She looked across to the two young men who had entered with Lucy. "Are you going to introduce me to your friends?" Jocelyn asked.

"Oh, sorry for being so rude. This is Charlie and Sean. The two I told you about from my course that are helping to iron out the bugs we found in the system."

Jocelyn rose from the chair and went over to shake their hands.

"Good afternoon Ms Harrold." said Charlie, whilst Sean smiled and nodded his greeting.

"Well if you are going to be working for me you can start by calling me Joy. I might get you to call me by my formal name when we are meeting clients. Okay?"

They both smiled and said "Okay."

Lucy spoke, "We've an hour or so before we have to go back to our late lecture so we thought we would look at the program again and see where the glitch is. We didn't think you would be back yet. We hope we won't disturb you."

"That's fine. I can always do any phone calls from the bedroom. But whilst you are here, and haven't settled down to work yet, I might as well have a chat with you both now, instead of tonight. Come over and bring a chair to the window." Jocelyn instructed.

Both Charlie and Sean picked up a chair she appraised both of them as they moved toward the window. Charlie's massive six foot four frame started to obliterate the bright sunshine that was streaming into the room. His tight T-shirt was emblazoned with a popular group, whose tour dates showed a long past memory, accentuated his rippling muscles. Jocelyn nodded in approval, and sat back down in her favourite seat.

Her eyes then moved to Sean, who was the complete opposite. Where Charlie was tall, broad, and muscular Sean was tall, thin, and willowy. Sean noticed Jocelyn scrutinising him and pushed his thick glasses back up his nose. He hung his head lower as he slunk his shoulders as he moved towards her. Charlie stood tall and proud, Sean tried to hide himself away. They put the chairs down opposite Jocelyn's. Sean sat whilst Charlie hovered.

"May I get a glass of water before we start?" Charlie asked. "Would you like one?"

"Please."

"Lucy? Sean?"

The two of them shook their heads. Charlie moved towards the kitchen area and found two glasses on the draining board. He proceeded to fill them. Lucy suddenly made a noise as Charlie poured water into one of the glasses and, having been startled, the water overflowed.

"Are you feeling nervous?" asked Jocelyn of Charlie.

He laughed, "No. I always give one hundred and ten percent." He came back with a smart quip.

"That's very good," retorted Jocelyn, joining in the laughing. "I like that. Quick and funny."

Charlie brought over the glasses and sat opposite Jocelyn. She took a deep glug of the water and said, "I want you both to tell me about yourselves. Pretend that Lucy hasn't told me anything. Tell me anything you think I should know or want to know."

"Shall I start?" He asked of Sean, who nodded, "Okay. My name is Charles Adams. Or as people call me, Charlie Adams. I'm nineteen but people think I'm older. I'm on the same course as Lucy and we both have the same tutor."

Lucy butted in, batting her eyelashes, "Yes the adorable Ms Davis."

Jocelyn gave Lucy a stern look, "Enough. All right. I have no interest in her, as well you know."

Lucy laughed, "But she still asks after you."

Sean muffled his mirth in his hand.

Lucy flapped her hand in front of her face and imitated her tutor's voice, "Lucy, when is your sponsor back from her trip? Flutter, flutter, flutter." Lucy pretended to be sick. "Gag, gag, gag."

This time, both Charlie and Sean tried their best to stop laughing, so much so that Charlie had a coughing fit to stop him spurting out the sip of water he had just taken.

Annoyed Jocelyn said, "Let's ignore her."

"You loves me really," Lucy snickered and wiggled her eyebrows.

Jocelyn shook her head, but a smile played on her lips,

Lucy's young boyish looking face smiled at her, with an ease that comes with complete trust. The cheeks had lost their gauntness and she was turning into a warm, beautiful, intelligent and caring woman. Her short, cropped locks had become a thick mane, the colour of burnt umber, making her face appear more rounded.

Jocelyn smiled and thought back to their first meeting when she had come across this wet bundle of rags, begging for money in the torrential downpour that had greeted her first day back in Bristol, after the years away. How their paths had crossed again, when she had waded in to stop Lucy receiving a vicious beating by three thugs. And again, when she realized that there was more to this young woman she had befriended. Intelligent, with the necessary skill set needed for her own new business venture. Jocelyn had seen Lucy evolve from a feisty, homeless individual into this funny, charming and sometimes feisty, young woman.

Smiling she turned to the two men sat opposite her, "Please continue."

Charlie continued, "I've had a few jobs as I have put myself through college, mainly menial, seasonal work but I love doing this. I've been on the same college courses as Lucy for the past few years, but it has only been the last couple of months that we have teamed up. I come at things differently to Lucy and Sean and I think we complement each other."

He paused, and Jocelyn asked, "Family?"

"I live at home with my parents. I have two older brothers who live and work abroad."

"Why do you want to work for me?"

"I have to give my parents some board and lodgings and want some money to socialise at the weekend." Charlie laughed, but then turned serious and replied, "I was working part-time in a burger joint to help me out financially. Having the opportunity to work on this project is brilliant. I have really enjoyed the challenge and thinking about the further challenges down the line really excites me."

Jocelyn nodded, "Yes. Lucy has shown me the work you have done."

"I won't let you down Ms Harrold, Joy, I promise."

"I would hope not." Jocelyn stared at him, tilted her head on one side, appraised him for a moment, and nodded. She looked at Sean, "What's your story? And why do you want to work for me?"

Sean cleared his throat, and quietly started to talk. Sean's quiet demeanour and his Belfast dialect made understanding difficult and Jocelyn strained to catch every word. "My name is Sean, Sean Connor. Lucy and I teamed up for lots of our assignments. My parents both live in Northern Ireland. I have three brothers and one sister who all live at home. Having no friends over here, I felt blessed to have teamed up with Lucy. I think we work well together. During the holiday breaks, I've tried to work the whole way through, to get together enough money to help me through my course. Until working for you I was dishwasher stacking in the kitchens of the big hotel on the corner." He pointed towards the centre of town. "I need to work because I have rooms in a shared house that I have to pay for. Things were a bit tight so Lucy telling me about this opportunity was a godsend. The extra money I get from working for you is the difference between eating properly, and living off baked beans."

Again, Jocelyn nodded. "Yes, you and Lucy do seem to work well together."

He looked over to Lucy who gave him the thumbs up. "Yes, we work so well together."

Jocelyn looked at both men in turn, "I'm going to ask you both a question, and I want a straight answer. Do you have any issues, at all, about working for me?"

Charlie smiled, "Before I answer that, perhaps I should ask you the same question."

"I have no issues with you. As long as you can do the job I pay you for, that is all there is to it."

"I totally agree. I will do my job to the best of my ability. But some people have an issue with the way I look." He pushed the dreadlocks that had fallen over his face back behind his shoulders. "I don't care whether you are gay or not. Lucy says that you are a great boss, so that is all that matters. I do not have an issue with that."

Sean whispered, shaking his head, "No issue at all."

Jocelyn shrugged, smiled and started to speak, "When you are working for me, as long your lifestyle doesn't interfere with what I want this company to achieve, I don't care if the colour of your skin is black, white, or sky blue pink. I get so angry when I hear any judgemental comments. So don't let anyone judge you on how you look especially if it different from you, or if they are a lurker, hiding in the dark shadows, coming out only long enough to hurl abuse and hurt. Confront these bullies, expressly if it's directed against someone who is struggling to cope."

"Neither do I care about your religion. Catholic, Muslim, Rastafarian, or anything in between. It's about what is in here," she touched her head, "and in here." She covered her heart with her hands. "If you have integrity, honesty, and humanity why should I care how anyone would live their life?"

She paused and appraised them again, to see how they reacted to her words. "Don't be afraid of fear. As fear of failure could stop you being the person you are meant to be. Don't let fear rule you, take over your life, otherwise twenty years down the line you could have many regrets. Don't allow the words 'I wish I had done this or done that' to be part of your vocabulary." She took a sip of her water and both young men were hanging on every word.

"Sometimes it's good to be afraid, especially when you are going into the unknown and changing something that you know, deep inside your heart, is wrong. But when you are afraid and have challenges to overcome, do not have the fear. Face the challenges head on and throw caution to the wind. If you think you will fail then you are halfway down the path to failure. Also, don't become too sure of yourself. Keep grounded and allow others to keep you grounded. Don't over celebrate your successes, nor wallow in your failures. If others have helped you thank them, acknowledge them. Listen to your instinct, grab your opportunity when it rears its head, and then give it your all. Lastly, be pleasant to work alongside and keep a sense of humour. A smile and a laugh will take you further than a sigh and a snarl."

She then continued, "I have four rules that I would like you to keep. One. Turn up for work when you say you will or when I've asked you. Two. Do the job you were paid for. Three. Respect the clients and your co-workers. And four. If you have any issues or want to try something different out just run it past me first. Do you have any questions or problems with that?"

"No Ma'am, I mean Joy. I can work within those parameters quite easily," replied Charlie.

Sean nodded his head.

"And I can see why Lucy wanted you both on board. I've seen your work and I'm impressed. Is the financial arrangement what you expect?"

"It is more than generous." Charlie said and Sean again nodded in agreement.

Jocelyn held out her hand, "Well then, welcome to the team Charlie?"

Charlie shook her hand and said, "You won't regret it."

Jocelyn winced, "You don't have to squeeze my hand quite that tight."

"Sorry." he apologised. "I'm always being told off about that." and he laughed his rich baritone laugh, whose deep timbre seemed to vibrate throughout her body.

Jocelyn warily took hold of Sean's hand and shook, "Welcome on board."

"Thank you." Sean said quietly but his eyes portrayed his pleasure.

Lucy shouted over, "Can we get back to work now you've had your little tete a tete? I was hoping we would iron out the gremlins before we have to get back to our next lecture."

Jocelyn got up and said laughing, "See how she bullies me. Anyone would think that she is the boss. Have fun kids. I've some phone calls to make so I'll leave you to it."

With that, Jocelyn walked towards her bedroom, but Lucy giving her a warm embrace stopped her. She asked, "Are you back for good now?"

"I am."

"I'm glad." she smiled, "Welcome home."

ꟸ

Chapter Two

Tuesday Evening

Jocelyn parked the car and walked the few yards to her brother's front door, but as soon as she was about to knock, the door flew open, and the familiar sight of her brother greeted her. He immediately pulled her into a tight bear hug.

"Hi Chunky, Punky, Dunky." Jocelyn said laughing.

"Hi back at you Dumps." He replied, giving her an extra squeeze.

Jocelyn batted at his arms, "Put me down. Why do you have to keep doing that every time I come back home?"

"Because I want you to know that I love you," he said sincerely. "I don't ever want you to feel unloved again."

"What? By squeezing the living daylights out of me."

"You wouldn't have it any other way, would you?" He grinned.

Jocelyn smiled. She looked at her brother after he replaced her on the ground. Duncan was a fairly good-looking man, about six feet tall. His shoulders were broad and he filled the sweater he was wearing. The jeans he had on were worn and torn in the right places.

"Couldn't you afford a new pair?" She teased pulling at the tear on his thigh.

"Oh, ha, ha. You're so funny." He grinned, with the laughter shining through his blue eyes, making the crow's feet around his eyes deepen.

His hair was slicked back, but an odd strand fell onto his forehead. He pushed it back in time-honoured fashion, as she knew he would.

Ushering her into the front room he asked, "So you managed to get it all sorted out finally?"

She huffed, "Who would have thought that selling an apartment in one of the newer blocks in town would cause such difficulties?"

"But it's all sorted now?"

"Yes. Finally. Three different estate agents and a drop of ten grand. But the place is no longer my problem." She shrugged.

"Ten grand?" he said, incredulously. "That's a big hit."

"It was either that or wait for another buyer. So I decided to cut my losses and run."

"Bad luck seems to follow you."

She shook her head, "Don't say that Dunc."

"Sorry. I bet you won't be sad about not doing that drive again. How long did it take? Four hours? Five hours?"

"Yeah at least five hours. I've lost count of the number of trips back and forth I've done. It was a shame that the first seller fell through the day before completion, especially after I had sold or moved out all of the furniture."

"I know, but it did make me laugh though, when your bed ended up being a blow up lilo and your three piece living room suite was a deck chair, a camping chair and a foot stool."

"Go on, laugh."

Duncan again burst out laughing. "You really know how to live in style. You hate camping and yet you lived like that for… was it three or four months."

"On and off for three months, one week and two days and twelve hours." She laughed, "Not that I counted every uncomfortable day I had to stay in the flat."

"Why didn't you stay in a hotel?" Duncan asked, "Even a one star hotel would have suited you better."

"I wanted to save my money for my fledgling business but I am never going to go camping, caravanning, or any kind of roughing it again."

Duncan gasped, "But you promised the boys."

Jocelyn looked worried, "I didn't, did I?"

"No, just teasing." Duncan let out a chuckle.

"You pig." she shook he head. "My head suddenly filled with all the ways I could get out of it."

Duncan replied, still smiling, "But I'm sure the boys would love it. They keep on wanting to make dens and tents."

"Well, you'll have to take them, won't you? I can see you roughing it."

Duncan laughed, "You said you wanted to spend more time with them. That would be an ideal opportunity."

"No way Jose. I would go loopy if I had to crawl around on my hands and knees, or fight with a sleeping bag or wake up in the middle of the night on the floor because the lilo had gone down. Again. And the thought of going to the loo in the middle of the night." She shook her head with a grimace. "It is all right for you boys if you're taken short in the night, you can go out and point it at the hedge. No such luxury for us girls." she said, shaking her head. "No way. Nh nh. There's no way I would camp again."

"I can imagine you, hopping around trying to get your wellies on, trying to be as quiet as you can, but waking every one up. You would then wonder whether you can make it to the toilet block, or find a place to go in the bushes away from prying eyes."

Jocelyn joined in the laughter. "Exactly what I mean." Smiling she continued, "I'm looking forward to having a bit of comfort, and spending time in Nan's place."

"So the old part of your life is over now, and the new phase of your life will start properly." Pausing for a moment, he continued, "How's the business going?"

"I'm nearly all set to go with my fresh venture. It has gone quite well. We have quite a few companies on board and interested, but until they have signed on the dotted line, we will never know. Lucy and her friends are ironing out a couple of glitches then we will be good to launch."

"I bet Trina is looking forward to you being back permanently."

"Yes. It's hard carrying on a long distant affair. Moreover, the longer I've been away, the more I've missed her. You are doing so much during the day but nothing exciting, nothing that is worth talking about, nothing that the other person really understands about or is interested in. You start to run out of things to talk about. I can't wait to spend some quality time with her and her two lovely kids." She smiled, "They are such sweeties."

"What do they think about you two being together?"

"At first we tried to hide it but then Peter asked why we jumped apart every time he came in the room. He then reminded us that his best friend Simon had two Mums," she laughed at the memory. "Cathy enjoys having another adult to read her stories."

Duncan nodded his understanding.

"But I'm not allowed to stay over whilst they are in the house." Jocelyn looked sad, "Trina doesn't want to confuse and upset them. All being well, now I'm home, that will change." She smiled a hopeful smile.

Duncan turned serious and said, "Dad's has taken a turn for the worse.

Mum is really struggling to cope."

"And you are telling me this because?"

"They are still your parents."

Jocelyn gave him a questioning look.

Duncan conceded, "Okay but they both brought you up."

"And we both know how that ended."

"Don't you think it's about time?

"As I've said before, they will have to make the first move. None of it was my fault."

"I know that Dumps, but Mum needs your support."

Jocelyn shrugged, studied the face of her half-brother, and shook her head. "Mum pushed away my overtures when I last tried, so it is not my call anymore. You can only be rebuffed and disbelieved a certain number of times."

"What if we went together?"

Jocelyn again shook her head and abruptly changed the subject. "How are those wonderful munchkins, you and Sharon somehow managed to produce?"

He laughed, "Running us ragged as they always do. Sharon has them playing a silly game in the garden. So, knowing them, they will soon get fed up and our peace will be shattered."

As soon as he spoke his last word two identical mini people came rushing through the back door and raced to see who could be first to jump on Joy.

Admonishing them, Duncan scolded, "Stop jumping on your aunt. Give her chance to breath."

Jocelyn pulled them both into a close hug. Each on either side of her and kissed both their heads. They both started to speak to her at the same time and Jocelyn pleaded with them to stop. "Boys. I only have one pair of ears so if you both talk at once I won't be able to hear either of you. So who is going to start?"

"Mum said that we could make a den if you helped us." Alfie said excitedly.

"Oh she did, did she?" Jocelyn asked, raising her eyes.

Sharon came and stood in the doorway then smiled, "David, what did I actually say?"

"Alfie asked if we could make a den and you said no, not today as Joy was coming over."

"So will you help us?" Alfie begged. "Please Joy. Please."

David joined in, looking beseechingly, "Pretty please? You're my favourite Aunt."

The instantaneous sound of begging filled the front room. Pretending to block her ears from the noise, she smiled. The boys looked expectantly at her.

"Sorry boys. I'm not staying that long." Jocelyn shook her head then looked at David and smiled, "And I'm your only Aunt."

Trying to take a different tack Alfie looked over at his Mum. "If you're hungry, Mum can make you something to eat. Can't you Mum?"

Sharon leant against the doorjamb and folded her arms. She gave Jocelyn a look that implied that it was up to her.

"Sorry munchkins, but I'm on my way to see Trina." She saw the disappointment on their faces and continued, "Boys, I promise I'll help you make a tent later this week. That's if it doesn't rain. I'll organise it with your Mum, okay."

Disappointment showed on their faces but they answered "Okay."

She patted the settee either side of her, "Come and tell me what mischief you've been getting up to.

"We don't get up to mischief." David stated.

Jocelyn raised her eyes in disbelief.

David continued, "Alfie does sometimes and drags me into it."

"I don't."

"You do. Ms Frend put me in detention because you pulled Chelsea's ponytail. And because you wouldn't own up we both got punished."

He gave David a look and said, "Tell-tale."

"Is that correct Alfie?" His father asked.

Alfie squirmed, and then nodded.

"Come here," he said to Alfie. Alfie stood before him and Duncan took hold of both his hands. "How many times do we have to have a similar conversation? If you do something wrong you must take ownership and not get your brother into trouble. It is not fair on David. Do you understand?"

Alfie squirmed, "Yes Dad. Sorry Dad." he turned towards his Brother and said, "Sorry David."

"What are you going to do to repay David?"

"Shall I do your chores for two days?" asked Alfie.

"David?" his Dad asked of him. "Is that acceptable?"

"Yes it is."

As Alfie turned around, David whispered, "We'll do them together. Okay."

Alfie gave a slight nod, which Duncan noticed.

"And whatever the two of you are planning it won't work. If I find out that Alfie hasn't done your chores by himself, you will both be grounded for two weeks. Do you both understand?"

They both nodded.

Jocelyn got up, kissed Sharon on the cheek, and said, "Hello and goodbye Sharon. I can't stay. I have to go. I promised Trina I would be around for tea. I'll phone you later and we'll arrange a meet up in a couple of days. What days are you working this week?"

"I'm free Thursday and Friday this week. What about coffee Thursday morning?" asked Sharon.

"Can I ring you tomorrow evening to confirm? I'm not sure of my plans until I've made some phone calls."

"That's fine. I'm looking forward to a good catch up without any interruptions." she nodded towards the twins who were playing with some toy cars on the floor.

"So am I Sharon. Hopefully Thursday then." Jocelyn again kissed Sharon on the cheek.

Duncan rose and pulled Trina into another of his hugs, "See you soon, Dumps. Give Trina my love."

"Will do."

"Boys, come and give Joy a kiss goodbye please."

The twins got up and both threw themselves into her arms.

"Bye munchkins. I'll see you both soon."

"Will you help us build our tent when you next come around?" David asked.

"Only if it's not raining. Deal." She bumped fists with both boys.

"Deal." they replied.

She ruffled both their heads and followed Duncan to the front door. After another of his hugs, she bade him farewell.

ꟾ

Jocelyn inhaled a sweet raft of baby talc and shampoo that wafted out of the bedrooms. She had willingly allowed herself to be roped into the children's bedtime routine. Even if it was only to remind Peter to wash behind his ears, and to read to Cathy. She quietly climbed down the stairs.

Finally, Jocelyn flopped down onto the settee. She picked up the glass of wine Trina had poured and asked, "How did I allow myself to be persuaded to read three stories?"

"Pushover." Trina grinned. "She was playing the 'you've been away too long and you must make it up for abandoning me' card. And you fell for it. You let her get away with too much."

"Only because she is as lovely as her mother." Jocelyn leant across and gave Trina a tender kiss.

She smiled at the woman who brought out these feelings of protectiveness. The intelligent eyes, deep set into chiselled cheekbones. Her shoulder length golden hair was now pulled back in a ponytail, instead of the normal framing of her handsome features. A long baggy T-shirt hung over her leggings, hiding her stomach that she found so hard to trim. Jocelyn noticed that she had lost a few pounds around her face, and she looked well on it.

"They've missed you. So have I"

"I've missed them." She smiled, "And you."

"How much?"

"This much." Jocelyn said, opening her arms as wide as possible, laughing.

Jocelyn shifted her weight and wrapped her arm around the beautiful woman sat next to her and Trina allowed herself to be pulled in a comfortable embrace. Enjoying the silence, they sat together in each other's arms, heads touching. Trina let out a contented sigh.

"This feels so good. I've missed this. Are you sure you are back for good?"

"I'm back. I have nothing left of my life back in Sunderland. Everything has been sold or boxed away in storage down here, until I know what to do with it all."

Trina smiled and fingered the pendant made of Bristol blue glass, that Jocelyn had given her eight months ago, when she had first came home. She had worn it every day since and treasured it with all her might. She pulled it up to her lips and kissed it in time-honoured fashion.

She turned and studied Joy's face, her cheeks, underneath striking blue eyes, were a little flushed. Her dark hair had grown since her last fleeting visit and framed the tanned face. A slight smile played across her face. As she noticed Trina watching her, one corner of her mouth turned up in the lopped sided grin she wore whenever she was somewhat amused.

"What is so funny?" Trina asked.

"You."

"Me? What have I done?"

"Nothing." The smile grew deeper. "You were just being you. And I love you for it." She paused for a moment and stated, "I'll have to get you some earring to go with that." she leant over and lifted the pendant to study it. "It really suits you."

"You're going all soppy on me again." Trina stated, and nudged her in the ribs.

"If I want to go all soppy, as you call it, I'll go all soppy. So what are you going to do about it? Eh?"

Trina pulled a cushion from behind her and flipped it towards Joy.

"Two can play at that game."

She pulled the cushion from behind her and started to attack Trina with it. Soon both were giggling like little children and soon their hands were exploring places that hadn't been touched for a while. Extraditing herself before things went too far Jocelyn sighed, "I must go. Tomorrow is going to be a busy day."

"You don't mind do you?" Trina asked with regret.

"I would prefer to stay over but I understand that you don't think the children are ready to wake up to me yet." Jocelyn's body language showed she didn't agree but didn't want another discussion. She raised her eyebrows, gave another deep sigh and asked, "We still on for Friday?"

"Of course. Mike is going to pick them up from school and will bring them back home on Sunday evening, so we will have all weekend together. I'm sorry. I promise I'll make it up to you."

"I'll keep you that." Jocelyn laughed.

ꕤ

Chapter Three

Wednesday Afternoon

Lucy let herself into the apartment, noticed Jocelyn sitting in her favourite seat, and sat down beside her. Jocelyn looked up and found that Lucy seemed distracted.

"Problems?" asked Jocelyn.

"A couple." Lucy blew out a long breath.

Jocelyn looked enquiringly.

Lucy continued, "Someone at college has complained about us doing some of the work in the study centre. They said we were disturbing them, so we were called into the Dean's study."

"When was this?"

"This morning."

"Why didn't you tell me? I would have come with you. Taken the flak."

"All three of us went in together. The Dean listened to why we were using the study centre; that we needed to use our friends to help with the research. He seemed to understand and said that it was a good opportunity for us but we have been told we won't be able to continue in there. So if we need to do anything else which needs input from people we will have to find another place."

"I was half expecting it to happen." Jocelyn agreed. "We have been taking a few liberties."

Lucy sighed and shook her head. "I think I know who complained. If it is whom I think it is, then she has been moaning and groaning for the past couple of weeks about wanting to help. She's been trying to get into the act but she is a real pain in the arse. Not the type of person you would want to work for you or with you. She's always butting in to our conversations, which we try to ignore. She then gives you a tirade of her thoughts. She doesn't talk with you she speaks at you. There is never a two-way conversation. The only opinion that is correct is her opinion, everyone else is wrong, and woe betide if you disagree. I've had to walk away from her so many times. She is so frustrating."

Shaking her head, she continued, "Then she suddenly shows that she has been listening to what you've been saying and shows concern about something you mentioned weeks ago. That's when you want to like her, but you can't. She is so frustrating."

Lucy sighed as Jocelyn asked, "Is she on your course?"

"Yes. We've been on all the same courses since I've been going to the college, but she usually works totally alone."

Jocelyn asked, "Have you ever asked her to work with you?" Lucy frowned and Jocelyn continued, "Has anyone?"

Lucy thought for a moment then looked embarrassed, "No to both questions"

Continuing Jocelyn said, "Has she ever asked anyone to work with her? I bet she finds it difficult to connect with people. I bet she is fighting her own battles."

Jocelyn hated seeing anyone sitting on the sidelines. She knew it stemmed back to the days when she was bullied for being out of place, different. It made her even more determined to look after the little person, to engage them, to make them feel important, wanted, of value. Whenever the occasion arose, she also tried to instil these values in others.

"Okay I get it. Yes, she always is the one at the back of the group. She never pushes herself forward. It's as though she doesn't expect to be picked, as though she is falling through the cracks of the groups' social life, as though she doesn't want to be seen as a failure."

"Does she have any special gifts? Is her work good?"

"I'm sure if she put her brain into gear before she opened her mouth she could be an asset. Because occasionally, and I mean occasionally, she sees things from a very acute angle, from left field, and her ideas are good. She always manages an A grade on all her work. If only she had some social skills."

Jocelyn sighed, "That's sad. I think she is lonely and to help her overcome her loneliness she does anything which will get her noticed." She made Lucy look at her directly then probed, "Does she ever come out for drinks with you all?"

Lucy shook her head, "Come to think of it, no she hasn't."

Raising her eyebrows, "Has anyone asked her?"

"I've no idea. I haven't." Lucy replied, shaking her head.

"Put yourself in her shoes. She looks around and sees people teaming up and working together. When she tried to join in the conversation she is dismissed, not listened to. Does she have any friends at all? People are allowed to be different, look at us, it doesn't make them weird, wrong or strange, just different. She might be shy and how she acts might be her way of trying to be more accepted by you all." Jocelyn raised her eyebrows questioningly at Lucy, pausing for effect. "Then groups of you go out and socialise. Have you ever tried to get to know her? You might be surprised and find out you like her."

"Hah. I shouldn't think so. And dobbing us in to the Dean was the last straw."

"But it's got your attention hasn't it? Why don't you ask her to go out with you all? Keep your mind open and try to be kind. Doing this might reward you in ways you never thought possible. "

She shrugged her shoulders, non-committedly, and said, trying to change the subject slightly, "It's a good job we've finished those questionnaires and surveys. I think we've ironed out the glitches. We don't need to ask our mates to be pretend customers anymore so we don't need to use the canteen anymore."

They sat in companionable silence for a while until Lucy asked, "Would you like a coffee?"

"Please."

Lucy started humming to herself as she waited for the coffee to percolate. After pouring the milk into the mugs, she walked back to the window and placed the mugs down on the small table. Lucy picked up her mug and cradled it in her hands. A faraway look came into her eyes, as though she was pondering over something else. Jocelyn noticed a plethora of emotions playing across Lucy's face. Jocelyn waited patiently.

Something had been on Lucy's mind all day. She hadn't known how to bring it up. She was so grateful to Jocelyn for taking her off the streets, giving a roof over her head, getting her back into college, and giving her a job. She didn't want to appear as though she was taking advantage of Jocelyn. She liked her too much to do that. Therefore, she decided to blurt it out.

Lucy finally spoke. "I'll be moving out soon, Joy."

"I knew this day would come, but are you sure?" Jocelyn asked. "Have you saved up enough money? You've only been here for six months."

"It's not about the money, Joy. You know I've been so grateful for everything you have done for me but Sean needs to find a new home. The lease on his place runs out in just over a month and he can't afford any of the ones he's looked at. So we've decided to cut the costs and are going to move in together."

Jocelyn nodded, showing her approval, and then asked, "That seems like a plan. Does that include Charlie?"

"Yes. But not at the start. He's going to be joining us as soon as he gets a full time job so that he can afford it. His parents have given their blessing. I think from what Charlie says, his parents want to downsize from the large house they live in to a much smaller one, but they won't whilst he is living at home."

Still nodding Jocelyn said, "A good idea. You all get on so well."

"Yeah, we are going to be looking at a three bedroom place tomorrow. It's a bit far out of the centre, so it will either be a long walk or bus to college for the last couple of months before we graduate. I hate buses."

Joy didn't say anything but tapped her fingers on her chin.

"Don't you want to know where we are thinking of going?"

Jocelyn still seemed distracted, "What? Oh yeah. Where is this flat?"

"It's in one of the big houses off the Whiteladies Road. We'll have the top two floors."

Jocelyn nodded. She pulled at her bottom lip. "You haven't signed anything yet, have you?"

"No. Why."

"Can you hang fire for a week or so?"

A puzzled look came over Lucy's face. "Why? We have to find somewhere before Sean's lease runs out."

"I'm working on something which I think could be mutually beneficial.

I'm waiting on a phone call."

"Okay." Lucy said, hesitantly.

"Still go and look to look at the flat. You know, to keep your irons in the fire but promise me you won't sign anything until you hear from me. I promise I'll get back to you by the weekend." Jocelyn smiled at her.

"Okay, you've intrigued me, but I'll have to run it past Sean."

ℰ

Chapter Four

Thursday Morning

"Hi Joy," Sharon said as she gave her a kiss on the cheek. She looked around the independent coffee bar that had sprung up in the new city centre developments. "It looks a nice place. Do you come here often?"

"Not as often as I would like. I hope that I'll find time after we manage to get the launch off the ground. At the moment I'm too busy and, because I'm working from home, I don't venture out much."

Putting her bags on one of the chairs she asked, "Another?"

"Please. A cappuccino."

"Cake or biscuit?"

"Neither thanks. I'm trying to look after my weight."

"Tosh, there is nothing of you."

"Not now. I tried hard recently to lose those last few pounds. However, you've twisted my arm. I'll have a danish. See, that's why I'm not losing any more weight. Too weak willed." Jocelyn laughed and Sharon joined in as she walked to the back of the queue.

Jocelyn studied her sister-in-law as she stood at the counter. Her strong build was slightly overweight, which accentuated her soft curves. Her dark brows and lashes stood out against her pale skin. Her wide mouth didn't seem out of place below the rosy cheeks of her oval face. Her red hair tumbled over her shoulders in waves that gave her a soft approachable look.

Jocelyn nodded and agreed with herself that her brother had made a good choice all those years ago. She gave the impression that she had a good head on her shoulders that you could speak to her, that she was interested in what you had to say.

Sharon carried the tray back to the table, scooted into the chair opposite, and took the cups and plates off the tray. Silence followed whilst they started to eat their cakes.

Jocelyn finished the cake with the last few bites. She wiped the crumbs from her mouth and tossed the crumple paper napkin on to the plate. "That was gurt lush." She said licking her lips. "I'll have to come back here again."

Sharon smiled, "I see you still relish cakes. I thought you would have chosen one of those cream ones." She said pointing to a cake on one of the neighbouring tables.

"I did think about it." Jocelyn owned up, she started to giggle, "I had one just before you came. So two would have been piggy," she continued giggling.

Sharon almost choked on her drink. "You haven't changed then."

"I'm trying." She replied, laughing. Jocelyn picked up and took a sip of her drink. She sat back, stretched out her legs, and let out a contented sigh.

"That was a big sigh."

"Yeah. I'm feeling content. Things are going really well."

"I must say, you do look content."

"And you? What are you doing now? Did you get that job you were going for? I forgot to ask when I saw you Tuesday." Jocelyn asked of Sharon.

"Yes. I got this little part time job about four weeks ago, which I share with another woman. She lives a couple of streets away from us. We cover the lunch period, in a busy office, from eleven to two. We normally work three days one week and four days the next. We do a bit of everything, covering reception, typing, filing, making tea and anything else that is needed. I've sorted out with my job share that she would work all the weekends now and I would cover the weekends during school time so I don't have to find as many baby sitters over the summer holidays. Your Mum has offered but I'm not too sure."

"Neither would I be." She said quietly and paused, "So you are not using your qualifications."

"No, I couldn't find anywhere to use my book keeping skills on the hours I wanted to do. I'll just have to wait until they are old enough to look after themselves."

"Keep looking. Don't give up."

"I am enjoying being back at work. The money's not bad and they do treat us well." Sharon nodded, "What about you? Are you any closer to launch day?"

"I've exchanged contracts on those premises I told you about a few weeks ago and if everything goes to plan it should be mine tomorrow lunchtime. It'll need a bit of decoration and some updating for the use of computers so, hopefully, a couple of weeks"

"Remind me where these premises are?"

"It's one of those old three storey places on the Hotwells Road. It has business space on the ground floor and a flat on the two floors above. There is limited street parking outside and four spaces around the back. It's been standing empty for a year so I can't envisage any last minute problems."

"Does it need much doing to it if it's been empty for that length of time?"

"A fair amount but nothing too drastic. I've borrowed the key to do some measuring up this afternoon. Do you want to come with me?

"I'd love to. Would you mind?"

Smiling, she said, "I wouldn't have asked you if I didn't want you to come, silly."

ઈ

Jocelyn and Sharon stood over the road from the premises.

"It's that one there, next to the small alleyway." Jocelyn pointed, "You go down there to get to our parking spaces. It is a joint entrance for all these premises and there will be quite a lot of passing local traffic. Moreover, with us being on one of the main routes out of the city it will be easy to find. Well? What do you think?"

"It's in a good position. It's close to the City Centre, but it does need some new paint work and decent signage."

"I agree. The brown paint isn't very inviting, is it? Shall we go in?"

"Would love to, but trying to cross the road will be the difficult part."

Laughing, Jocelyn took hold of Sharon's arm. They waited for a gap in the traffic and they ran across the road, giggling like schoolgirls.

"Do you want to see the work premises or the flat first?" Jocelyn asked.

"It's got to be the working area first."

She put the key into the key and turned it. She tried to open it but it stuck. She pushed harder and as it suddenly opened, she flew into the small entrance hall. She burst out laughing, recovered her balance, and removed the key. She said, "Now that's what I call an entrance. Welcome to, hopefully, my new business premises."

Sharon stepped across the threshold.

Jocelyn continued, "As you can see, this doorway to the left leads into the office. And this one ahead leads up to the flat."

She changed keys and opened the office door, this time without mishap.

"Try to ignore the grimy carpet and the rubbish furniture. It's all going."

"What are you going to do to the place?"

"I want to divide this bottom space into three integral areas, reception, working, and conference. I need to get the measurements so I can work out the optimum size for each."

"Do you want to move the tables and whatnot into this corner so it's not so cluttered?"

"Would you mind helping me to shift some stuff? Then I could do some measuring."

After a while, the broken tables and chairs were stacked in a corner.

"I take it that the reception area will be here." Sharon held out her arms indicating a rough area.

"Yes up to about here. I want a desk there," Jocelyn pointed, "and about three or four easy chairs over there."

"What about a small, low coffee table. And have you thought about a coffee maker?"

"I have thought about it but it all depends on space and what is available, once we have got the rest in." Jocelyn looked at the flooring and made a disgusted sound. "I'm not looking forward to pulling up this carpet. You can only just see the pattern in places, but it looks as though it was a burgundy and yellow colour. I'll have to come tooled with gloves, masks and a sharp knife."

"Rather you than me on that one." Sharon looked towards the back of the room and asked, "Do you want me to hold anything whilst you take some measurements?"

"Would you? I know what workstations I want to buy but I need to see whether they will fit in and whether my quick plan for the downstairs will work."

Taking the measure and sticky tape Jocelyn, with Sharon's help marked out the three areas. When finished she stood back and contemplated their work.

"I think it will work. I'm going to divide the room up using moveable interlocking partitions, along the lines of the tape." She said pointing, "reception, work, and conference section. We've room in the work area to bring in more workstations for when we expand."

"What about facilities to make coffee or to go to the loo?"

"Already here. The toilet is through that door."

Sharon poked her head around the door. "That's fully serviceable. Just some bleach and elbow grease needed."

Jocelyn directed Sharon through the other door, "And here is the kitchen area and back door leading to the parking lot."

Sharon had started to pull open and examine the sink and cupboards. "This all looks fine. Again, some elbow grease needed. Perhaps some new door and drawer fronts, as the carcasses of the cupboards look solid." She looked around, "Will you be putting some easy chairs over there?"

"I should imagine so. On a sunny day, the sun must stream through these windows as it faces the same way as my apartment. I can imagine drinking coffee and relaxing over there."

Sharon laughed, "I suggest you don't make the chairs too comfy or you'll never get any work done."

They continued to poke about in the remaining cupboards until Sharon looked at her watch, “You’d better show me the flat before I have to go.”

“Come on. Let’s go upstairs.” Jocelyn led the way through the other door and climbed up the stairs saying, “The carpets on the stairs and throughout the flat are not too bad. It’ll do for the time being. I will order one of those industrial cleaners and give it a good going over.”

Three doors led off the landings and another set of stairs dog legged around and continued upwards. Turning left, they walked into the living room, which made its way to the front of the building. A couple of settees and a chair faced one of the walls, towards the evidence of where a TV set had once sat.

“This is a good sized room. And I like how it’s almost open plan with the kitchen back there.”

Walking back onto the landing Jocelyn said, “There’s a small toilet and shower room in there and one of the bedrooms in through there.”

Sharon poked her head through both doors.

“And going upstairs there are two bedrooms and a more substantial bathroom and toilet.”

They continued climbing higher, “I’ll tell you the truth, I’m glad I don’t have all these stairs to climb every day.” She puffed and took a deep breath at the top. After a moment, she looked around upstairs, poking her head into all the nooks and crannies. She nodded her head showing approval, “All three bedrooms are a decent size and there’s a good living room kitchen area. You’ve fallen on your feet here.”

“I think so.” Jocelyn agreed.

“When will it be officially yours?”

“Lunchtime tomorrow. I’m so excited. I can’t wait.”

“I hate to put a dampener on your enjoyment but I really have to go now.” They both started to walk down the stairs. “Let us know if and when you need anything. Duncan’s not very good with a paint brush but he’s good at helping to rip things out and moving things around."

They reached the bottom of the stairs.

"Are you hanging around here for a little while?"

"No I have to get the key back. Shall we walk back toward the centre, bus or catch the ferry?"

"Let's catch the ferry. I hadn't done that for years."

"I'll go and make sure everything is locked up. I'll be two ticks. A small path leads from the parking area down to the river, so we won't have a big detour. I'll catch you up."

ꕤ

Chapter Five

Friday Morning

Jocelyn watched her three employees walk towards her. Never had she seen such an unlikely combination: The small, butch dyke, the handsome, black man mountain and the skinny goofy geek. Yet they seemed to fit together. Each brought to the table something that was missing from the others. They complimented each other like missing pieces to a puzzle. In that moment, she realized that she needed them and she hoped they needed her.

She started to scrutinize them all. Charlie had a day's growth of beard that accentuated his thick lips. Those lips formed into a smile as they approached her. He waved an acknowledgement. Black jeans and a crisp white shirt gave him a smart casual air. His broad shoulders tapered to slim hips, and even with his young years, he walked with a confidence born through success. His laugh was a deep, rich baritone. Its sound made you feel good; made you want to join in, even if you didn't know why.

Lucy walked in the middle, and was dwarfed by the two men on either side of her. She had a young boyish looking face and a petite frame. Her eyes portrayed restlessness, eager to finish new projects as quickly as possible. Her thin legs poked out from short shorts. A baggy T-shirt hung off one of her shoulders making her small frame seem even smaller. A rose tattoo poked its head out at the top of her arm as though in search of the sun. She walked quickly trying to keep up with her two friends.

Sean's red curly hair framed his thin face. His green eyes were a little too sunken in the gauntness of his chiselled cheeks. Although tall he hunched his shoulders as he walked, bowing his head to look at the path in front of him. His knees poked through the holes in his jeans, and his short-sleeved patterned shirt was opened at the neck to reveal a tuft of chest hair.

They stopped beside her.

Charlie asked for all of them, "Why did you ask to meet us here and not in the pub over there?"

"We could go in there after but first I wanted to show you something." She turned and opened the door, outside which they stood. She stepped aside and ushered them into to the front room. "These are our new offices. Yes, I know it needs a lick of paint and some work to get it Ship Shape and Bristol Fashion. But imagine this: I've put some tape on the floor."

The three of them cast a critical eye around the room. It was a good size. Most of the original features had been removed, but the architrave and cornices looked original. Jocelyn started to communicate her ideas and as she was speaking, the three friends began looking around and felt Jocelyn's infectious enthusiasm.

"Imagine it all spruced up with fresh paint. The reception desk will be here with a small table with easy chairs here." She moved to another place in the office. "A small partition will go right across the room here and down here. We will have our four interlocking desks on this side with the ability to make another four over there. On this side of the partition, we shall have six interlocking desks, which will be used as a conference area. We shall have a projector up there and an interactive white board on the wall there."

She walked over to the left and pulled open a door to a space that would be under the stairs. "The toilets are in here." She said, "Don't look too closely as it needs some a good clean." She paused "and, if you follow me." she walked through a door to the back of the building. "Here will be a little kitchen and our staff area."

Jocelyn looked at them and gauged their reaction. All she saw was small positive shrugs, which she took as a good omen. They each were wandering around the room deep within their own thoughts.

"Well? Comments please."

Lucy spoke, "It's a good space. I can see it working."

"It goes without saying that it needs a paint job to spruce it up, but yeah, I like it." Charlie nodded in approval.

Sean just nodded and said, "Yes, it works."

"So the only question I have to ask you all now is, are you prepared to work for me when you leave college in the next month? The contract we have now finishes at the end of your course. I will pay you above the going rate for your qualifications. You know what I want to achieve and how I want to achieve it. And I know how you work. You don't have to answer me now but I would like an answer early next week."

Lucy piped up straight away, "You don't need to sell it to me I'm in."

Jocelyn thought of Lucy like a daughter, she hoped that with her being on board it would nudge the other two towards working for her full time.

Charlie was about to speak but was halted by Jocelyn, "Please don't make a rash decision, take a couple of days to think about it. I want it to be right for you, and for you to want to work for me for the correct reasons."

She moved towards the front door. "What I am going to show you next

I don't want to have any bearing on your decision to work for me or not."

They looked quizzically at each other. She turned to them and opened the door to the flat upstairs. "Follow me."

The three of them followed Jocelyn upstairs and she showed them the flat. "I have bought the office downstairs with a three bedroom flat above."

She started showing them around the various rooms and at the end of the tour Jocelyn said, "Lucy has told me what the rent is for the flat you looked at off the Whiteladies Road, and I will be asking the same rate. I could rent it out to anyone or I could rent it out to the three of you. It doesn't really matter to me."

She paused to gauge their reactions "If you decide you want it then I will give you the first month rent free on the proviso that you spruce it up. You know, a paint job to your own tastes, as long as it is not too garish. I will hire an industrial cleaner for the carpets, and get you anything else you will need. You can have it furnished or unfurnished. Unfurnished the rent will be slightly less."

Charlie suddenly asked, "Why are you doing this, helping us?"

"Why am I doing it?" she asked, retrospectively, "That's a good question. Believe it or not, I'm doing it for myself as well as for you. If I rent it out to you lot, I won't have to worry about some of the regular landlord, tenant problems. Like not telling me if something is not working or if there is a leak. You know the normal problems that could crop up."

Sean spoke first, "I don't know about you two but I think there is more scope here than the last one we saw. And it's not because I'm desperate." He laughed.

Jocelyn was taken aback as this was the most words she had Sean say since their first meeting.

Charlie turned to Jocelyn and asked, "And you mean it when you said that it is not dependent on the job offer?"

"No it's not dependent on the job offer but I would be lying if I said I didn't want the two to go hand in hand."

"Okay count me in. The same rent as the last place?" Charlie pressed

Reaffirming the offer Jocelyn merely said, "Yes."

"And it's a yes from me." Lucy agreed and gave Sean a hug and jumped into Charlies arms, grinning from ear to ear.

"Would you like it furnished or unfurnished? If you decide furnished, each bedroom would have a bed, chest of drawers and wardrobe. In the living room, you would have the furniture already there or if it is too ropey I will provide a couple of two seaters and a couple of easy chairs. The kitchen I will provide an oven, microwave, and a fridge. Any questions?" Jocelyn asked. "No? Okay, I'll meet you downstairs in a little while. Take your time, have a good look around sit on the chairs etc."

After a quick discussion, the three of them decided on furnished, and the furniture in the living room would suffice.

Lucy looked at her two friends and said, "You two can have the top rooms with your own bathroom. The bedroom at the top of the stairs is going to be mine then I can have my own shower room and keep all my girly stuff safe from your prying eyes."

Charlie and Sean rolled their eyes.

"I want my own toilet. I don't want the two of you peeing on the seat, or leaving the seat up or, heaven forbid, missing the pan altogether."

Sean looked aghast. "I wouldn't do that."

Lucy shook her head as Charlie smiled, "Perhaps not when you're sober, but after a couple of ciders who knows. And if you do pee on the seat I'll scrub it with your toothbrush"

Sean was aghast, "You wouldn't"

"Gonna try me."

Charlie smirked, "We'll agree to our own bachelor pads upstairs. I think there will be enough room on that landing area to have a games console and screen. And up here we can be as slobby as we like and missy prissy can keep down here as clean as she wants."

Sean saw Lucy pained look and butted in, "We're not slobs. We'll keep the living room clean and tidy. Promise. We'll try not to leave smelly socks lying around, won't we Charlie?"

"Of course, I'm just teasing about our cleanliness. My Mum would kill me if she thought I would live like a slob. She would say," Charlie put his hands on his hips and spoke with a Jamaican accent 'Charles Adams. I have brought you up good to be a God fearing boy who helps with the chores. Not a slob who lounges around all day. Nh nh no sir, now get up them stairs and clean the place.'"

Lucy and Sean burst out laughing. They had met Charlies Mum and his impression was spot on.

"I suggest some sort of rota for different things that will need to be done, like the bins and things." Sean said, "That's what we did at the place I'm staying in now and it seems to work most of the time. Agreed?"

The others nodded, "Agreed."

Lucy said, "Come, let's go and speak with Joy."

The walked down the stairs and re-joined Jocelyn.

"Everything Okay?" Jocelyn asked.

"It's great Joy." Lucy spoke as the others nodded, "We would like for it to be furnished, but the chairs in the living room are okay."

"No problem. Sean, when do you need to leave your place?"

"I have to be out before the first week of next month."

"I'll have something drawn up for Tuesday, but you can start on decorating as soon as I get some keys cut."

Sean asked, "Will you be buying the stuff for us or what?"

Jocelyn thought for a bit and replied, "I'll get all the kitchen stuff. Either

I can buy all the rest, or you can get your beds and I'll get the rest or you can get it all. Your choice but there will be a limit on what you can spend.

Charlie again asked, "Why are you doing this, helping us? Why do you want us to work for you? Why haven't you looked elsewhere for other people?"

"The three of you work so well together. And as you know by now, I have been relying heavily on you all, so why would I want to look elsewhere. I believe in rewarding loyalty. If you are loyal to me then it will be reciprocated many times over. We've run through all the trials and I've offered you full time jobs after your college course has finished. You all have really impressed me with your work ethic and why should I look elsewhere when you have ticked all the boxes. You have gained my trust on the work you have done for me. Trust is an important fact that I look for in people."

She paused for a moment, "We have potential customers ready to come on board. Now all I have to know is that if I can trust you implicitly. I think I already know the answer to that. The projects will require discretion. There is a chance that you will see financial details of our clients as well as some of our financial information. So I will need complete confidentiality from you all. I will need complete honesty."

She looked at their faces, "This is your opportunity to set yourselves up, the chance to prove yourselves in the real world. It will be a challenge. So you have to decide if you want to come along for the ride."

"For a start everyone deserves respect and kindness, both monetary and well-being. You have so far been loyal, trustworthy, hardworking, and good at your jobs. I like you all and I respect you all. The better you feel about working for me, the more energy you put into your work. The more energy you put in for me, the more is done. The more that is done the sooner our clients are pleased. The sooner our clients are pleased the bigger your bonus will be. The bigger the bonus the better you feel about for me. And so we go full circle."

She paused and looked closely at Charlie, and continued, "That is why I always try to respect my co-workers. I will always try to look after them. That is why I will always pay a decent wage. Something that will allow you to enjoy yourself outside work, there must be a balance between work and play. And talking about the work and play balance, let's go for a drink in the pub over the road."

ဢ

Chapter Six

Friday Afternoon

Lucy was putting the finishing touches to her penultimate assignment. She looked around the study centre and noticed only one other person. At the same time, the other person looked up and their eyes locked. Lucy immediately felt her hackles rise. The other person drummed nervous fingers on the surface of the desk and threw Lucy a cautious look.

Lucy took a deep breath and in her familiar fashion she blurted out, "Rose. Why did you go to see the Dean?"

"I haven't been to see the Dean. Why?" Rose stuttered.

"You know why." Lucy replied tersely,

"Why would I know why?" Rose frowned and looked away.

"Oh come on. What have you been doing the past week except tutting every time you walked past us in the canteen? You knew we were doing and made it obvious that you disapproved."

Rose sounded jealous as she said, "I might have tutted and yes, I didn't approve of where you were working but I thought it was a brilliant opportunity for you all."

Lucy shook her head, "You have a funny way of showing it. So it wasn't you who dobbed us in."

"Why would I dob you in?" she asked turning away in her seat.

"Because you were jealous and wanted us to fail." Lucy responded.

Exasperated, Rose replied, "Oh don't be so stupid."

Incredulously Lucy again shook her head and raised her voice, "Stupid. You're calling me stupid."

Rose shrank into herself, "No. I know you are not stupid, but the idea that I would go to the Dean is daft. Why would I do that? It definitely wasn't me."

"Humph" Lucy gave out a disbelieving noise.

She shook her head, "Honestly it wasn't me. But from your reaction you don't believe me."

"Humph"

Hands on hips Rose looked at Lucy and said, "I do actually know who it was."

"So who was it?"

"Don't know his name but he's on one of the engineering courses. I heard him in the canteen telling one of his mates that it wasn't right and he would report you all."

"So you don't know his name."

"Sorry I don't but I could point him out to you."

"Okay. Do that."

"Only if you don't let on it was me. I don't want any more hassle from anyone."

"Who's hassling you?"

"Everyone hassles me. But why should you care?"

"You don't have a very high opinion of me, do you?"

"What have you done for me to have any opinion of you?"

"I do care, you know. And if you get to know me better you will find that out." Lucy looked directly into Rose's eyes, "You must admit sometimes you are a bit full on. You butt into people's conversations and lecture them."

Silence followed for a few minutes. "It takes a lot for me to speak out and then to be ignored is rude. I deserve to be listened to as much as the next person."

"Agreed but listening to someone is different than being lectured to. A conversation is a two way process. We are having a conversation now."

"Yes and there are only two of us."

"All I'm saying is to think before you speak. Choose the battles you want to win; you will not win every one. Having different views and perspectives is what makes the world alive. Appropriately challenging the views and perspectives of others is part of what makes life interesting. Know when it is right to join in and when it is best to keep quiet. That's what I do."

"But you're really well liked. You have loads of friends. When you speak people listen."

"You've hit the nail on the head. You said when I speak. I listen more often than I speak, especially when in a larger group.

"People usually talk about me, judge me and criticise me. It is not very pleasant"

"When that happens it says far more about them than it ever says about you. Moreover, friendships, anyone can have friendships, but it is about those who are there when you need them. It can sometimes take years to have those types of friends, other times it can just happen. But remember this, be your own best friend, because some days that is all you'll have."

Rose felt that something special had happened between them. That someone had told her that her soul was good enough for them, and that the feeling was reciprocated. She felt a warm glow spread between them, filling them both with hope, and understanding for the future.

Rose thought on Lucy's words for a moment and then spoke, "Lucy, may I be candid."

"Be as candid as you like."

"I'm worried about you, Charlie and Sean?"

"Why are you worried? You've nothing to be worried about."

"Lucy, please. You know I would love to be doing what you're doing but I think you, Charlie and Sean are being taken advantage of."

"Why in the world do you think we are being taken advantage of?"

"Oh come on. When you are not doing college stuff you are forever working."

Lucy raised her eyebrows, "And the problem with that is?"

"I think your girlfriend is asking too much."

Lucy burst out into an uncontrollable fit of the giggles. When she had control she asked, "What did you just say?"

In a huff she said, "I said, I think your girlfriend is asking too much."

"That's what I thought you said. Not that it is any of your business but Joy is not my girlfriend." A smile continued to play across her face.

"Thank goodness for that 'cos she is much too old for you. She could be your mother."

Laughing, Lucy said, "I told her that when I first met her. She'll love you when I tell her what you said." Another fit of giggles overtook her.

"Well, she could be. So what is the deal between the two of you?"

"Again none of your business but Joy is my sponsor." Lucy studied Rose and decided to open up to her. "She befriended me when I had nothing or no-one. She gave me a roof over my head and she is sponsoring me through college. In exchange, I give her fifteen hours of my time. For which, by the way, I also am paid handsomely. If I work anymore, I have to run it past her first. She always makes sure my college work gets done before anything else."

Rose leant toward Lucy, taking in all she was told, "I agree. Your college assignments and getting your qualifications should take precedent over everything."

Nodding her head Lucy continued, "I realised Joy wanted and needed more to be done and that there was way too much for me to do alone, and some aspects others were more qualified to complete, that's when Charlie and Sean got involved."

"Okay. My mistake." accepting Lucy's words. "If that is true then you are not being taken advantage of. She sounds like a good person to have as a boss and as a friend." Quietly she said almost to herself, "I'd love a friend like that."

Lucy only just heard what Rose had said. She studied Rose and it was as though she was seeing her for the first time. Rose began to shrink away from Lucy's gaze as though she was trying to make herself as small as possible.

"Why do you do that?"

"Do what."

"Shrink down. Make yourself look small."

"Do I?"

"Yes you do."

Rose shrugged and gave a shy smile. Lucy suddenly remembered Joy's words and decided to include Rose in her plans for tonight, saying. "A group of us are meeting up at the pub later on. Would you like to join us?"

Rose gasped, "You want me to go out for a drink with you all?" she shook her head, "The others won't want me around."

"I wouldn't have asked if I didn't want you to come and anyway it is up to me who I ask to join us. We're meeting in the pub behind the Hippodrome about half seven. Please come."

"I'll think about it."

"What are you doing for dinner?"

"Nothing planned. I was going to pick up an Indian on the way home."

"So instead of having a take-away why don't you join me for an Indian in Millennium Square? Then we can go to the pub after." She paused, "Well? What do you think?"

Rose set her mouth in a straight line as though she was weighing up her options, "I've got about ten minutes more work to do. After that, if you are sure, and only if you are sure, I'd love to join you for an Indian. I don't know about the drink though."

"Charlie, Sean and the others won't bite. Moreover, it will be good to have another girl in the crowd. They forget sometimes that I am a girl and I have to whack them when their comments get a little too lewd. Nevertheless, you don't have to make up your mind now. Let's have that Indian and you can walk to the pub with me. That way you'll have me to walk in with and will be able to leave whenever you want. So is that a yes."

Rose beamed, and took on a completely new persona, "Let me finish off here, then we'll be off."

ഽ

Chapter Seven

Friday Evening

They sat on a bench on Brandon Hill, just below the Cabot Tower; the place she sat on the day her Nan's will was read. To her it was a sad place but also it was one of the most joyous of places. Even though it was part of a public park, it felt as though a piece of her resided here, and it was here she felt like she had truly come home.

People of all shapes, sizes, and creed walked the paths of the oldest city park and climbed the tower. Huffing and puffing their way up the extremely steep hill. She tried to think back to bygone years when washing was hung on tenterhooks and laid out to dry on these steep slopes. She could imagine her Nan and her great friend Meg sitting here in the aftermath of the war and having all their hopes and dreams stretching out before them.

Jocelyn loved to while away the time sitting and watching, making up stories for the different scenarios that played out in front of her. Her attention was suddenly taken by shrieks of children's laughter. Looking down the hill she saw two young mothers sitting together whilst their offspring played on the swings in the fenced off playground.

She turned her head and placed a kiss on Trina's forehead, "You mean the world to me." she said and pulled Trina into a closer embrace. "Your Cathy would love it here, playing on the swings, and rolling down the hill. She is becoming quite a little tom boy."

Trina gave out a deep sigh, which contained a smile. "That she would and Peter would be urging us to climb the tower."

Jocelyn asked, "Do you want to climb the one hundred or so steps up to the top of the tower? Or are you content to sit here?"

Trina looked towards the tower and replied, "I haven't been up there for years, and yes I would love to do it again, even if my knees and thighs would protest. But can we wait and let the kids come with us."

"Of course. I love your kids, but I'm really enjoying spending the time with you, just the two of us. So I can kiss and cuddle with no interruptions."

Jocelyn tried to give Trina a kiss, but before Jocelyn had the chance, Trina abruptly sat up and pointed. "Look. Balloons."

Jocelyn turned to where Trina was pointing and saw four balloons of different shapes and sizes rise from the grounds of Ashton Court and begin to float high above the trees. As the one that looked like a beer can, floated nearer, Jocelyn and Trina heard the gentle whoosh as the burners heated the air in the balloon. They looked up and could make out a group of people waving to anyone looking. They waved back as the balloon's peaceful journey continued eastward.

"They are like gentle giants, but I don't think I would like a trip in one. I'd be worried about the landing." Trina owned up.

"I'm the opposite. One of these days I'll do it." Jocelyn replied.

"You'll have to see if there is any room during the Summer Balloon Fiesta. Do you want me to see if there are any places left? I could get it for your birthday that's coming up."

"You've remembered it's my birthday. I didn't think you would." Jocelyn challenged. "And if I'm going to go up in a balloon then you'll have to do it with me."

"We'll see. And the date of your birthday is etched on my brain. You kept on telling me when it was and made me remember it all the time we were growing up. I bet you can't remember mine?" Trina replied.

"I know it is sometime in September cos you were always the oldest in our year group and I was one of the youngest."

"You are correct, it is September 23rd. Anyway going back to this balloon flight, I'll look on the website for availability. I'm sure Lucy would love to do it with you."

"Scaredy cat."

"I'd rather be a scaredy cat than be frightened to death. No. Get Lucy to go up with you if I can arrange it. Me and the kids will wave from the ground and take pictures."

"I love you," said Jocelyn as she pulled Trina into another warm embrace.

"I know." Trina got to her feet and pulled Jocelyn with her. "So shall we go and have that early dinner and a bottle of wine. Then we can go and have that early night we deserve. There's a great Italian on Park Street."

Jocelyn grinned, "Lead on MacDuff."

ꟹ

As they left the restaurant, darkness had fallen. The dreariness of the day had turned into a crisp cloudless night. The clear sky twinkled, and the city lights allowed only the brightest of stars to shine through. The moon started to appear over the tops of buildings. They walked down Park Street arm in arm, laughing at inane comments. The pulse of the city seemed to beat there and accompanied them during their short walk down the hill. As they approached College Green, Trina stopped and searched the sky.

"What are you looking for?" Jocelyn asked.

"For Orion's belt. On a clear night, Mum and I always looked at the stars. I don't know many of the constellations but I can recognise Orion."

"Come on let's sit down and search. I can usually find Cassiopeia, the W, and Ursa Major, the big dipper."

They sat down on a nearby bench, tilted their heads back, and started examining the sky.

Jocelyn was the first to speak, "There's Cassiopeia. Can you see it?"

"No."

Jocelyn stood up and walked behind her. She placed her arm over Trina's shoulder and pointed, drawing out the W.

"Oh yes. There it is."

Jocelyn draped both her arms around her and kissed her affectionately on the cheek. Trina looked over her shoulder and smiled tenderly. She glanced back up at the sky and said, pointing, "There's Orion. You can just make out the belt. I don't think it is dark enough yet to see the other stars clearly."

Jocelyn went back and sat next to Trina, "Give it half an hour and it will be."

They sat, drinking in the sights and sounds of the city, in companionable silence. Gradually the night became darker and other bright stars could be seen. Trina got out her phone and googled the night sky, and they spent time trying to find the constellations, wrapped in each other's arms, gazing skywards.

Trina sighed and said, "I think the city lights are hampering us. I'm giving up. We'll have to go out into the countryside to see the sky clearly."

"Let's do it. We'll take the kids away for a weekend. Then we can all gaze at the stars together. Somewhere like the Forest of Dean, not too far but away from the bright lights." Jocelyn nodded.

"Okay." replied Trina.

"I remember camping there with guides and being able to see the Milky Way. It had an amazing effect on me. I began to think that there must be something or someone else out there. We can't be the only planet with intelligent life form, surely?"

"I wouldn't say that everyone on this planet is intelligent. Look at you." she laughed loudly.

"Oh ha ha. Very funny. But don't you ever think about it?"

"I can't say I have, but if all the stars are suns and each sun has planets orbiting around then there must be billions and billions of planets out there so the chances that life will arise on one of them is not really so remarkable."

"That's what I think as well."

Trina gave a slight shiver.

"Are you cold?" Jocelyn asked.

"Not really, but I think we need to move."

Jocelyn got up and asked, "Do you want to a drink first or go straight back to mine?"

"Let's have a wander around the harbour-side instead. It's not often I get to walk around at night time. There might be something going on in the square, and then it'll be back to yours and spend some quality time together."

"Sounds like a plan."

Both women jumped and Trina said, "You're either vibrating or you have a text."

Jocelyn shrugged.

"Are you going to look at it?"

"It won't be anything important."

"You'll never know until you look."

Jocelyn stood up and took her phone out of her pocket. A smile spread over her face, she shouted "Yes." And picked Trina up and spun her around.

"So it was good news. Now put me down before I become dizzy." Trina laughed.

ஐ

Chapter Eight

Friday Night

"Hi guys." Lucy plonked herself down on a seat next to Charlie, opposite Sean, Mo, Jake and Gabe. She spoke to Sean and Carlie, "Rose is joining us. Okay?"

They all looked at each other. Charlie said, "If that's what you want."

"It is."

They sat in silence for a few moments until Lucy spoke, "It wasn't Rose who complained to the Dean."

"And you know this because..." Sean left the question hanging as he pushed his glasses back up his nose.

"Because I asked her."

"So she lied to you." Charlie stated bluntly.

"No. I believe her. She was told that it was someone on the engineering course."

Out of the corner of her eye, she saw Gabe shift in his seat. She looked towards him as he turned his head away.

Rose came over to them carrying two pints placed them on the table and sat next to Lucy. "Hi all." She said looking around at all of them. She let out a gasp. Trying to mask the gasp, she picked up her pint and said, "Cheers."

They raised their glasses in response.

Lucy leant in and spoke into her ear, "What's the problem?"

"Nothing. Okay."

A tune suddenly blared out through the speakers, making small talk for the next few minutes impossible. Some people in the room shouted out, "Turn it down." The barman found the volume control and apologised.

Lucy again leaned in to Rose and said quietly, "Come with me to the ladies." and because Rose suddenly stiffened and worry flashed across her face Lucy said, "I think you have something to tell me. But you don't want to speak here. Is that correct?"

Rose nodded.

Lucy said, "Excuse me boys but nature calls."

"I'll come with you. I don't know where the loos are in this pub."

Charlie laughed, "That's a lame excuse if you ask me."

"Ha ha." Lucy replied giving Charlie a withering look.

They found their way to the loos and Lucy asked Rose, "What was the gasp for?"

"I didn't gasp."

Giving Rose a disbelieving look said, "You gasped and Gabe looked shifty. So what is going on between the two of you?"

"Gabe? Is that the one in the denim or checked shirt?"

"Denim, as well you know."

Shaking her head, "I didn't know that was his name."

Lucy waited.

"The one in the Denim shirt, who you called Gabe, is the one I heard talking to the one in the checked shirt in the canteen. You know. The one who said he would complain to the Dean."

Lucy raised her eyebrows, and said, incredulously, "Are you sure?"

"Don't you believe me? I knew this was a bad idea." Rose tried to move past Lucy.

"Wait." Lucy took hold of Rose's arm. "I do believe you. It's just that we've been going out drinking with Gabe and Mo for the past six months."

"Don't do anything or say anything please. I don't want any hassle," pleaded Rose.

Still holding onto Rose's arm she agreed, "I won't do or say anything to hurt you."

"But you've already told them it was me."

"I think you listened to my words but didn't hear what I said. You were too far away to hear the whole sentence. I said, 'you were told that it was someone on the engineering course'."

"Oh! Okay."

"So let me get this straight. You heard denim shirted Gabe say to checked shirted Mo that he was going to complain to the Dean."

"Correct."

Lucy thought for a while and said, "Don't worry. I won't do or say anything tonight. Let's go back out there and enjoy our evening."

"Okay. But whilst we are here I might as well go."

Lucy laughed, "Yeah might be a good idea."

When they got back to their table, Gabe was missing.

Lucy asked, "Where's Gabe. I thought he was out for the duration?"

Mo replied, "He suddenly remembered he promised to meet someone else. He told me to say goodbye."

Lucy shrugged.

Charlie nudged Lucy, "You were gone a long time. Good was it?"

Rose turned bright red and Lucy walloped him, laughed, and said, "You have no idea. Eh Rose? What makes you think there wasn't a long queue?"

"Oh puhlease. Count how many women are in here?"

"Charlie," Rose found her voice, "I don't like what you are insinuating. Do not start rumours about Lucy, or about me. It doesn't become you." She sat back and folded her arms across her chest.

Lucy burst out laughing, "That told you." As the others joined in the laughing.

"We were having a girlie chat. That is why we were so long. Would you rather we talked about women's things with you."

"Good grief no." Jake said, "Lucy puts up with all our macho chat. So if she wants some girlie time then so be it." He continued, "I know I would rather you talk about girlie things in the loos rather than out here with us."

Mo stood up. "On that note I'm off. See you all on Monday."

Jake downed his pint and stood as well, "I'll be going as well. See you."

Lucy waited until Mo and Jake had left, and spoke, "Rose didn't complain to the Dean. It was Gabe."

"Gabe?" The two men stuttered, "Why Gabe?"

"I have no idea, but I will find out. Didn't you see him squirm when I said it was someone from engineering? It wasn't until Rose came over did the penny drop. He left pretty quickly after we arrived."

"I can't see it myself. He always comes out for drinks with us." Charlie frowned.

Sean piped up, "Do you think he was jealous of us. You have me thinking. How many times has he bought you a drink?"

Charlie replied, "I'll stand anyone a drink."

"So will I." agreed Lucy.

"And me, but he is always the last to go to the bar. Always finds an excuse to leave early. Don't you think it odd?"

Rose lifted her hand, "May I say something?"

"It's never stopped you in the past." Charlie stated.

Lucy gave Charlie a glare. He shrugged.

"Gabe and Mo were in the canteen queue a couple of days ago. I didn't know them from Adam. All I knew was that they were both on the engineering course. I overheard them both slagging you off Charlie. I made a note of their faces so I would know them again, because it wasn't right what they were saying."

"So what were they saying and what made you jump to the conclusion that it was Gabe who was the culprit?"

"They were moaning about something that happened at a club you went to last weekend. The conversation ended when Gabe told Mo that he was going to the Dean and that was the last time you were going to act superior to him."

"Sounds like the sort of thing he would say." Sean said, nodding.

"I didn't go out with you guys last weekend. I was getting the flat clean and tidy for Jocelyn's return. What happened? Where did you all go?" asked Lucy.

Charlie took up the story, "We all were going to ST4RZ but Gabe started being a plonker in the queue and annoying a couple of girls in front of us. I think he had already had plenty to drink before we all met up. We kept on telling him to stop but he crossed the line. The girls told the bouncers and they wouldn't let him in. Sean and I told him that he wasn't going to spoil our night by his stupid behaviour so we went in without him."

Sean resumed, "When we saw him on Tuesday he didn't mention it. We all continued as though nothing had happened."

Lucy began to get angry, "I will ask Gabe why he did it, and whether Mo knew anything. It's a good job we had finished what we had needed to do. I don't particularly want to drink with him again if he did that. You don't do that to your friends, no matter why."

"If it's true," said Sean, reasonably, "and I always think innocent until proven guilty, but thank you Rose."

"But you have to admit that it is a bit of a coincidence." Lucy's tone had calmed down, but she forced her point, "You and Gabe having a disagreement and then the Dean finding out. If it was Rose, then why wait until we were almost finished.

"Because Rose wanted to be bloody minded." Charlie looked pointedly at Rose.

Rose shook her head, "Not true."

Ignoring her, Lucy pressed, "What has Rose to gain from this?"

"She's out with us. That's a first." Charlie replied quickly

Rose lowered her chin and gave a smile that Lucy had come to appreciate in such a short while. And with that quick all or nothing manner which Lucy had also come to admire, Rose said, "I am here, you know. But let me state my case. When the course finishes next month I'm looking at going into computer graphics. Mainly logo design and taglines. I have three months' work experience lined up, and if at the end I have impressed, then there is a post waiting for me. So Charlie, apart from sabotage, which I could have done months ago, why would I suddenly get involved? I have nothing to gain. You decide whether I'm guilty or not. Go and ask the Dean if you want. That would be the quickest way to find out."

Rose leant back and again folded her arms across her chest.

Sean responded by agreeing, "She's got a point. She could have complained months ago. The whole course knew what we were doing. We asked them all to help us and she was one of the first to offer."

"Okay, I'll concede, but there is still the nagging doubt."

Rose looked directly into Charlie's eyes and said, "Charlie, I know that you doubt me. I understand that. I know you don't really like me. But that is fine as well. I am not going to change for anyone. I am me and if you don't like it then tough." She finished her pint and nodded towards the bar. "Want another one? Lucy, Charlie, Sean. Is it two lagers and a cider?"

They nodded, and Rose walked towards the bar.

"Well you're a dark horse." Charlie smiled.

"What do you mean?" Lucy asked.

Charlie prodded, "How long have the two of you been seeing each other."

Lucy gave a deep breath, "We're not."

"Doesn't look that way. You are both sitting way to close to each other." Charlie teased.

"Honestly. There is nothing going on. Today was the first time we had a proper conversation." Lucy huffed.

Sean butted in, "You know she's gay?"

"Nah. She's not. You're mistaken. My gaydar would have picked it up months ago."

"I bet you she is." Charlie reached for his wallet.

"Okay. A fiver."

They both got out a five pound note and passed them to Sean.

Lucy smiled, "I'll ask her when she gets back. It'll be good to get another one over you?"

"Don't be so sure. I can't wait to wipe the smug smile off your face."

Sean laughed. He loved how they bounced off each other. He felt blessed to be part of the friendship. "Changing the subject, are we going to start the decorating of our flat tomorrow. If so, how are we going to get the paint there and what time shall we meet.

Charlie replied, "Mum said I can borrow the car for us to get to the DIY store and bring it over to the flat. I have to get the car back by two, as she is going to see my aunt."

Sean said, "I'll meet you there as it's easy for me to get there."

"Okay." Charlie nodded, "Lucy, I'll pick you up from the car park outside your place about half ten."

"Will you be up by then?" she laughed, "That's a Saturday morning, especially after a few sherberts tonight."

"Don't worry about me. I'm an early bird as well as a night owl. Sean, is that sort of time alright for you?"

Sean shrugged, "It will have to be."

"Joy said she was getting some keys cut today. Otherwise, I'll see if I can borrow hers. Talking about Joy, have you both decided whether to take up her offer of work?" Lucy asked, and then laughingly continued, "I've repeatedly told her she can't get rid of me."

Sean answered quickly, "I had a chat with Mum and Dad on the phone last night and they told me to go for it. I'll tell Joy tomorrow."

"Charlie? And you?"

"Of course, I can't break up the three amigos." He was smiling, fit to burst, "Come on, let's tell her now."

Lucy quickly sent a text, telling Jocelyn the good news. After a little while, her phoned pinged as she received one back welcoming them to the company. All three of them stood up and as Rose came back, they were all hugging and laughing. "Why are you having a group hug?"

"Celebrating getting a proper job when leave college. Joy offered us all full time work and we've all just agreed."

"Congratulations. That's worth a celebration." Rose picked up her pint and said, "Cheers." She raised her glass and toasted, "To you all, and your venture into the world of work."

They clinked glasses, "To us." And they all drunk a large amount of their pints

Lucy put her drink down and looked intently at Rose.

"What?" Rose asked. She rubbed her hand over her face and then looked at both hands, then down at her clothes. "What's wrong?"

Sean smirked and said, "Nothing's wrong. Honest."

"Then why is Lucy looking at me strangely?"

"Because she has to ask you a question." Charlie laughed.

Lucy took a deep breath and asked, "Can I be candid with you, like you were candid with me?"

"Sure. What's on your mind?" replied Rose.

"Well it's like this." She paused, "We were wondering."

Charlie coughed.

"I was wondering."

"Oh for goodness sake. Spit it out." Rose said annoyed.

Lucy stroked her chin with her fingers, "Umm. Well."

Charlie butted in, "Come on Luce. We're waiting." He turned to Rose and said, "Lucy won't believe that you are gay and she is trying to ask you whether you are."

Lucy smiled and asked simply, "Well are you?"

"Am I what?"

Lucy rolled her eyes, "Rose, are you gay?"

"Yes. I thought everyone knew. I haven't hidden it."

"Pass the cash, Sean," laughed Charlie. He turned to Lucy and said, "Told you."

Sean handed over the two fivers.

"That was naughty of you." Rose said and then sat open mouthed. She shook her head and continued, "You've taken a fiver off Lucy. How could you?"

"Lucy, everyone found out that I was gay when I had a massive argument with my girlfriend outside college. How come you didn't hear about it?"

"Was it last November?" Lucy thought back to the days and weeks she found herself sleeping on the streets, before Jocelyn had befriended her and turned her life around. Jocelyn had sponsored Lucy, which allowed her to get back into college, to continue her studies and get her where she is today.

Rose thought for a moment and replied, "I think it might have been."

Charlie was one of the few people who knew about her dark days, "You pig." Lucy walloped him on the arm. "You knew I wouldn't know. I'll get you back." She nodded, "And you know I will?"

Charlie tipped his head back and laughed his rich laugh. His baritone voice filled the air, "I know you will. But I couldn't resist. Your gaydar is usually spot on but you were so way off. I've been waiting months for this opportunity." Again, he burst out laughing, and soon they were all joining in.

Lucy asked of Rose, "So are you still seeing her?"

"Nah" Rose scoffed, "I haven't been with anyone since that day."

Sean gave Charlie a knowing look. As they were getting towards the bottom of their pints Charlie spoke, "Sean and I are going to ST4RS. Are you both going to join us?"

Lucy replied, "It's about time the two of you got hooked up with some lovely ladies. They usually think I'm your girlfriend and I don't want to cramp your style any longer."

Rose looked at Lucy and asked, "Do you fancy coming to Fairies with me for a few drinks?"

Lucy felt Sean give her a nudge under the table. He raised his eyebrows, and gave a slight nod towards Rose. Lucy gave a sigh and gave a small shake of her head.

Charlie butted in, "Go on Luce. Go and enjoy yourself. You can't live like a nun forever."

"Since when have you been my dating agent?"

"I wouldn't dare. But you've never been to a gay pub in all the time I've known you. I just think it's about time you did. And what better way than to go with your new friend." Charlie laughed again.

"Is he always like this?" Rose asked of Lucy.

Lucy nodded, "Always and if you are going to come out with us more you'll have to get used to it."

"So?" Rose smiled, and asked, "Are you going to come to Fairies with me?"

"I might if I knew where it was." Lucy said.

Rose frowned, "You know, The Lord Fairfax."

Lucy shook her head. Sean laughed, and said, "Even I know where Fairies is. You really are out of the loop aren't you? That's hanging around with us too much."

"It's around the back of the City Hall, so not too far from here. Well?" Rose looked questioningly.

"Okay. Okay. If it gets the two of them off my back. But only for one."

ഗ

Chapter Nine

Saturday

Trina wondered if Joy ever watched her as she slept, as she was watching Jocelyn now. This idea she found enticing and was greeted with a fluttering in her stomach. She allowed her smile to deepen. Pressure built behind her breastbone. For this single moment in time, she was truly happy. There had been too few times in her life when she could completely surrender to pleasure.

She sighed and settled back into the pillow, leaning on an elbow keeping Joy in her sights. A peaceful expression lay on Joy's features, her breath came out in a steady rhythm, a smile started to play on her lips. She was a woman with a backbone of steel and ethics to match. Someone who had had disappointments and grief but they hadn't broken her, Jocelyn had never given up and she fought back from any adversity with everything she had. Jocelyn was exactly the person she was looking for and felt blessed that Joy had chosen her to share her life.

Trina looked at her watch and was surprised to find that it was only six o'clock. She felt a headache beginning to form and not wanting it to spoil her day she decided to take a remedy. She quietly got out of bed, wrapped a robe around her, and padded silently to the kitchen area. She poured herself some water and downed a couple of tablets. As she leant against the sink, she heard fumbling at the door. Trina picked up the bottle of wine that was standing on the counter top. In her other hand she picked up a fork that was lying around. She made her way towards the door, lifted the bottle over her head, and held out the fork.

The door suddenly flew open and a figure staggered forward, cursing.

"Oh it's you." Trina let out her breath that she didn't know she had been holding.

Lucy quickly said, "Bloody hell. You frightened me to death." She burst out laughing, as she looked at what Trina was holding. "So what were you going to do? Eat me and wash me down with a nice Chianti?" She slurped in, mimicking Anthony Hopkins.

Trina laughed as well. She placed the objects back on the counter and said, "It was all that was to hand."

Continuing to shake her head, incredulously, Lucy started to frown and asked, "Why are you up so early?"

"I could say the same about you."

"You first."

"I woke up with a bit of a headache so I have taken some tablets. And you, why are you up so early or should that be, why are you up so late?"

Lucy cringed a little, "Well I actually fell asleep on a friend's settee."

Frowning, Trina stated, "You don't usually stay over at Sean's. He lives too far out. And how would you get back from there at this time in the morning?"

"Not Sean's."

"I thought Charlie lived with his parents."

"He does. And it wasn't his settee."

Trina clapped her hands together, smiling, "You've got yourself a girlfriend."

Lucy put her hands on her hips and rolled her eyes, "No, just a friend."

Trina continued as though Lucy hadn't spoken and said, "Come on. Tell me all about her. Where did you meet her? What's her name?"

"She is not my girlfriend." Lucy emphasised.

"So it is a she." She continued to clap her hands together, "You stayed overnight in a woman's pad. Brilliant. So pleased for you." she gave Lucy a big hug.

Jocelyn, yawning, came into the room, pulling down an extra-large T-shirt. "I thought I heard voices."

"Lucy's got a girlfriend. Moreover, she was about to tell me all about her. I'll make us all some coffee and then Lucy can spill the beans." Trina switched the kettle on and proceeded to put granules into three mugs.

Lucy let out a deep sigh and shook her head again, "She's not my girlfriend. How many more times have I got to tell you?"

"It's milk, no sugar, isn't it?" Trina asked, again ignoring Lucy's protestations.

Jocelyn laughed, "You're not going to win this discussion Luce. So you might as well tell her what she wants to know. The sooner you tell her the quicker you will get to bed. And the quicker we will as well." She smiled seductively at Trina.

Lucy again sighed, this time in resignation.

Jocelyn settled down on the settee and said, "Anyway I want to know all about her as well." She turned towards Trina, "Is that coffee ready yet. You know I can't concentrate until I've had my java and I think I'll need to concentrate for this."

"This isn't fair Joy. The two of you joining forces against me. Anyway it's not as you think."

Both Trina and Jocelyn looked at each other and raised their eyebrows. Jocelyn piped up, "Whatever you say."

"Okay. Okay. I give up. I'll tell you but it's quite boring really." Lucy plonked herself down in the beanbag and moulded it into her body.

Trina brought the cups of coffee over, set them down on the coffee table, settled next to Jocelyn, and pulling her feet under herself, snuggled in as Jocelyn wrapped a protective arm around her shoulders. They both took a sip of their scalding hot coffee and looked at Lucy expectantly.

"I finished my college work that needed to be done, found out who dobbed us in to the Dean, had a quick Indian, them met the others in the pub, went to Fairies and fell asleep on a sofa in a flat not too far from here." Lucy went to pick up her drink and continued, "See I told you it was boring."

"Not good enough." Trina smiled and shook her head, "We want all the gory details. Now what is your girlfriends' name?"

"Her name is Rose and she is not my girlfriend."

Jocelyn laughed quietly at Lucy's annoyed look. "So her name is Rose. Where did you meet this Rose?" she asked, trying to keep a smirk off her face. "I've never heard you mention her before."

"Joy. I told you about her a couple of days ago. She's the one I thought had complained to the Dean."

"Oh. And had she?"

Lucy went on to explain what had happened in the study centre and early evening in the pub. The two women listened intently but interrupted Lucy with questions and innuendo.

"So you and Rose went to Fairies?" asked Trina.

Jocelyn butted in, "Where is Fairies?"

Trina looked at Jocelyn strangely, "You don't know where it is?"

Lucy replied, "Don't worry Joy. I had no idea where it was either. You might know it as the Lord Fairfax, back of City Hall."

"Oh. I know it. Didn't know it was a gay pub. Well it wasn't back in the day. What is it like?"

"It's not bad. Sells drink, a bit of music. What more could one want."

"We could try it out tonight," Trina said to Joy, "as Mike still has the children."

"Sounds like a plan." nodded Jocelyn.

Lucy yawned and began to stand.

Trina put a hand on her leg. "No you don't lady. You still haven't told us what happened between going to the pub and getting home."

Lucy rolled her eyes. "Okay. After we left Charlie and Sean, we walked to Fairies. The place was buzzing so we had a couple of drinks. The time flew by and knowing that I was meeting Charlie and Sean at ten this morning." She looked at Jocelyn, "You have had some keys cut, haven't you?"

"Yes there are three sets in the bowl over there."

"Thank you."

"And?" Trina butted in. "Stop drawing the story out and tell me about your night with your new girlfriend."

"She's not my girlfriend," repeated Lucy.

"If you want her to stop teasing you then just ignore her. That's what I usually do. Ow. What was that for?" Jocelyn protested as Trina swatted her with a cushion.

Lucy laughed at their antics but continued, "I asked Rose where she lived and she lives with her parents in that old block of flats by the roundabout, so we walked along Anchor Road together. We were just getting to the awkward moment when we were going to have to say goodbye when she explained that her parents were away. She still lives at home by the way, and she didn't like going into the flat by herself. So gallant me offered to see her to her door."

Jocelyn smirked and said, "Oh yeah. That's a new one." and ducked as another cushion flew her way.

Ignoring the comment Lucy continued, "As we got to the door Rose asked me in for a coffee. So I went in. And before you start smirking between you, nothing happened. She asked me to take my shoes off as her parents had just had a new carpet laid."

"Which place did she use? Did they do a good job?" Jocelyn asked.

Lucy shook her head, "I'll ask her, and to my untrained eye they did."

Trina looked exasperated, "Look the pair of you. Luce, get on with the story and Joy, stop butting in."

Jocelyn and Lucy gave each other a smirk and Lucy continued, "So I kicked my shoes off in the hall and plonked myself down on the sofa. Well you know me. I like to make myself at home, so I lifted my feet up and kind of spread out. I remember Rose shouting from the kitchen if I wanted milk and sugar." Lucy gave a quiet giggle, "then the next thing I knew I was waking up underneath one of those snuggle blankets and a stone cold cup of coffee on the little table in front of me. So what was I to do? I looked at my watch and it was about ten to six. So I looked around for a piece of paper, scribbled a note of apology and my number, and said I would phone her later. I tiptoed out of the flat and made my way back here.

"So nothing happened, apart from you falling asleep on your girlfriend." Lucy gave her a look, as Trina continued. "Or should I say host?" Trina sounded disappointed.

"No nothing happened. And I'll have to make it up to her. I'll give her a ring when it's a more reasonable time."

"So you have her number?" Jocelyn asked.

"I have everyone's number. And I won't disturb her now with a text."

Lucy replied, and then chuckled, "Anyway I have to recover from being greeted by a mad woman brandishing a fork and a bottle of wine."

Jocelyn looked at the two of them frowning, "I don't understand."

"I thought we were about to be robbed. So I picked up the only two things at hand, that I thought I could do damage with."

Jocelyn burst out laughing.

"And if I would have been an intruder I was more likely to laugh than be frightened away."

Trina huffed, but smirked at the same time, saying, "It was better than nothing."

"True. But I've got to get to my bed." She glanced at her watch. "I've another three hours before Charlie is coming to pick me up."

"What are you planning to do?" Jocelyn asked.

"Charlie is borrowing his Mum's car; we are meeting Sean and going to the DIY shop get some paint. We might make a start later on. That's why I wanted to know if you had the keys cut, otherwise I would have asked to borrow yours."

"I've picked up some catalogues which I'll leave out so you all can have a look through. See if anything takes your fancy furniture wise."

"Okay. Catch you both later." Lucy replied as she went to her bedroom.

Jocelyn sighed and looked lovingly towards Trina, and said, "She's getting better with the teasing and opening up. One day I hope all the pent up hurt and distrust will go, and she will be able to become the truly loving person she is."

"When that happens it will be down, in no small way, to the nurturing you have given her. You have allowed her to develop a good, honest caring young woman. She is no longer rebelling against all and sundry."

"I just gave her a helping hand along the way, by setting her on a path which was right for her. She had the will to succeed and be different from the life her Mother had chosen. At some point in everyone's life a choice has to be made."

"And on that point, I choose that we go back to bed and make the most of our time together."

ထ

Chapter Ten

Monday

Lucy gazed into the eyes of the woman sat a few seats from her. She had enjoyed spending time with her on Friday night. She was glad that Rose had taken her phone call on Saturday morning and accepted her apologies for falling asleep. Lucy smiled and she saw tenderness, empathy, deep interest and a steady personality in the face that looked back. The wavy hair made her want to touch it, to wind her fingers through it, to draw the head closer to kiss; to smell the delicate scent emanating from it.

Rose seemed to have substance and no matter what she told herself, she really did seem to be the total package. Her lips did a slow slide into a crooked smile, her shyness making her unsure that she should. Rose hardly looked anyone in the eyes. She needed someone to believe in her to allow her confidence to grow and with it her ability to grow into society and allow her talents to shine through. It was as though her shyness was holding back her artistic ability.

A classmate asked Rose a question. When Rose spoke, her hands moved in unison, as if her words alone didn't portray their full meaning. Lucy smiled at her. Rose nodded an acknowledgement, giving her a mischievous grin. It was a new look and a look that sent her nerves tingling.

Lucy looked back to the computer screen, reminded herself that she had work to complete and Rose was not a distraction she needed. A while later Rose walked behind her and squinted at her screen and, as an afterthought, she remembered her reading glasses tucked into her shirt. She shrugged and rubbed her eyes with the heels of her hands in that now familiar way of hers and replaced her glasses on her nose.

"Everything going well?" Rose asked.

"Yes. It's looking good." Lucy felt flustered.

"Anything I can help you with." Rose placed a hand on Lucy's shoulder.

Lucy shook her head, "No. Not at the moment."

Rose gave her shoulder a slight squeeze. Lucy shook her head again. She couldn't stop the way she was beginning to feel. She needed to go, and go quickly before she did anything she would regret and humiliate herself. Lucy knew that Rose would find her lacking in more ways than she wanted to think about. She tried to deal with the situation in the best way she knew how. Lucy suddenly felt nervous in her company and tongue-tied. She wanted to start a conversation but instead she shut down her computer and said, "I'm off now. I'll catch you later."

Lucy had noticed the grin on Charlie's face and wasn't too sure she liked the smile. As if he knew something that Lucy didn't. Lucy pondered the look, and thought if Charlie thinks that there is something going on, something of a romantic nature then he is wrong very wrong. Lucy had no wish to get involved with anyone again. Being burnt once and taking a beating for it was enough for her. She thought back to that evening when she ended up in hospital. She was shaken from her reverie when Rose spoke again.

"Pardon." Lucy said, missing the words.

"I said don't go. Not yet."

Her presence made Lucy flustered and she stopped in her tracks.

"Have I done something to upset you?" Rose asked with unease.

Charlie butted in. "Lucy wants to ask you out for a drink but is too frightened to ask you herself."

Lucy gave Charlie a look, as Rose stared at Lucy.

Lucy cleared her throat and asked, "Well will you? Will you go out for a drink tonight?"

"I would love to. I was going to ask you myself, but you've been giving out strange vibes all morning and this afternoon session."

Lucy was stunned by this assertion. "I think I'm feeling a little embarrassed after falling asleep on your settee."

"Nothing to be embarrassed about. You looked tired in the pub. I'm sorry I persuaded you to come in. So, are we going for this drink straight from college or later on?"

"We, that is, Sean, Charlie, and myself, are going to do some more decorating on our new place whilst the light's good. We could meet up in the pub opposite."

"Or I could come and help. I'm good at stripping wallpaper, or painting emulsion on walls, or gloss on skirting boards."

"Here's the address." She scribbled down the address on some paper and handed it to her. "It's up to you. Alternatively, I'll ring you when I'm finishing off. Don't worry; it will be only the two of us in the pub. I'll make sure Charlie and Sean leave us alone, so we can have a chat."

ꟃ

They walked back towards their respective homes, arm in arm, and chatted amiably. The evening had passed by quickly as they worked on the living room of the flat, then relaxed in the pub later. Walking past a recessed doorway Rose pulled Lucy into an embrace, and as their lips met, a shudder flowed through them.

Moments later, as they took a breath from what had happened, Lucy pulled away from the embrace. She faltered at the twinkle that came into the eyes looking at her. A surprised look came over both their faces at what had passed between them.

"You okay with this?" Rose asked, concerned.

"I liked it."

Rose smoothed a rogue strand of hair away from Lucy's face with her fingertips.

"Good. So did I." her voice melted through the shadows of the night, with the sounds of the passing traffic.

Rose saw the buried vulnerability in the depths of Lucy's eyes, half hidden behind a brave front. She pulled Lucy into a comforting hug. Rose leant in for another kiss but Lucy shook her head and gently pushed her away. A variety of emotions flashed across Lucy's face. "You are meant to be the shy one. The one who doesn't know how to say the correct words or how to react. Yet I'm the one feeling unsure and shy."

Rose smiled, "We are all complex people. I am shy in a group. I find it difficult in large social situations. That is why I'm full on. I try too hard to overcome my shyness. I also know that because of this, I annoy people. Like I used to annoy you."

Lucy was about to butt in but Rose wave away her protests.

"I'm not stupid. I saw the looks between you and Sean or you and Charlie. I know what you thought."

"I'm sorry. I didn't think."

"Most people don't. We are not all like you. We don't have the confidence to put it out there."

"I'm beginning to understand that now." An apologetic look was in her eyes as she continued, "I am truly sorry."

"Yet one on one, I'm fine. I don't get flustered if I get the words wrong, and I can laugh with the other person when I do. Don't forget there is always more to us than meet the eye." She held Lucy at arm's length, "For me, it is trying to be more comfortable around strangers. For you." She stopped and wondered whether she should continue.

Lucy studied Rose as a challenging look flitted across her face. "You were about to say?"

"Okay." Rose started to bite at the quick of her thumb. "You have to step out of your comfort zone and start to trust people, and I don't mean your close friends. I mean you have to spread your wings."

"Oh do I?"

"Yes. You can start right now." Rose leant in for another kiss.

Lucy shook her head, "I don't think I can do this."

"You just have." Rose looked at her and asked, "Why are you hiding from yourself?"

Her softly spoken words lingered in the air.

"I'm not. This is the real me."

"No the real you is the person I see every day at college. The person who knows what she wants and, overall, gets it. This isn't the real you. Shrinking away from any sort of emotional attachment."

"How dare you. You don't know me at all." Her voice rose, and ended in a shout. She batted Rose's hands away.

Rose continued in a quiet soothing tone, "I'm thinking you don't know yourself."

Lucy looked away. Her emotions bubbled under the surface. How could she tell Rose that she knew herself very well and that she was frightened to death to get close to anyone? That any hint of intimacy, of anything more than a kiss, that she would run a mile. Wasn't that the reason that the real reason Rachel had finished with her. She tried to believe that it was because of her circumstances, but was it that she was frightened of not being in control of her emotions, that showing emotions would be a sign of weakness. A weakness that she couldn't afford, if she were to survive the day to day struggle of everyday life.

Through gritted teeth Lucy replied, "And as I told you. You don't know me."

With a slight shake of the head, Rose continued, "I see the real you, the determined you, the funny you, the empathetic and caring you, the 'throw some more shit at me' you, but there is something that is making you scared of this, of us." She paused, "And I think there can be an us."

Lucy closed her eyes and breathed in a deep sigh, "It's complicated." She stared at Rose and willed her to stop questioning, being caring.

Rose took hold of Lucy's hands, "Try me. If you want to take this further, one day you'll going to have to tell me. And I'd rather it be sooner rather than later."

Rose was pushing her too hard and she couldn't understand, "Why? Why do care?"

Rose sighed, "Oh Lucy, you seem to be carrying the world on your shoulders. I've respected you from afar for too long for this," she waved her hands. "Whatever this is we have between us, to fizzle out to nothing. I have too much admiration of you to allow you to push me away without knowing the true reason. Is it me? Have I come on too strong? I think we could have a good thing going, but something is holding you back."

"You want to know why? Do you really? Well I'll tell you why. Because everyone I have ever known, and loved all through my life, have all left me. Until Joy, Trina, and to a certain extent, Charlie and Sean, no one has really cared about me. My Dad left me when I was little, my Mum is an alcoholic, and into whatever drugs she can get her hands on. She only wants me for any money that will fuel her habits. I've had abusive 'uncles'. My only girlfriend left me when I wouldn't take it further than kissing, because I was scared of giving too much of me away. I've lived on the streets, been beaten up, and been in fear of my life."

She paused, collecting her thoughts, "Now here you are; pushing me into something I'm not comfortable with, so no, you don't know me." She looked past Rose, into the night, and blinked at the unexpected and unwanted threat of tears.

"But I want to know you."

Rose looked deeply, tenderly, into Lucy's eyes, but then apprehension took over, "When were you living on streets?" Rose asked, her voice full of concern.

"Earlier this year."

An incredulous look came over her face, "Is that when you stopped coming to college."

Looking embarrassed, Lucy nodded.

"And is this when you got beaten up."

Again, Lucy nodded.

The concern on Rose's face radiated from her as she asked, "Do you know why you were beaten up or was it just a random attack?"

"Oh I know who had me attacked and I can even give you their names and addresses."

"But why? Have you gone to the police?"

"What's the point in that?"

"It's a hate crime."

"And, after I bared my soul again to strangers, the outcome would still be a severe letting off or with them being told, 'you were a naughty boy. Don't do it again." with a tap on the wrist"

"You don't know that."

Lucy gave Rose a look that shouted, 'Please. Are you serious.' but instead shook her head.

"So you won't go to the police with their names." Rose spoke, not expecting an answer.

Lucy pinched her lips together and silently agreed.

"But you do know why you were attacked?"

"Yes." She said quietly.

Rose gently took hold of Lucy's hand, "So tell me."

"You won't let it drop will you?"

"I will if you want me to but I think it has had a profound bearing on you."

"All right." Lucy took in a deep breath. "My ex-girlfriend's Dad had forbidden her to see me. Rachel was pushing me to take our relationship further, but I didn't feel the time was right. You see, I thought she was too young. I wanted our first time to mean something, not a quick fumble, and a notch on the bedpost. She was impetuous and told me that if I wouldn't, she would find someone who would. Therefore, we split up, or to be more precise she finished it with me. Even though we had split up her Dad must have found out that she was gay, thought that she was still seeing me, and paid some local louts to rough me up."

"Have you seen her since?"

"Oh yes." Lucy shook her head at the memory. "About a month after the beating she was in town, hanging on to the arm of an older woman. And no, it wasn't her Mum. She smirked at me. Then as if to make a point, she began to play tonsil tennis with the woman. Looking over the woman's shoulder directly into my eyes."

"What did you do?"

"I shook my head and continued on my way. I had more to think about than mind games."

"And about this time is when you teamed up with Joy." Rose stated.

"Joy came into my life and saved it. She stood up to the thugs and stopped me taking more of a beating that day. She then took me under her wing. She allowed me to stay in her spare room and has sponsored me through this year. If it hadn't been for her, I don't know what I would be doing now. I don't know if would still be alive. I owe her my life, my everything."

"I gathered that."

"She found out who had attacked me. And yes, she did try to persuade me to go to the cops. She tried really hard but I didn't see the point then and I still don't see the point now."

They stood in silence for a few minutes. Each engrossed in their own thoughts. Rose gave Lucy a small smile but the look on her face was far away as though she was trying to form correctly her next words.

Finally Rose spoke, "So you are going to let these unfortunate incidents take over your life, where you are too scared of getting close to people? To trust again." Rose said gently, taking her face in her hands.

She shrugged and let the phrase unfortunate incident go, instead, she replied, "I trust Joy and Trina. I also trust Sean and Charlie."

"I know you do, but they are not a threat to you. You are not hoping to have a meaningful, loving relationship with them." Rose continued, in a soothing tone and pulled Lucy towards her. She gently raised Lucy's chin and placed a soft kiss on her forehead.

In a voice barely above a whisper Lucy said, "Don't you think I despise myself for my weakness? Why do you think I'm always part of a group? That my two best friends my age are straight men. Do you honestly think I enjoy pushing people away, but for me, I always come back to the realisation of my life, that I will always be alone because I can't handle rejection, I push people away, and that I should get used to it."

"Come here." Rose pulled Lucy tight.

Lucy melted into Rose's embrace, let out all the pent up emotions and allowed the tears to fall.

Rose waited for the sobs to stop and the tears to dry and said, "Lucy that moment back a while was everything I dreamed it would be. Your lips felt as if they have always been there. As though they were meant to be kissing me. You felt so right in my arms."

She paused and studied the reaction on Lucy's face. Liking what she was seeing she continued, "Yes. I would like to take you to bed, to love you, as you deserve to be loved. However, I also know that it will happen if, and when, the time is right. I will never push you into doing something you don't feel safe with. I will wait until the time is right. Going out and enjoying each other's company, getting to know each other and feeling safe and secure, and perhaps sneak a kiss." She laughed and looked into Lucy's eyes. "That is all I ask."

Lucy suddenly looked vulnerable. A look so alien that Rose experienced a deep feeling inside her, a feeling that she hadn't faced before. She knew she wanted to protect Lucy from any more pain and suffering that she had experienced in her short life.

Rose looked lovingly into the eyes of Lucy, "Is that a deal? However, you must promise me this. Try not to let your past become your excuse for the future. Open up the door that has been closed for so long, and let me see the chink of light that is longing to break out. A sign of hope for the future."

"I'll try, but I cannot promise that I will not have those feelings. They have been a part of me for most of my life. We could see where it goes, to try to build something. I will warn you. Don't push me too hard 'cos I will walk." She looked away, feeling that it was easy for Rose to tell her how to handle the situation when she hadn't lived it. Yet Lucy felt a wave of relief flow through her, as though an important milestone had been reached, that the last block of her new life had been put into place.

She turned to Rose and said, "Thank you." Lucy leant into Rose as they both stepped into the most exquisite kiss they had ever experienced.

ꟹ

Chapter Eleven

Friday Morning, Almost Two Weeks Later

Jocelyn was looking out of the front room window in Trina's house hugging a cup of coffee. The hustle and bustle of getting ready for the school run invaded her ears. Trina silently came up behind Jocelyn and wrapped her arms around her waist, and kissed her on her cheek.

She asked, "What do you want to do on your birthday weekend? Don't forget we have the children on Sunday. Bloody Mike. He promised he'd have them for the whole weekend."

"Never mind about him. We will still have a great time. What about a quick drink in the Three Graces tonight. I haven't been in there for ages." She thought for a moment then continued, "A fairly lazy day tomorrow. I said we would pop in to see Duncan, Sharon and the boys in the morning. Perhaps some retail therapy in the afternoon, followed by an early meal." Joy then enquired, "How about an Italian?"

"An Italian sounds good. We could go to that one on the Waterfront."

"I've never eaten there. Is it good?"

"Well I like it."

"That's good enough for me, let's try it." She paused, "I said we would meet Lucy and Rose for a birthday drink in the evening. So we could meet up in the Fairies after. Lucy so wants us to meet Rose. I think she is smitten."

"Sunday, I thought we could go up to the Downs, to the area by the Suspension bridge."

"Okay." Trina frowned and sounded doubtful. "I know there is a children's area there but I've seen better."

"I'm not talking about the children's area. We'll take a ball and have a picnic. And then we'll take them on the limestone slide, go into the Camera Obscura, and down into Vincent's Cave."

Trina looked at Jocelyn as though she was speaking a different language. "Apart from the first part with the ball and picnic, I heard what you said, but I don't know what you said."

"Didn't you go to these places when you were a child?"

Shaking her head, Trina said, "No."

"Right by the suspension bridge there is a slab of limestone. Over the years it has been rubbed into a shiny slide by countless generations of children's, and not so young, bottoms. Mum used to take Duncan and me there sometimes when we were little. We used to come back with bruised bums, but it was worth it. It was such good fun. I hope the council haven't altered it on health and safety grounds." she sighed.

"Never heard of it or seen it."

"There is a path you climb from the road leading to the suspension bridge that goes right by it. You used to have to scramble through the railings to get to it. I bet you can't do that now."

"Is the Camera Obscura in the Observatory? I know where the Observatory is."

"Yes and so is the entrance to the cave. The Obscura is in the room at the top. A set of lenses project a live image of the ground outside onto a circular screen. You can turn the camera around and see 360 degrees surrounding the building. It is better on a sunny day as the image is clearer and you can see much further. When I'm on that part of the Downs and see the Lens on top turning around, I wave like mad when it is pointed in my direction and dance around like an idiot."

Jocelyn gave an impression and started laughing raucously. Trina joined in Jocelyn's laughter.

"You are daft, but I love you." She pulled Jocelyn into an embrace and kissed her tenderly. She smiled and asked, "So what about the cave?"

"The cave is at the bottom of a tunnel leading from inside the building. It comes out half way up the rock face of the gorge. Quite close to the Suspension Bridge."

"I hate heights."

"So do I, but it is perfectly safe. There are high railings keeping you secure. I usually keep on the cave floor. There is a platform jutting out you can stand on, and from there you can look out over the gorge. There are great views of the suspension bridge and the River Avon from there."

"If that's what you want to do then let's do it. I'm sure the kids would love it. Especially as the cave sounds a bit scary."

"When I was a kid, it was being scared that made it fun."

Before Trina could respond, Peter walked into the room and said, "Hi Joy. Did you stay over?"

"Yes Peter. Was that okay?"

"I'm glad you stayed the night. I told Mum not to be so stupid not letting you stay. Yvonne lives with Dad, so I don't see the problem. Will you still be here when I get back from school?"

Jocelyn smiled at Trina with a look that said 'I told you not to worry' and replied to Peter, "I don't know. Depends on whether the work commitments I have to do are finished on time. I'll try to get here before your Dad picks you up, but I can't promise."

"Okay." Peter replied, "Stay there a minute. I'll be back."

Jocelyn looked at Trina questioningly, who shrugged her shoulders. After a short while, they heard Peter bounding down the stairs again. He held out an envelope and said, "In case I don't see you. Happy birthday for tomorrow."

"Thanks Peter. Can I give you a hug?"

He shrugged but allowed Joy to wrap an arm around him.

"It's from Cathy as well." He said as he walked back out of the door.

As if on cue Cathy ran into the room and hugged Jocelyn's legs, and asked, "Are you taking me to school today with mummy?"

"I don't know." she looked at Trina, and enquired, "Am I mummy?"

Trina turned to her young daughter and asked, "Do you want us both to take you?"

Cathy nodded, "I want you to meet my teacher. Mummy has met her. She's nice."

Jocelyn made a face over Cathy's head.

"I told Mrs Wright that you were mummy's girlfriend."

Trina looked amazed, "Did you? When was this?"

"Ages ago." She replied.

"Was it whilst Joy was living a long way away or when she came back." asked Trina.

"Don't be silly Mummy. Joy can't be your girlfriend when she wasn't living here."

"Joy's not living here." replied Trina

"I know Mummy, but you see her all the time." Cathy looked at her Mum and asked, "Mummy?"

"Yes?"

"Sally said, that her Mum said, that you were a lethbeen. Are you?"

Trina looked at Joy's smirking face, and replied, "I suppose I must be."

"Good. I told her that you weren't and now I can tell her that you are."

Jocelyn started a coughing fit as she tried to swallow her coffee and laugh at the same time. Trina gave her a look that implied, stop enjoying this. Jocelyn managed to get the coughs under control and smiled sweetly at Trina, who batted her on the arm.

Cathy had started to dance around the room, she stopped and asked, "Joy, do you like my new shoes."

Joy looked at Cathy as she stumbled into the settee, and said, "They are very nice but should you be wearing them to school?"

"Mummy can I wear them to school?"

"No Cathy. They are your party shoes. We don't want you to spoil them."

Cathy ran out of the room, Trina shook her head and Jocelyn smiled. "So am I your girlfriend?"

"It appears so."

"So are you a lesbian?"

Trina let out a sound between a grumble and a growl.

Jocelyn grinned at the expression on Trina's face, as she pulled her arms tighter around her, and asked, "Does that mean we have to live together?"

"One step at a time, my love, one step at a time."

"I love you Mrs. Rennet."

"And I love you Ms. Harrold."

༻

Chapter Twelve

Friday Evening

Trina walked into the Three Graces with Lucy in tow. She gave Jocelyn a hug and a kiss on the cheek. "Look who I bumped into on the way here."

Jocelyn gave Trina a kiss and acknowledged Lucy, saying, "Hi. Are you stalking me?"

Lucy gave Joy a friendly nudge. "Funny."

"Have you finished all the decorating yet?"

"I've had enough for today. There's no rush for me, that's why I've come for a drink."

"So give me an update."

"The lad's bedrooms are finished as well as the stairs. They have the doors on the landing to finish. I've almost finished my bathroom and my bedroom. Just a few bits of touching up to do there. The kitchen is almost finished. The only thing left to do is one door and one wall in the lounge."

"So you want the carpet fitter booked in for next week?" asked Jocelyn

"Please. Sorry about having to get a new carpet in the living room, but when we tried to clean it up, it started to disintegrate." She paused then asked, "Does it tie in with downstairs?"

"That's no problem I half expected it. Not quite, but it doesn't matter. I'm aware that Sean has to move out tomorrow. I've persuaded Duncan to help finish getting the office ready next Saturday. The painters and decorators are booked in for next Thursday and Friday. I've the carpet fitters coming for downstairs and the entrance hall the following Tuesday"

Lucy asked sheepishly, "Would you mind if we have a few friends around for a couple of drinks next Saturday evening."

"As long as we're invited." she smiled with affection.

"Joy, I think you should leave off on the new carpets until after then," laughed Trina.

"That might be a good idea." Lucy chuckled. "I'll tell the others that they will have to wait another week for the carpets."

"Don't forget our launch is the Friday after."

Lucy shook her head laughing, "As if we could ever forget that date. It's all you have been talking about for weeks."

Trina took hold of Joy's hand, and smiled into her eyes, "I love seeing you so excited."

Lucy saw a couple of college friends over the other side of the room. "Excuse me my lovelies, some of my mates are over there. See you later."

Trina smiled, "Go and enjoy yourself. You don't want to hang around a couple of old fogeys like us."

Trina whispered into Joy ear, "I got to go to the loo. I'll bring back some drinks. Is it another lager?"

"Please."

As soon as Trina wandered off, Jocelyn felt someone take hold of her hand. She turned around and saw a face that looked familiar.

"Hi Joy. Remember me?"

Jocelyn squinted at the woman in front of her, thinking back to years gone by. "Marie?" she asked.

Marie smiled and nodded.

"Marie Stockton? Good to see you. You are looking well."

Marie held onto Jocelyn's hand for a while longer than would be seen as polite. Her brown eyes took on a sense of anticipation as she leant in for a full-bloodied kiss and, stunned, Jocelyn pulled away, saying, "What was that?"

Confused Marie replied, "I just felt…"

"Felt what?"

"I just felt that we had a moment. Something more than it obviously was. I'm sorry."

"We're acquaintances."

"I thought you were gay."

"What difference does that make?"

"No difference at all."

"Just because you want something, it doesn't mean that you can take it."

"Sorry." She shrugged.

Jocelyn shook her head, "You were never sorry back in the day. You tormented me all those years ago. You tried to take away a part of my spirit, and you almost succeeded."

"I was only trying to have a kiss."

A hard look came into Jocelyn's eyes, "No. Not again. Never again." Jocelyn continued shaking her head, "No one is going to take advantage of me ever again."

Marie rolled her eyes, "For goodness sake it was only a kiss."

"No. It is not about a kiss. It isn't right that you think you can take something that isn't yours to take. Not then, not now."

"From your reaction, I realise that now."

"You tormented me."

"I'm not the person I was at school. I know that I'm gay like you. I was frightened and confused back then."

"You are nothing like me. And I wasn't frightened and confused back then?" Jocelyn replied incredulously. "I knew I was gay. I needed some support."

Marie shook her head in sadness, "If you were that upset I'm truly sorry for what I did all those years ago, how I treated you. But you never really showed your displeasure, and anyway it was only a bit of a laugh."

"Did you ever see me laughing? Or any of the others you and your cronies tormented? You were just another one of those people who took delight in watching others suffer. I just hope that you have changed but somehow I don't think that you have. Otherwise, you wouldn't have tried to pounce on me. Do you still try to bully people?"

Marie shook her head and spoke quietly, as though she was trying to convince herself, "I never bullied you. I wanted to be like you."

"Hah. You damn well had a funny way of showing it. Oh just go away. I can't be dealing with you now." Jocelyn said dismissively.

"What? Like you couldn't be dealing with Sam all those years ago."

"What has this got to do with Sam?" Jocelyn asked, incredulously.

"Nothing. Everything. The way you walked out on her. Like she meant nothing to you." Marie shrugged.

"She meant the world to me."

"But you still walked away. It was as if you had no feelings for her."

"It wasn't like that."

"So what was it like?" She asked pointedly.

"I loved her." She said, emphatically.

"I don't think you ever loved her or thought of her again."

"I thought of her a lot. I thought of her every day for weeks, months, years, then again recently. Especially after I first came home. But I will ask again what has this got to do with Sam?"

"Nothing. I'm sorry I brought it up." Marie said as she walked away. She turned back to Jocelyn and said, "Do you know what? You are still so up yourself."

Giving Jocelyn one last look, she disappeared into the crowd.

"Who was that?" Lucy asked incredulously, as she sidled up. "She was gorgeous."

Lucy then saw the pained expression on the older woman's face. Then it was gone as quickly as it had come.

"An old school friend and someone much too old for you, you tart." Jocelyn smiled at the younger woman.

Lucy silently questioned Jocelyn by raising her eyebrows.

Jocelyn continued, "No. Friend is not the word I should have used, more like school tormenter. Anyway, she tried to kiss me. Then she started to question me about Sam."

"Sam? Your ex Sam? Awkward or what? Are you going to tell Trina?" Lucy asked.

"Of course. She made me realise why she bullied me all those years ago. I think she thought that she was gay back then but was ashamed and scared. Marie didn't want others to feel uncomfortable around her, so instead I was the scapegoat, the butt of their jokes. I became the pariah amongst the popular young things. It was amazing how quick it took before these gits to turn from friends to tormenters. Trina was incensed and put a stop to it, but by then it was too late. People who I thought were my friends were instead a shallow impression of themselves. They were pleasant to my face, but had no depth."

Jocelyn let out a big sigh, "Trina was so supportive. She was my rock. I wasn't getting the support at home. In fact, I think home was worse. Trina was there for me. We should have got together all those years ago." She gave a small laugh, "but things happen for a reason. The time wasn't right. We were too young and didn't know what we wanted out of life. And if we had got together then she might not have had those two gorgeous children."

"Trina seemed like a good friend to you back then as well as now."

"She was and still is. I love her to bits." Jocelyn paused, "I had become so angry with the world. I felt as if no one, apart from Trina, truly understood me. That is until Sam came along. She showed me I wasn't different, and I wasn't evil and I wasn't alone. She made me believe in myself. To become the person I am today. She gave me the strength to be able to walk away on the worse day of my life, even though it meant turning my back on her."

Jocelyn became lost in thoughts of years gone by. Lucy studied Jocelyn, looking at the whole gamut of emotions flash by in a few minutes. Breaking into the older woman's reverie, she touched Jocelyn's arm.

"Where is Trina?" asked Lucy, looking around.

"She was dying to go to the loo and said she would pick up some drinks on the way back. She might be gone a long time. You know how long these toilet queues are, but she has been away a long time."

Lucy looked around and spotted Trina at the bar waving a twenty around. "There she is. She's trying to get served." Lucy pointed at a frustrated Trina, who was getting more exasperated by the minute as the different bar staff ignored her.

"I'd better go and help her," said Jocelyn, as she noticed the telltale signs. "Do you want another?" she asked of Lucy.

"No. I'm good."

"Anyway must dash and help her ladyship." Jocelyn said with a laugh. "Otherwise I will die of thirst."

As Jocelyn walk away Lucy notice Jocelyn's old school friend talking animated to another woman. They gave each other a high five and burst into laughter. They both looked in the direction of Jocelyn. Some more words were spoken, followed by hugs, as though a plan had come to fruition. They downed the rest of their drinks, turned and left the pub. Lucy shook her head, feeling troubled by the interaction.

Jocelyn looked at Trina as she walked towards her. Trina was running one hand through her hair and leaned one elbow on the bar, waving the twenty pound note. She could hear the sigh of frustration from five yards away, even over the continuous thump of the music.

Jocelyn sidled up behind her, wrapped her arms around her and made Trina jump. "Need any help."

"They all seem to be ignoring me," she said through clenched teeth, the frustration only just being held in check.

"Here let me." Jocelyn took hold of the note and straight away one of the bar staff came over and took their order.

"How do you always do that?" Trina asked disbelievingly, and started swatting at Jocelyn arm.

"You either got it or you haven't." Jocelyn burst into a cackle of laughter.

"Did you pay them to ignore me? I wouldn't put anything past you." Trina huffed.

The barman put the drinks down and took the money. Jocelyn handed Trina her drink and took a large swig of her own, then retrieved the change that had been put in front of her.

"And that change is mine." Trina stated, still annoyed.

Jocelyn returned the change to Trina, and laughed. Trina started to get annoyed with Jocelyn laughing at her. And in time-honoured fashion, Jocelyn pinned Trina's arms by her side, then sealed her lips over Trina's, who immediately disappeared into the kiss. The din of the pub faded away as Trina became intoxicated with desire. Trina reluctantly pulled away and looked at the strong, caring woman in front of her. Laughter and pure enjoyment of their closeness, oozed from her whole being.

"I love you Trina Rennet."

Trina smiled and felt content.

ഇ

Chapter Thirteen

Saturday Morning

"Joy." Alfie and David shrieked as they ran down the hallway.

"Hi boys," replied Jocelyn.

"Happy Birthday." They spoke in unison. Alfie handed Jocelyn a card that had stickers and pictures on it and said, "Here's your card."

She made a point of looking at the pictures stuck on the outside, opened it up and read the greetings, "Thank you, Munchkins. Did you make this especially for me?"

They both grinned and nodded.

"Well thank you very much. I'll put it on the shelf when I get home. What are you up to today?"

"Mummy has to work this afternoon so Dad said we could play pirates," replied Alfie.

David joined in, "We are going to make a den that looks like a pirate ship. Do you want to help? We could start it now." He started to pull on Jocelyn's hand.

Duncan and Trina walked back into the house after putting some bags of old sheets into the car.

Trina spoke to the boys, "Hi Alfie, Hi David."

"Do you want to help us, and Joy, make our pirate ship?" Alfie asked Trina.

"Boys. Let Joy and Trina have some peace. Go off in the back room and finish what you were doing. We'll make the pirate ship this afternoon. Okay?"

"Okay." they replied, dejectedly. They both looked at the grown-ups and pouted.

Duncan looked at them and said, "I don't have to help you this afternoon. I can see what extra homework I can get you to do. Maths, English or Science, what will it be?"

He walked down the hall towards them.

"No Dad we're good." they scurried into the back room.

Laughing he turned back to Jocelyn and asked, as they moved into the front room and sat down "Are you sure you don't need any more old sheets?"

"Those should be fine. I only want them as dustsheets in case the office furniture arrives before we finish the decorating."

"How's that coming along?"

"Good. But why do things always take longer than it should? The electrics, plumbing, and heating are finally finished. We're waiting for the plaster to dry. They completed skimming the walls yesterday. I've the decorators in first part of the week. Then the carpet fitters later. If all goes to plan, we'll be able to move in next weekend, so we'll have a week to be sorted. All I need now is a snappy name for the company."

"You haven't got a name yet?" he asked incredulously. "You do need time for the print run on your business cards to be finished."

"I keep on changing my mind. I have my old cards that just say my name and number, and yes, I do know that they are not professional enough. The printer said it would take a couple of days after I email them the design. I still got almost two weeks before the launch. That's if everything goes to plan." She stated wistfully.

Trina piped up. "You've done everything else to the last detail. Invites sent out, replies coming in, presentation completed, work colleagues briefed, caterers sorted, wait staff employed."

"Sounds as if you have all bases covered, Sis. What could possibly go wrong?"

Jocelyn didn't sound as sure as she replied, "Yeah. I'm waiting on one major company to reply. I'm hoping they will land us a big contract, which would see us sorted for the whole of next year. I'm meeting with one of their representatives in the week to finalise details. So fingers crossed that they will dot the I's and cross the T's."

"You'll pull it off. I have complete faith in you." Trina gave her a loving and caring smile as she said these words.

"Thank you love."

Sharon entered the room, drying her hands on the apron she wore around her waist. "Happy birthday Joy." She gave Jocelyn a kiss on the cheek and then looked around. "Hasn't he offered you a tea or a coffee? What would you like?"

Duncan gave a shrug and mouthed 'sorry' to Trina and Jocelyn. Trina stood up and said, "Sit down Sharon, I'll make it. Is it coffees all round?"

"Duncan have you given your sister her card and present yet?"

"I was just about to get it."

Sharon looked at her husband, "Men. Can't live with them, can't live without them."

Jocelyn laughed, "I wouldn't know about that Sharon."

Sharon blushed slightly and replied, "You know what I mean."

Duncan came back into the room and asked, "What's so funny?"

"You." came the reply from the two women.

"Looks like I'm out-numbered. I might have to join the boys in the back room."

"It makes a change from me being the one that is ganged up on." Sharon laughed.

"You love it really, babe, having three men to take care of you."

To which Sharon huffed.

He handed Jocelyn a present and said, "Happy birthday Dumps."

Jocelyn unwrapped it, and took out a gorgeous scarf and top.

"How did you know I had my eye on that top?"

"I had help." Sharon replied.

"It's lovely. It will go so well with the trousers I'm planning to wear at the launch. Thank you Sharon."

"It's from me as well, Dumps."

"I know but it was Sharon who organised it. If it were left to you, all I would get would be money or a cheque. Or have you changed since I been away."

Duncan grunted and Sharon laughed, "No. He hasn't changed."

Trina came back into the room with the coffees and, placing them on the table, she asked, "What have I missed?"

Jocelyn wrapped the scarf around her neck and held the top against her. "How do I look?"

Trina looked at the top and scarf, and said; "They so suit you."

Sharon looked pleased and asked, "What are your plans for the rest of your birthday weekend?"

"Shopping, dinner, pub, in that order. And tomorrow we're taking the kids up to the Downs near the Observatory for a picnic."

Duncan asked, “Are you taking them on the slide?”

“Of course.” Jocelyn smiled as she remembered.

“They were good times with Mum when we were little.”

“I was telling Trina about it. I still can’t believe you never went down it when you were a child.”

Sharon spoke, “It’s only a couple of years ago that I had been there, but I didn’t go down. I had a short skirt on.” She laughed.

“Not the best item of clothing to wear to go down.” laughed Jocelyn.

“The boys loved it, and the not so small boys.” She looked lovingly at the handsome man sat in the other armchair.

Trina butted in, “Why don’t you and the boys join us for the picnic tomorrow?”

Jocelyn smiled, “Yes, why don’t you join us.”

“I’ll pack a picnic enough for all of us.”

Sharon looked at Duncan, smiling and nodding.

Duncan said, “It’s about time the children met. What time?”

“How about twelve thirty near the Observatory?”

“The kids will love it.”

ဢ

Chapter Fourteen

Saturday Early Evening

Trina and Jocelyn lingered over a pleasant dinner. The food was delicious and the atmosphere was congenial. Their conversation was light-hearted and about nothing special, except the gentle teasing that accompanied their time together.

"I can't believe we spent all that time in town and all you wanted me to get you for your birthday was a plain pair of lace up shoes. You can get those anytime."

Jocelyn lifted her feet and said, "And very comfortable they are too."

"Oh don't be so old fashioned."

"Oi." Jocelyn acted as if she was hurt by the words but her grin showed she wasn't.

She continued, "I needed a comfortable pair. The sole on my other favourite ones had worn through. You know I have some decent dressy ones. Ones that hurt my toes, for when I'm meeting customers. I have my everyday trainers, some beach sandals, and my walking boots. What more do I need?"

Trina shook her head in disbelief. "You can't only have five pairs of shoes."

"Yes. What is wrong with that?" Jocelyn frowned.

Trina continued shaking her head in disbelief.

"What?" said Jocelyn.

"I have a whole big box full of shoes underneath the stairs, a pair for every occasion."

This time Jocelyn shook her head, "But you can only wear one pair at a time."

"My love, you're going to have to change your thoughts on shoes if you want to stay with me."

Jocelyn leant over the table, took Trina's hand, and smiled, "Not gonna happen."

"Do you mean staying with me or changing your ways?"

Jocelyn looked shocked, "I meant changing me." She stammered, "Why on earth would I not want to stay with you?"

"I'm only teasing you my love."

"Don't do that. Well at least not about us splitting up. You had me worried for a second. I thought you had enough of me." Jocelyn scolded.

"Never." Trina shrugged her shoulders, crinkled her nose, and said "Sorry."

Jocelyn smiled at Trina and said, "I love you Trina Rennet."

After a few moments of silence, Jocelyn spoke, "I took out Nan's letter today. I haven't read it for a few weeks. She was such a wise woman. I want her to be proud of me.""

Trina grasped Jocelyn's hands in a firmer grip, "She was always proud of you. Even when you annoyed her to distraction."

"I never annoyed her, or if I did she never showed her displeasure."

"She wouldn't. She loved you too much. She told me once that your sense of doing what was right would be your downfall. That everything was black or white, and that you needed to see the shades of grey."

Jocelyn smiled at the truth. She sighed deeply, "Now my Grandad was a different proposition. He always showed his displeasure. His anger came fleetingly, but that was because of the events he had experienced. He was a prisoner of war. He never spoke of it but I remember his nightmares whilst I was growing up, and stayed over with them." Jocelyn paused and Trina could tell she was decided on whether to continue. Trina knew the signs and allowed the silence to develop.

Finally, Jocelyn said, "I've had some nightmares recently."

"And you are only telling me now." Trina said trying not to let her annoyance show.

"I didn't want to worry you."

Trina gave Jocelyn the eyes that said, 'now you have really worried me.'

Instead, Trina asked quietly, in a voice full of concern, "Can you remember what happens in the nightmare?"

Jocelyn didn't speak for a while but her face told a story of the thoughts that were going through her mind. Trina waited patiently knowing that if she pushed then Jocelyn would clam up and would not share her innermost thoughts. That she would retreat inwards and go into self-protection mode, building a wall that would take patience, understanding, and plenty of time to break down. So she continued to wait. Finally, Jocelyn noticed Trina waiting in anticipation.

"I only remember snippets but it always the same theme. That I am being chased or that I am covered in bruises."

"Do you know who is chasing you? Hurting you?"

Jocelyn looked off into the distance and gave a small nod.

Trina gave her hand another squeeze, "Do you want to tell me?"

Jocelyn took in a deep breath and said, "I never see his face but I think it is a manifestation of my Dad. He's the same size and shape, but when I try to look at him he is always in shadow."

"Why? Why do you think it is him if you can't see his face?"

"I think I smell him, but it could be my heightened senses imagining it. Every time I have that nightmare I am flung back to that awful night all those years ago."

Trina's face was a picture of concern.

"Why don't you go and see someone. Talk to them; see whether something can help. I know you don't like talking and you have bottled up those feelings for years. Perhaps moving back has caused them to raise their head again."

"I'm not mad, I'm not a crazy woman and I'm not going to a shrink." Jocelyn shook her head.

Trina looked deeply into Jocelyn's eyes, "I'm not saying that you are mad." She squeezed her hand. "I'm saying that perhaps you need to talk to a professional. Someone who is trained to listen. Having nightmares can really affect your everyday life by not allowing you to have a restful and peaceful night's sleep."

Jocelyn saw the love shining through her words and said, "I'll think about it."

"Promise?"

"Promise." Jocelyn agreed. "Let's talk about happier times."

"Okay." Trina picked up her glass and said, "Happy birthday my love. Cheers."

"Cheers."

They both took a drink. Trina looked at her watch and asked, "What time are we meeting Lucy and this Rose that has gotten her so smitten?"

Jocelyn too glanced at her watch, "Plenty of time yet. Shall we have one their speciality coffees before we wander over to the pub?"

"A good idea. That will give me time to let the meal go down; otherwise I'm going feel bloated and will be uncomfortable all night."

ᏈᏍ

Chapter Fifteen

Saturday Late Evening

Trina and Jocelyn walked arm in arm towards Fairies. They passed by the various imposing looking bouncers, dressed in dark clothing, loitering in the different doorways of numerous clubs and pubs. They gave the impression of plain clothed detectives searching for known felons. As they reached the entrance to the pub, they exchanged a few words of banter with the bouncers who guarded the entrance to the pub. The volume of music appeared too loud for the time of evening, too loud for talking at normal volume. They luckily found some seats near where they normally perched.

The pub was still fairly quiet in the early evening. They knew it would be heaving by the end of the night. They looked around the bar and couldn't see Lucy.

"What would you like to drink now birthday girl?"

"I'll have a lager please."

"I'll go and order but come and rescue me if I get ignored."

"I don't know why anyone would ignore you love."

"Because I'm short."

"And sweet and fully formed."

"And flattery will get you everywhere." she smiled and walked to the bar.

As she walked towards the bar, Jocelyn felt the butterflies in her stomach surface, as her love for this woman fought to overcome her emotions. She could hardly believe her luck at getting together with Trina. She definitely couldn't understand what Trina saw in her. The spark between them was obvious from the moment she had come back into Trina's life and it hadn't diminished all the time she was resolving her life back in Sunderland.

It was a huge step for her to take coming home, with all the associated problems with it, but she relished the opportunity to reignite the friendship, and now something deeper, with Trina. Jocelyn realised that Trina brought so much to their relationship that had been missing from her life. It wasn't just companionship and love, but understanding. Trina knew what make Jocelyn tick, what she needed, ages before Jocelyn had an inkling anything was awry.

Lucy startled Jocelyn as she wrapped an arm around her, and gave Joy a kiss.

"Happy birthday. Did you find my pressie?"

"You made me jump."

"Sorry. You did have a faraway look in your eyes, but I thought you'd seen me."

Jocelyn shook her head and smiled, "I was daydreaming. Yes, I did find the present. Thank you so much. How did you know that's what I wanted?"

"Every time the advert came on the telly you made a remark. So I told Trina I was getting it."

"So that's why she didn't take my hint. I thought she was being obtuse and didn't like it. Again, thanks a lot." She paused for a moment and said, "Trina's at the bar if you fancy a drink."

"Okay." Lucy went off to catch up with Trina at the bar.

They came back carrying the drinks.

"A half. I've never seen you drink a half before." Jocelyn teased Lucy.

"I want to impress Rose with my wit and sophistication. And if I drink too much I usually make a fool of myself."

"So when are we going to meet Rose?"

Lucy looked at her watch, and relied, "She should be here in half an hour."

"We're looking forward to meeting her."

Their conversation and teasing continued for the next half an hour, and just when they were ready for their next round of drinks Rose entered. Lucy waved and gave her a smile as Rose walked over to them.

Her soft curly hair was swept back from her face in gentle waves. Her eyebrows peaked through a half fringe with a casualness that made you think she styled it using her hands. Her eyes were an alert, piercing grey, a little too close together, but did not seem out of place in her long thin face. Her nose had the air of roman about it and her thin lips looked troubled. She tilted her head down and to the right, and looked out through her lashes as though they would hide her shyness and discomfort. But the most striking feature was the myriad of tattoos that ordained her arms.

Jocelyn did a double take but remembered that sometimes the most supportive people are covered in tattoos and the most judgemental go to church on Sundays. She didn't want to judge Rose, as she didn't know much about her. Only what Lucy had told her. She now tried not to appraise individuals by the opinions of others, but instead would bide her time until she had gathered enough information of her own. She thought about times in her past when she had misinterpreted the signals, sometimes to humiliating effect.

Rose gave Lucy a quick kiss and wrapped an arm around her waist. Lucy introduced Rose to Jocelyn and Trina, as she leant into Rose's light embrace. Jocelyn looked sceptically from one to the other. She saw the way that Rose looked at Lucy and seeing the beginning of something growing between them. She could sense the chemistry between them so she let her face split into a wide grin.

"Good to meet you, Rose." Jocelyn said as she shook her hand. "I've heard a lot about you."

"All good I hope."

Trina replied, teasing, "Well…."

Lucy looked at Trina shocked, "Trina."

"Of course it's all been good. Apart from the time when she thought you had gone to the Dean. That wasn't what a lady should hear."

"But you're not a lady." replied Jocelyn smiling. "Ow, why did you do that?" she rubbed her arm.

"Are they always like this?" Rose asked Lucy.

"Always. I sometimes don't know when they are teasing or meaning it." Lucy replied.

"We always mean it, even though we're teasing. Don't we Lady Trina of Horfield?" Jocelyn countered but scooted away out of reach.

"You're lucky it's your birthday or there would be no favours for you tonight." Trina laughed.

"But how could you ever resist my charm?"

Trina let out a noise, and then smiled lovingly at Jocelyn. "Easily." She countered.

"Ha." Jocelyn got up and nodded towards the bar. "Anyone want a drink?"

"No. it's your birthday. Let me." Rose responded.

Jocelyn replied, "No. I insist. Please join me in a birthday drink."

Coming back with the drinks, Jocelyn and Rose were stood side by side. Grabbing the chance to get to know her better, Jocelyn started to ask about her family and life. Rose replied to the questions in her normal candid way. Jocelyn began to like what she heard and warmed to her. She was intrigued by the tattoos she could see, and tried to study the details. Jocelyn had been trying to glance at them without being seen.

Rose caught Jocelyn looking and said, "Do you like them?"

"I'm unsure. I've never wanted one."

"I've nine different tattoos. Some are big and some small. Do you want to look closely at some?"

"Yes, okay. I would never have one myself, but I find them on other people fascinating. Is there a reason behind the ones you have?"

"You make your mind up." Rose replied.

She showed the inside of the forearm of her left arm "These are the names of the people who are special to me." She showed Jocelyn an intricate design, which covered her whole forearm. Inside were the names written in the Arabic script, "My Mum and Dad's first names are here and here. And my sister, bless her soul, is here. Notice that there is space for when I find the woman of my dreams."

Rose turned the inside of her right wrist 'Believe in your dreams' was written. "I look at this every time I have something important to do, or something I want to achieve."

"A good inspirational quote."

"Above the arch on my left foot is written, 'best foot forward', and on my right is 'one step at a time', which is how I try to live my life. Finally, I have five different roses on various parts of my body. The only one you can see, and the largest is this one on my right arm. It's a single rose poking through a mass of thorns.

"Does this have a meaning and if so, what does it represent to you."

"I had it done just after I split up from my girlfriend. To me it represents that my future is in my own hands. That it is me against the troubles surrounding me. That I have to fight through the obstacles that are put in my way. Like a rose, that pushes its way through the thorns that protects it. If it wants to be seen, and allow its beauty, and aroma, to shine through, it must push its way to the front. At the bottom the words say 'through pain comes strength and gain'."

"That's rather profound."

Rose gave a small laugh, "There's more to me than meets the eye."

"I've gathered that. In just the short time I've been in your company and the small snippets that Lucy has spoken to me about you."

"Lucy thinks the world of you. I think she loves you."

Jocelyn caught her breath, shocked.

"No. Not as a lover, but as if you were her Mother."

"I don't know if that's a compliment or not."

"I meant it as a compliment. You care for her as no-one has ever done. And for that I know she will be forever grateful."

"She's a good kid. And yes she is almost the right age, I could be her mother."

Jocelyn took a swig of her drink and asked, "I don't want to be intrusive but what about the other tattoos?"

"Don't ask to see them because I won't show you." She laughs. "But one is on my right shoulder blade. Another over my heart and the last is on my left hip."

Trina slipped her arm around Jocelyn's waist. At the same time, Lucy did the same to Rose.

"Have you been putting the world to rights?" Trina asked.

Jocelyn laughed. "Nothing quite as profound as that. Rose was explaining some of her tattoos."

Trina looked at Rose. "They are rather striking."

"That's a polite way of saying you don't like them." Rose smiled, "I realise it is not everyone's cup of tea."

Trina smiled apologetically, "Sorry."

"No problem. My body, my choice. I don't expect to have anymore, except one."

"Which is?" Trina asked.

Rose indicated the space and said, "Something to go in there."

"What are the symbols?"

"Arabic script of family names."

The conversation changed tack several time and Trina and Jocelyn noticed that Rose seemed to have a quick wit about her, and an intelligence to match. Jocelyn understood the attraction Lucy felt. Looking at the two of them, she could see the warmth between them, and expected the relationship to flourish.

Jocelyn stood back and studied the interactions between the other three of them. She felt love and warmth flowing between them all. She felt blessed with her life and hoped that this moment be frozen in time. She felt complete. She sighed with contentment.

Later, when Jocelyn and Trina were alone at the apartment, Trina turned to Jocelyn and stated, "I like Rose. She seems very level headed. When she first walked in, I was unsure. All those tattoos, you know how I dislike them."

"Same here. Nevertheless, you can see why Lucy is so smitten. She has a lovely sense of humour. Let's hope the relationship between them can flourish. Lucy deserves some happiness in her life.

"I've a good feeling about it."

ꕥ

Chapter Sixteen

Sunday

Trina held onto Cathy's hand and carried a couple of waterproof car blankets under her other arm. She spread them out on the ground. The sun was shining on the lush trees, and the green of the grass seemed to shimmer. Jocelyn struggled up the hill, plonked the cool bags down, and lay out on one of the rugs, "What have you packed in there. They were so heavy."

Trina looked at Peter, enquiringly.

He spoke, in his defence, "I did ask Joy if she wanted some help, didn't I Joy?"

Joy nodded in agreement, "He did." She then looked at Trina, "Are you feeding the five thousand?"

"You would be the first to moan if you didn't have enough to eat."

Peter asked, "Mum can I go and try to climb that tree over there."

Trina studied the area and then gave a dubious look.

"I promise to be careful. Please Mum."

"Okay, but only that tree. Don't go any further. Promise."

"Promise."

"But first, I want you to look at those information boards and come back and tell me three things you find out."

"Mum, must I?"

"If you want go and climb the tree then yes."

Peter huffed but went off to read the information boards.

Cathy sat down next to Jocelyn and was playing with her dolls, "Joy?" she asked.

"Yes?"

"Do you want to play dolls with me?" Cathy looked at Jocelyn sincerely.

"I'm not good at playing dolls Cathy. I've never played dolls." Jocelyn said.

"Never played dolls?" Trina replied amazed.

Cathy took hold of Jocelyn arm and said, "I'll help you. You can have Rudy to play with."

"Rudy?"

"Don't ask." Trina shook her head with a smile.

Cathy handed the doll to Jocelyn. "Peter named her."

"Peter? Okay." Jocelyn tried not let any surprise show, but her voice displayed her thoughts.

"Cathy kept on removing the clothes so Peter said it was her rudy nudy doll. So hence the name Rudy." explained Trina.

Jocelyn smiled, "Oh."

Peter came running back and plopped himself down, saying, "The building was once a snuff mill. What's a snuff mill?"

Trina replied, "You know what a mill is?"

"Buildings like they have in The Netherlands with those big sails on them, which go around."

"That's correct. The sails turn a millstone that grinds different grains into powder. I think snuff is a type of ground up tobacco. In olden days people used to sniff it up their noses."

"Ugh gross." He said and screwed up his face in disgust. "How can anyone do that?"

"So you don't want to try some."

"No way." He shook his head. "I'd be sneezing all the time." He then continued, "The building now holds the only Camera Obscura that is open to the public in England. I know what a camera is, but what is an obscura? The board said something about a lens but I didn't understand what it meant."

"Obscura is a strange word. But don't worry. You'll soon find out what it is. We'll be going to up to look at it after lunch." Jocelyn pointed upward, "Do you see that box that is turning around slowly on the top?"

"Yes."

"Well there is a quite a big lens in there. Behind the lens is a mirror and it reflects the view down onto a screen. Next time it comes around, we'll wave at it. And the people up there looking at the screen will see us waving at them."

"Cool." Peter replied

Cathy gave Jocelyn a small nudge, "Joy, you are not playing." She huffed, "Rudy wants some food"

Feeling as though she had been told off, Jocelyn replied, "Okay. Sorry Cathy, sorry Rudy." and pretended to give the doll something to eat. Cathy giggled.

"What else did you find out?" Trina asked of her son.

"In the olden days the gorge was meant to be home to two giants but I can't remember their names. They lived in a cave. There is now a tunnel that goes down to the cave from the building."

"Do you want to go down the tunnel to the cave?" Jocelyn asked.

"Can we?" Peter pleaded.

"Yes. We'll do it after lunch as well. It sounds like fun."

"It does. I wonder if it will be dark in there. We haven't a torch."

"I'm sure it will be lit by electricity. We will not be going back to cavemen days." Jocelyn laughed.

Peter joined in laughing, and then asked, "May I go and climb the tree now please Mum? You promised."

Trina nodded. "Be careful. Don't over-reach and don't climb up too high."

"Thanks Mum. I'll be careful. By the way, there are peregrine falcons that live in the gorge." Peter ran off towards the tree.

Trina watched her son climb onto the first branches and gasped when he stood up.

Jocelyn touched her arm and said, "He's a sensible lad. I know you are like a Mother Hen but let him have some fun."

"It's difficult."

"I know. I know you are not going to relax until he's back on firm ground so scoot over so I can lay my head in your lap."

Jocelyn lay down and tried to make herself comfortable, "Your hips are bony. I need a cushion."

"Stop moaning."

Cathy looked at Jocelyn and asked, "Don't you want to play anymore with Rudy?"

"Can I play again in a little while? I've a bit of a headache."

Trina smirked and said, "I wonder why. Anyone would think it was your birthday yesterday."

"Mum?"

"Yes?"

"Don't you have anything in your bag to take away Joy's headache?"

Jocelyn butted in, "I only need to close my eyes for a few minutes Cathy."

"Okay."

Jocelyn felt Trina relax and soon Peter was plonking himself down on the blanket.

Trina asked of her son, "Was that fun?"

"I couldn't climb as high as I wanted because I couldn't quite reach, but it was. There are some rocks over there. Can we go and scramble over them, later."

"It depends. We'll see how the time goes. Okay?"

"Okay."

Jocelyn spoke with her eyes closed, "There is a rock slide which we are going to play on."

"Why do you have you eyes closed?"

"I've a bit of a headache, Peter."

"Did you drink too much yesterday? Daddy and Emma often have headaches on Sunday."

Trina stifled a laugh.

Jocelyn lifted her head up, "A little, but it was my birthday. I've an excuse."

She noticed her brother and family coming up the hill towards them. The twins were kicking a ball whilst Duncan and Sharon walked hand in hand, with Duncan carrying a couple of chairs. Jocelyn thought it was lovely seeing her brother show his feeling for his wife in this very public way.

"We've got company."

As the twins moved closer to the blankets where Trina, Jocelyn and the children were sat, Duncan called out, "Don't kick the ball anywhere near your Auntie and Trina. Pick it up now please."

Jocelyn stood up and pulled Trina to her feet. They greeted Duncan and Sharon. Trina introduced Peter and Cathy to the twins.

"So what is the plan for the afternoon?" Duncan asked Jocelyn.

"We thought we'd spend some time here and let the kids run off some energy. After lunch, we'll pack up and take the stuff back to the cars. We'll go up the Obscura, then the tunnel to the cave, and finish off with the rock slide. Peter also said that there are some rocks to scramble over and I know there is also a children's playground."

Duncan nodded and said, "Luckily, today it is a relatively bright day. I don't think the reflected picture would be so good if it were overcast."

"No. We are lucky."

Duncan spoke to the boys, "Why don't you play football over there whilst us grown-ups have a sit down and get the picnic ready?"

Sharon said, "After lunch, I think I'll wait down here when you all go into the observatory and see the Obscura and tunnel. I'll stay with all the gear. It will save making a trip back to the cars.

Trina said, "I'll go up to the camera but I don't want Cathy to go down into the tunnel. So I'll come out afterwards and join you."

"Are you sure?" Jocelyn asked of Trina.

"Sharon and I will be able to have a good catch-up without you interrupting." Trina smiled

Sharon laughed, "It would be good to find out what a pain you really are, and whether my first impressions were correct."

"Oi." Jocelyn replied laughing. "Sharon, how did you manage to get time off work?"

"My job share needed time off for a doctor's appointment so we swapped. It has worked out quite well. Duncan loves spending time with his sister.

ꟹ

Sharon asked the twins, "Was it good fun?"

Alfie said, "We saw you Mum but you didn't wave to us."

"I waved a few times when the box faced this way. I must have missed it when you were up there. How was the cave?"

"You wouldn't like it Mum. The cave tunnel to the cliff face is quite long and Dad and Joy bumped their heads a couple of times."

Jocelyn rubbed her head, "It hurt."

Trina rubbed Jocelyn's head, "And it doesn't help that your head is so delicate today." but then she laughed, "However, it might have knocked some sense in you."

"Funny." She nudged Trina.

Duncan spoke, "At the end it gets very steep and low, but the view at the bottom is great. I loved it. It was cheap to do both so well worth it."

Peter spoke excitedly, "When you get to the bottom of the tunnel there is a small cave. You can step out onto the metal grid and watch the cars and lorries driving by on the Portway below. They look like the little toy cars we had when we were small."

Alfie joined in, "We waved at some people who were on the bridge and they waved back. It was cool."

Both Trina and Sharon looked worried so Duncan stepped in. "It is no different than being on a balcony, but with a metal grid floor and high railings. It was perfectly safe. Absolutely brilliant views, and it was high tide so the river mud was covered, but it is not for the faint hearted."

Trina asked, with a smirk, "So how long did you stay out there Joy."

David, Alfie and Peter burst out laughing. Duncan wrapped one of his arms around his sister and asked, "Yes Dumps. How long did you stay out there looking at the views?"

Jocelyn mumbled, "Didn't"

"I didn't hear what she said, did you Sharon? Boys? Cathy? Did you hear what Joy said?"

Cathy jumped from one foot to the other, and said, "She said she didn't." Cathy looked confused, "What didn't you do Joy?"

Peter replied, with a smile, "Joy wouldn't come out on the balcony. We tried pulling her out but she wouldn't."

Jocelyn closed her eyes and shook her head. "It made me feel sick. I tried, but I couldn't step out. I started to feel woozy. I didn't know I was frightened of heights."

"So the balloon flight is out of the question now." Trina smiled.

Laughing, Jocelyn said, "I think so. Right, let's pack up and go over to the rock slide."

ꟸ

Later that evening, after the children had gone to bed, Jocelyn looked at Trina, as she made the instant coffee. Jocelyn loved the way she moved. How she shifted her weight onto her left hip. How she raked her hand through her hair, all the time humming an old tune slightly off key. Less than a year ago Jocelyn was in the north-east of England, feeling alone and depressed. Now she was home, and everything had changed for the better.

The warmth of the smile and the look in her eyes, accompanied with the touch of humour that drifted below the surface, battled with the innate shyness inside Trina and in that moment, Jocelyn didn't think she could love her more.

"I've had a wonderful weekend. Thank you." Jocelyn said, once they had settled down in the living room.

Trina said nothing but held Jocelyn's hand as she sat next to her on the settee. Jocelyn snuggled in and closed her eyes, as her senses took over: the delicate smell of Trina's perfume, the intimate touch of her thumb, circling her hand, the sound of the rhythmic beat of her heart. Trina's hand moved and brushed over Jocelyn's wrist. Jocelyn's pulse leapt as she gulped in a lungful of air. She could taste Trina. She opened her eyes and smiled at the beautiful woman before her.

"I love you."

Trina smiled back and pulled Jocelyn closer.

ജ

Chapter Seventeen

Friday Evening

Lucy and Rose joined Jocelyn and Trina. They had been out with the others celebrating the end of their course, but had moved on to Fairies after they had all gone different ways.

Jocelyn teased, "So how does it feel joining the ranks of the working population?"

Lucy gave Jocelyn a grimace. "Ho ho ho."

"Yeah. Funny. Ha, ha, not. You know both of us have been working ever since we could." Rose smiled, knowing Jocelyn was, in fact, congratulating them on achieving the grades they did.

"I know, but you are not students anymore. You have to make your own way in the world. And buy a round."

"So am I going to get a pay rise now I can work full time?" Lucy asked, with a look of innocence.

"Let us get the launch out of the way and we'll see how it goes." Jocelyn countered.

Trina came back carrying two drinks. "How's two of my favourite people? Did you enjoy your last day at college?"

"Yeah. It was good. A little bit sad as I know there will be a few people that I will never see again." Rose smiled, "And some who I hope never to see again." She then gave out a raucous laugh, nodded towards Lucy and said, "But she keeps on following me wherever I go."

"Yeah and you're very funny as well." Lucy drew Rose into an embrace and looked intently into Rose's eyes.

Jocelyn pulled out a couple of twenties from her wallet and said, "Have a few drinks on me tonight. You both deserve it. Well done on getting the grades you did."

"Thank you." Lucy gave Jocelyn a smile so full of gratitude. Rose, smiled and nodded her thanks.

Time passed and Jocelyn noticed that Lucy and Rose were becoming secretive. Initially it seemed no more than college related chit-chat, but gradually Jocelyn sensed that something else was going on.

"What's the secret you're not telling me about? That's twice now you've shut up when you think I'm listening."

"Vivid imagination you have there, Joy." Replied Lucy.

"I know when you are not telling the truth. You scratch your nose. So are you going to tell me?"

"All right." Lucy shrugged, defeated.

"You know that woman who came up to you and I said was gorgeous."

"Yes."

"Well she is in here again."

"It's a gay pub; she's gay so what's the big deal."

"No big deal."

"I don't think she will bother me if that's what you are worried about."

"I'm not worried. Anyway, she is with someone. I think it's the same woman she was with before." Lucy replied, "We," she nodded to Rose, "were discussing whether or not to tell you."

Laughing Jocelyn replied, "Let me know if she starts to come over, so I can disappear into the crowd."

Trina came back from the toilet and disquiet seemed etched on her face.

"You okay?" Jocelyn asked with a worrying frown.

"I thought I saw a blast from the past, but she was gone before I could react and check."

"Anyone I would know." Jocelyn asked but her voice was carried away as a new song blasted out through the speakers.

A little while later, Jocelyn made her way to the bar to get Trina and herself another drink.

"Hi."

It was a female voice, speaking loudly to overcome the thud of music, which was invading their senses. Jocelyn knew it was her, the moment she smelled the perfume. It made her stop mid-step. She heard the familiar voice, even though it was gruffer, but she couldn't turn around to look at the face that spoke that single word.

There were too many memories in that face. Jocelyn's heart started to flutter as she stole a glance. Something broke deep inside of her: Something that had lain dormant in her for years. These years melted away as she remembered every single time she had been kissed by her, touched by her. Jocelyn let out a massive sigh. It transported her for an instant to times past, but she didn't have time to take in her thoughts as the woman stroked Jocelyn's arm.

Jocelyn turned slowly as the woman again said, "Hi."

She studied Jocelyn and slowly looked her up and down, appraisingly, "I didn't know you were back in town. Are you staying?"

Jocelyn's attention was immediately drawn to the woman's face. A strange sensation coursed its way through her body as she looked at her. It hypnotised her, seduced her. Not trusting her voice Jocelyn nodded. She had wanted Sam all those years ago; they were going to spend the rest of their lives together. Now all she felt was pain. Not the tangible sort but the sort of broken hearts, of silent screams in the night.

"Can we talk?" asked the woman.

Her voice broke through Jocelyn's musings. She tilted her head on one side, her mouth felt like cotton wool, but still no words would come.

"Shall we go somewhere quieter?"

It took Jocelyn a few moments to process the words spoken to her. The woman sighed in irritation and started to walk away, but still looked at her. Jocelyn, unsure whether she should react, nodded and followed the woman out into the night.

The woman walked down the small alley by the side of the pub and stopped in the shadows, turning abruptly to face Jocelyn.

She tore into Jocelyn, "Why did you leave. No reason. No word. You just disappeared. I thought you felt more for me than that. I thought you were dead."

Anger boiled within Jocelyn, as she spat out against this tirade, "Good to see you as well Sam. Are you blaming me for your indiscretions? I wasn't the one who was having an affair."

"Affair." Sam laughed a hollow, dismissive laugh, "Affair. I wasn't having an affair."

Jocelyn shook her head, "So if you weren't having an affair why were you both playing tonsil tennis?"

Sam shook her head as well and sighed, thinking back to that fateful night. "Leslie turned up at our place all teary eyed asking to speak with you. She waited until she heard you open the door then pounced on me. I tried to push her off but it was too late. You were gone."

Anger continued to bubble under the surface, "I challenged her, after I got back from chasing after you. She said that she had been bet by your work colleagues that she couldn't break us up. And because you ran off you allowed her to succeed. That night was the last time I saw Leslie, and you," she emphasized, "until tonight. You disappeared into thin air. So that night I too lost everything. A place to live with the woman I loved. I looked for you everywhere. I badgered your friends and family for weeks, months. I thought they were lying to me when they said they didn't know where you were."

Sam paused, as though the memory was too painful. She continued, "I thought you were ashamed to be gay; ashamed to be seen with me; and that you changed your mind. So why were you in such a state when you came into my flat? I think I deserve an explanation."

Jocelyn said, "I understand that you were hurt. Of course you were hurt, but you also have to see it from my side. I saw it as a betrayal. I walked in and all I saw was the two of you locked in a passionate embrace. After everything I had just gone through with my parents, the last thing I needed was seeing the two of you together. I wasn't to know that my so-called friend was setting you up, trying to break us up. All I saw was red mist. My life had been turned upside down. Everything that meant anything to me had gone."

The anger Sam showed dissipated, allowing Jocelyn to study Sam. A few lines had appeared around the eyes, and there was touches of grey at the temples.

Sam leant in and Jocelyn became acutely aware of the increasing pressure of Sam's body against hers. She couldn't escape the touch without physically moving away, but she was finding it increasingly hard not to enjoy the contact. She backed up a step feeling a little unsteady. She waited for Sam to speak, as the butterflies in her stomach played a haunting tune.

She looked across at Sam and felt a tremble start deep inside. Her face blushed a deep red, as her mind wandered, as thoughts of what it would be like to feel that caress and those lips again on her body. Sam reached out again and touched Jocelyn's arm. Jocelyn tried to keep her eyes averted as she couldn't chance Sam looking into them and seeing her inner feelings and have her guess her thoughts. Sam leant in and gave Jocelyn a chaste kiss on the lips. Trina's smiling face came into Jocelyn's mind, as she thought foolish, foolish woman. She pulled back from the kiss and brushed Sam's hand away, "I have to go."

Sam replaced her hand over Jocelyn's, smiled and said, "So soon, we've only just renewed our friendship."

Jocelyn shook her head and tugged her hand away. She shook her head again knowing she needed to go before she did something that she would regret, and said, "You're looking good, but I need to go."

Sam brushed the back of her hand against Jocelyn's cheek and said, "I'm glad you're home. You were gone for too long and one day soon, I will find out why. I know from your reaction you didn't leave because of me, but I'll let it go for now."

Sam took a card from her wallet, containing her address and mobile. She pulled Jocelyn into a gentle hug, slipped the card inside Jocelyn's bra and tapped where it was held, lingering too long for comfort. She smiled her charming smile, took hold of Jocelyn's hand and said, "So you can find me. I expect a call." and as she began to walk away from the pub she turned and said, "Soon. Don't take too long. I know you want me."

Frowning, Jocelyn pivoted on her heel, and headed for the pub doorway.

Sam shouted across to her, "You will get in touch. I know you will."

Jocelyn glanced over her shoulder. She tried to keep her face bland as the words rattled around in her ears. Sam was once a temptress and, apparently, she still was tempting.

Sam laughed, "You won't be able to keep away." and with those parting words and with a wave of her hand she disappeared into the night, leaving Jocelyn perplexed. Sighing, she re-entered the noisy, crowded bar.

Jocelyn imagined Trina's reaction when she told her that she had spoken to Sam. Little did she realise that Trina had watched the meeting between them, had followed them and had seen the interaction. Jocelyn knew that it would be a difficult conversation something to be shelved to a better time.

Trina, who still stood in the shadows, felt an icy fist clenching at her heart. Her world was falling apart again and she was powerless to stop it. She silently walked back into the pub, and wiped away a rogue tear.

ꕥ

Chapter Eighteen

Saturday

Duncan pushed the door open, walked over to his sister and gave her a kiss on the cheek and a big bear hug.

Holding her at arm's length he said, "Hi Dumps. What do you want me to do?"

"Could you carry on putting gloss on the skirting boards, please?"

"Sure, no problem." Duncan eased himself to the ground accompanied with a variety of moans and groans.

"You sound like an old man." Jocelyn teased.

"I played walking football last night and I used muscles that haven't been used in years so I'm aching all over."

Jocelyn smiled and said, “You’re a bit young for walking football.”

“It was a works do. Walking football allows everyone to join in.”

“So did you win?”

“It was more about taking part rather than winning.”

Jocelyn laughed, “So your team lost every game.”

Duncan joined in with the laughing, “Yes, all but one. The office staff won every game. And four of their six were women.”

Jocelyn gasped, “Stop being sexist. Women can play just as well as men.”

“I know. What I meant was they had never played walking football before. They were good. Am I forgiven?”

“Just this once.” She gave Duncan a hug. “Now you are here I can start on the ceiling. I didn’t want to go up the step ladder until someone else came.”

“Remind me again, why are we doing this?” Duncan waved his arm around the room.”

“My decorators let me down in the week. The main man broke his arm so they are behind schedule. I need to get it finished before the carpets go down.”

“Have you managed to rope anyone else in to help?”

“Charlie, Sean and Lucy said they’d help, but I haven’t heard any movement at all, so your guess is as good as mine. Trina is taking the kids to Weston for the day to build sandcastles on the beach.” She sighed.

“Weston-super-mud. That brings back memories” he sighed as well. “Remember how we used to go there on the train with Nan. She would sit in deck chair with her cardie wrapped around her, no matter how hot it was.”

“That’s right and she would have that floppy, flowery hat on her head.”

“We’d see who could make the tallest sand castle, have fish finger sandwiches, go and clamber over the rocks by Anchor Head. Finally heading to the pier to go on the dodgems, then eating either a toffee apple or candyfloss, as we walked back to the train station.

"I would always have a candyfloss. It always lasted until the station approach. Yummy."

"I hope the tide is in so they can have a paddle."

"We had good times there." A faraway look came into her eyes, and then she laughed, "Cathy promised to bring me back some candy floss."

Duncan joined in the laughter, "It will be a gooey mess by the time it gets to you. Right, we'd best crack on if you are going to get it finished on time."

Lucy pushed open the door to the office, laughing over a shared joke, followed closely by Rose.

"Hi Joy, Duncan. I see you've started without us."

"Whilst I have my brother's undivided attention I thought I best getting him working."

She won't trust me with anything other than the skirting boards. I don't blame her." He laughs, "You're up early or out late."

"I stayed at Rose's last night. So up early. I'll go and get our step ladders and persuade the lazy so and so's out of bed to help."

Moments later a woman's scream could be heard, then a muffled apology. Lucy walked back down the steps carrying the stepladders.

Jocelyn gave Lucy an enquiring look.

Lucy looked embarrassed but was smirking, "I was looking for the ladder. I couldn't remember who had them last or whether we had stored them in the loft. I looked in the living room, and then went up to the boys' area. Sean was in the shower so I had a quick peek in his room. I heard the water stop so I shouted to him about the ladders. He told me Charlie had them" She gave a little laugh. "I checked the door handle for the tell-tale red ribbon.

"Red ribbon?" Duncan asked.

"If one of us has someone staying we tie a piece of ribbon to the door handle."

"Oh. Good idea."

Rose replied, "Yes. It stops any embarrassment. So what happened?"

"As I was saying I checked for the ribbon and there wasn't any. So I listened at the door and could hear gentle snores. I opened the door a crack and saw a glint of the ladder near the window." Lucy tried hard to suppress the laughter that was rising in her.

"Go on." Rose said impatiently.

"Well you know that Charlie likes those black out curtains."

"Yes."

"And you can hardly see a thing."

"Yes."

"I tiptoed over to the window to get the ladders and was making my way towards the door when I tripped. The ladders crashed to the floor and I landed on the bed." She started to smile. "Suddenly this woman sat upright in bed and started screaming blue murder. I scarpered out of there as quickly as I could."

Rose rolled her eyes and both Jocelyn and Duncan shook their heads, smiling.

At that moment, Sean came downstairs, wearing an old pair of shorts and eating a piece of toast, and said, "So you met Charlie's girlfriend I hear."

"You could have warned me."

"I did, about the same time as the screaming started." He laughed.

Footsteps could be heard coming down the stairs and then the voices got louder.

"Stacey stop."

"Why should I. How dare you sneak another woman into your bed."

"Stace please. It was only Lucy and she wasn't in my bed."

"I don't care who it was. I'm not into anything kinky. If you want a threesome then count me out. I thought you were a decent bloke."

"Stacey, you don't understand."

"Oh I understand all right."

With that comment, the outside door banged close.

Charlie walked into the office carrying a bra.

"Not quite your size, mate." Sean stated.

Charlie gave him a withering stare.

"Nor your colour." continued Sean.

"If you know what's good for you I suggest you shut up."

He then turned his attention to Lucy.

"What did you think you were doing?"

"I needed the step-ladders and I could hear you snoring so I thought I could sneak in and get them." She grimaced, "Sorry."

"Didn't you see the ribbon?"

Lucy shook her head, "There was no ribbon on the door."

"I put it there."

"I didn't see it when I went to take a shower," stated Sean.

And with that, Charlie stormed back upstairs.

Lucy muttered, "I'd best go and try to smooth things over, I'll be back down in a mo."

She caught up with Charlie as he was entering his room.

"Charlie. I'm sorry. I would never have done anything to hurt you, or to show you up."

Charlie turned around saying, "I know. The ribbon wasn't on the door. I don't understand. I'm one hundred percent sure I put it on."

He walked into his room and pulled the curtains open, as Lucy hovered in the doorway. She pointed by the side of the bed, and said, "There it is."

Charlie walked over to it and said, "It must have come off when I went to the loo. Bloody hell."

"I'm sorry Charlie."

"You weren't to know."

"Why don't you go after her?"

Charlie shrugged, "I will when she's calmed down a bit."

"Was she the girl you've gone out with a few times?" asked Lucy.

"Yeah. She finally succumbed to my charms, and then you butted you in." he smiled, sardonically.

Lucy went over to Charlie and gave him a hug, "I really am sorry."

"I had invited her to our party tonight. I was going to introduce you and Rose properly then."

Let's hope you still can. Give her a little while and get in touch. She might just have been embarrassed. I can't apologise enough."

"I know." He took in a deep breath, and when he spoke again his tone had changed. "Aren't we supposed to be helping Joy this morning? I'll grab a quick shower and follow you down."

"Okay." Lucy turned and began to walk out of the room, "I am sorry."

"Will you stop apologising? What's done is done. If it was meant to be then it will happen." Charlie laughed, "Now scoot, before you get an eyeful of something you'd rather not see."

"Ew. Gross."

༄

Jocelyn and Duncan sat beside each other devouring their cakes and sipping their coffees. Jocelyn was transported back to their early teenage years, when life was simpler and times were happier. She enjoyed the special time she spent with her brother. She was glad that they were back in each other's lives.

Jocelyn gave him a friendly nudge, as they did when they were still teenagers. She was glad that he hadn't judged her and accepted her for who she was. Trina and the children had been welcomed into the family for which she was truly grateful.

They sat in a companionable silence then Duncan spoke, "That was a nice touch earlier."

Lucy frowned.

Duncan continued, "Stop being modest. It was a nice touch organising with the local pub those bottles of booze, crates of beer and some glasses."

"Well you can't have a house warming party without some alcohol."

"I know, but it was a nice touch."

"See, I can be pleasant when I want to be." She smiled across at her brother. "We did a good job today. Thanks for the help to finish getting the office ready."

"I'm only too pleased to help. I know I'm no good with wallpapering and the like, but skirting board painting and tidying up after you is my forte." He laughed.

"A sister couldn't ask for a better brother than you. I'm sorry for the break in our relationship, and I'm glad we put the past behind us and return to the loving, and teasing, rapport again."

"Aw Sis. I'm sorry too. I should have listened to your side of the story all those years ago. Us Harrold's should stick together, even though we are only half-siblings." He gave a small laugh, "But remember I never stopped loving you." His voice partly indicated humour, and partly shame.

"I know." she said as she again gave him a playful nudge.

"None of what happened was your fault. I was a total idiot for not recognising what was going on. Since you told me your side of the story, I realise that I should have seen the signs, the indicators that not all was right. Thinking back the warnings were all there. I just didn't grasp their meaning."

"Stop it now, little bruv. What is done is done, and nothing can turn back the clock to another time, another place. We have to deal with it in the way that is correct for us. Please don't feel guilty, Punky Dunc. I would not be the person I am today if those things had not happened in my life. I do not want the past to spoil my future."

"Okay. But I think I had better tell you that Dad is getting worse. He asked to see you."

Jocelyn raised her eyebrows.

"He did. It's not a ruse to get you to go in and see him. I was there and he asked me to ask you."

Jocelyn shook her head, disbelievingly. "Was Mum there?"

"No. She had gone to get a drink."

Jocelyn continued shaking her head.

"Joy, come in and see him with me. You might live to regret it if you don't."

"I'll think about it."

Duncan was still unsure whether his words had got though. He knew that if he pushed it, and demanded that she go in and see their father, then Jocelyn definitely wouldn't. He hoped that her kindness and humanity would overcome the loathing she felt for him.

"Don't take too long. Okay."

༄

Chapter Nineteen

Sunday

She bolted upright in bed, her pulse racing. Jocelyn blinked but unsuccessfully couldn't make out anything in the dark room. She sat perfectly still, with feelings that seemed to be crowding in on her. She willed her breathing back to normal, praying that the dream was just that, a dream, not an insight of things to come. Gradually shapes seemed to appear out of the gloom. Her pulse slowly began to beat its normal rhythm and some of the tension left her shoulders and neck.

She got up, walked into the kitchen area and had a long drink. She then splashed water over her face and neck, and willed the disturbing thoughts to be washed away, along with the water. She walked back into the bedroom, straightened the sheets and climbed back into bed.

Sleep slowly took hold of her and when she awoke, she was tangled again in her crumpled sheets. Jocelyn closed her eyes and turned onto her back. A stream of sunshine acted as a spotlight on to her body and she stretched out like a cat who had found their favourite place. Feeling the warm glow of the sun, she finally opened her eyes.

Jocelyn wondered why she would still be having these dreams where her pulse is racing and her chest is so tight that she can't breathe. Where she would feel the weight of his body and wake up screaming and drenched in sweat, wanting to be sick.

She rubbed the sleep out of her eyes with her fists, and then massaged her cheeks and neck. Becoming more awake, she slung her legs over the side and padded quietly to the bathroom.

After showering and her obligatory two cups of coffee, she felt awake enough to face the world. Jocelyn was struggling to understand her reaction and emotion to this dream. She wondered whether she should have had it out with him. She needed to talk with him without her Mum around, accusing her.

She looked at her watch and knew that Trina would now be awake. She picked up her mobile and pressed her icon. The phone rang a few times and then she was greeted by Trina's voice.

"Hi love. You're up early. I'm sorry I couldn't stay longer last night. I didn't like to leave the new baby-sitter too long. I'm just about to go in and rouse the kids." Trina became aware that Jocelyn hadn't said anything. "Are you okay?"

Trina heard a big sigh from the other end of the phone.

"What's the matter? Has anything happened?"

Jocelyn shook her head, and said, "I had that dream again. So I'm all out of sorts."

"Do you want to talk about it?"

"Yes. No. I don't know."

"Don't close yourself away, Joy. You know that things become worse when you close yourself away."

"No, love. Things haven't become that bad. I'm good, really."

"Are you? Joy, these nightmares are becoming more regular. You need to talk."

"Honestly Treen. I'm fine."

Trina tutted down the phone and sighed which portrayed. 'I don't believe you.'

"I'm good. Honestly. I wish I hadn't told you now."

"That's exactly what I mean. Talk to me or talk to someone professional."

"Hah, you think I'm crazy."

Trina shook her head and said one word. A word that described all her own anxieties, "Missy."

Missy or Mister, was the word that Trina used when she wanted to say, 'you've crossed the line, but I love you so won't make a fuss.' It meant, stop right there, don't do it again or take it further, or, you know I'm right and will do as I ask.

Even though she couldn't see her, Jocelyn smiled an apologetic smile that said she understood the warning. She acquiesced and said, "I love you. I will phone the number of that shrink you gave me"

"Good." Trina said in a voice that would tolerate no other outcome.

At least she was going to receive some counselling. And she hoped that it would work. But how do you kill ghosts? Especially ghosts that are still alive.

"So when do we expect you over. If all goes well, lunch will be at one."

ꟾ

"I'm glad Charlie and his girlfriend sorted out their problem with Lucy falling onto them yesterday." Jocelyn smiled as they washed up the dishes.

Trina wiped up the final pot and replied, "Not as glad as Lucy, I expect. It sounded so funny when you told me. It could only happen to Lucy. The ribbon idea sounded like a good idea. Shame it didn't work."

"I think they were talking about rigging up a board with sliding panels which showed red or green."

"I'm sure they'll find something that works for them."

"You spent quite a while chatting with Stacey. Any juicy gossip I should know about?"

Trina flicked her with the teacloth. "You're incorrigible. If you want to know any gossip you should ask her yourself."

"But you are so much better at it than I am." Jocelyn replied, with a winning smile.

"Okay." Trina sighed, but a smile spread across her face. "Stacey works for one of the large department stores in Broadmead. She started working there when she left school. She has worked her way up to be an assistant manager. She works in what she called the fuddy duddy department." Trina paused, and then added, "You ought to go and see her."

Jocelyn shook her head, and smiled, "You are so hilarious. I'm not fuddy duddy."

Trina sniggered.

Jocelyn ignored her and continued, "And we're the same age."

"No we're not. You are ancient."

"Funny ha ha. There is only two months between us."

"So I'll always be your toy girl."

Jocelyn wrapped her arms around her, "And what a lovely toy girl you are."

When they parted from a deep and meaningful kiss Trina asked, "So how long did you stay with the guys last night?"

"Not long after you left. I walked along the harbourside path, then sat and watched the twinkling street lights reflected in the water. Even though I was in the heart of the city, it was so quiet, so peaceful." She laughed, "Ha. Then a group of young men obvious the worse for wear staggered by and my peace was shattered. For a moment, I thought one of them was going to fall into the harbour and I didn't fancy jumping in after them. So I wandered home and had an early night, not that it did me any good."

Trina pulled her closer, "Which nightmare was it this time?"

"I had two. The first one I have no idea. I had a fleeting memory but then it was gone. All I know I felt frightened. The second one was the usual one. Mind you, Duncan had asked me to see Dad earlier, so that could be my subconscious kicking in, with my old supressed fears rising to the surface. Treen, do you ever think I will get over his abuse?"

"I don't know love. But you promised me that when you got settled you would speak to someone."

"I will."

Trina put her hands on her hips and gave her a sceptical look.

"I will."

"You've been saying this for ages."

"I know and I will. I couldn't sort anything out today, as it is a Sunday. I promise, tomorrow first thing."

Trina shook her head and gave an unconvinced shrug.

"You don't believe me, do you?"

"Now what gives you that impression?" Trina again shook he head but a smile played on her lips, "I've known you too long. If you don't want to do something you make all the excuses in the world to put it off. But every minute your conscience is telling you it's the correct thing to do, you get yourself even more worked up. So for once in your life don't put something like this off."

"I love you Trina Rennet. You are and have always been my voice of reason."

ꙮ

Chapter Twenty

Monday

Jocelyn sat in a tiny waiting room and nervously looked around the room. As with all waiting rooms, there was the obligatory pile of magazines, looking dog-eared and well read, heaped together on a corner table. The different pieces of artwork on the walls, designed to be calming, had lines and squiggles that was an assault on her eyes. She much preferred prints that meant something, showed something, that told a story.

Jocelyn began to feel overwhelmed. She closed her eyes and tried to control her breathing. Why was she here? She knew why. The nightmares were getting worse. They were undermining her confidence. She was waking up tired and fractious. She knew that she needed them to stop, especially with the launch coming up. She took another deep breath.

"Jocelyn Harrold?"

A woman in her thirties appeared in the doorway. Jocelyn stood up.

"Yes." she responded.

"Would you like to follow me?"

As they left the waiting room, the woman introduced herself.

"Hi. I'm Doctor Alice Fortune."

"Oh hi Doctor. Thank you for seeing me at such short notice. I hope I'm not wasting your time."

"You were lucky you phoned when you did. One of my clients cancelled at the last moment." She opened the door to her office. "Please take a seat."

Jocelyn looked around and on the left hand side of the room; she saw the obligatory desk and a bookcase filled with a variety of tomes. Three easy chairs arranged in a triangle, with a small table between them were toward the right. They looked like the kind of chairs she could easily fall asleep in. She sat down in one facing the window. On the table was a box of tissues.

"Comfortable enough. May I get you something? A glass of water, cup of tea?"

"I glass of water would be good."

Alice poured two glasses of water from the jug of iced water that contained slices of lemon, placed them on the table and sat on her right hand side.

Alice asked, "Do you mind if I make an audio recording of your visit. I find it easier than taking notes. And to put your mind at rest, the only people to have access to the recordings would be just you and me."

"Okay."

Alice looked at the clipboard she held in her hand and noted the personal details Jocelyn had filled in whilst waiting in the reception. She looked from the paper and appraised Jocelyn, saying, "I know this might be difficult for you, and your anxiety levels might already be sky high but do you feel able to explain why you wanted to see me, talk to me this morning?"

Jocelyn shifted uncomfortably in her seat. She rubbed her hand over her face as though she was washing away all the thoughts that were flowing through her body.

She took a sip of the water, breathed deeply and said, "My girlfriend thought it would be a good idea to talk to someone."

Alice replied, "So you don't think it is a good idea?"

"I didn't say that."

"You might not have said it, but you implied it. So do you think it is a good idea?"

"I don't know." The words came out as no more than a whisper.

"People who come in here for counselling are all made differently. They all have different needs, different experiences. Sometimes talking to a stranger is all you need. You may find by verbalising your worries and fears, you may be able to put things into perspective. To understand what it is you are experiencing. However you may need a little helping hand to work things through."

Jocelyn sat with her head bowed. Alice sat patiently and waited. Moments ticked by and then minutes. Jocelyn picked up the glass and took another sip. She spoke, "Aren't you going to ask me anything?"

"No." Alice said with a shake of her head.

"I knew this was going to be a waste of time." but, instead of getting up and walking to the door, Jocelyn continued to sit in the chair.

Again, moments turned into minutes and the silence weighed heavy between them.

Jocelyn's resolve failed, "Do you ever speak?"

"Only when asked a direct question or if it is appropriate."

Silence again stretched between them. Jocelyn squirmed in her seat, and again sipped the water, whilst Alice waited patiently and considered the woman in front of her.

Finally, Jocelyn leant forward, apparently having resolved the issues she was fighting, and spoke, "I've been having bad nightmares again. They are making me tired all the time. These nightmares are causing my anxiety levels to rise to a place where I don't feel comfortable. I'm getting snappy and difficult to be around, and now, I do not have the time or energy to go into meltdown. I'm about to launch my new company on Friday and I need to have all my wits about me to cope. At the moment I feel as if I am being pulled in too many directions."

She sat back in the chair and let out a sigh of relief as she thought 'that's the hardest bit over'.

Alice asked, "At the start, you said 'I've been having bad nightmares again'. Would you go into more detail about what you mean by the word again?"

"Did I? Oh, okay. I had the same, or a similar, nightmare years ago, whilst I was living in Sunderland."

"Would you like to tell me about the nightmare you used to have all those years ago."

Jocelyn looked at Alice and frowned, "Why? What relevance does it have now?"

"I have no idea so would you please humour me."

Jocelyn looked sceptical but said, "I am being chased by a person or persons unknown. They are in shadow so I don't know whether it is male or female. I am caught and held with my arms pinned to my side. I fight back and try to suffocate them. Then I wake up."

Jocelyn shuddered at the memories of the bad dreams. She closed her eyes and was transported back to Sunderland, waking up to crumpled sheets and unease.

Alice spoke quietly, "I can see that the memory of that nightmare upsets you greatly.

Jocelyn nodded, not daring to speak.

Alice again spoke in hushed tones, "And your nightmare now?"

Jocelyn took her time and after a few deep breaths she said, "Again I am being chased but this time I am in agony. Suddenly, I'm running on the spot. Someone comes to me and forces me down on the floor and I feel the weight of their body. I attack them as if my life is depending on it. Biting is involved, I think I am being bitten, but I don't know. Everything is happening so fast but also in slow motion. I try to suffocate them to wipe them out of my life. Finally, I am alone and covered in bruises feeling deep hurt."

A deep wracking sob escaped, and a box of tissues was placed in her hands. When then sobs subsided and Jocelyn returned to some semblance of her true self, she spoke, "I'm sorry. I don't know where those tears came from."

"Perhaps it was something you needed to happen. Tears are a good release for your emotions."

"What do these nightmares mean?"

"What do you think they mean?"

"I think I know what the nightmare I used to have meant."

Jocelyn paused. Alice waited.

Jocelyn gave a small laugh. "You're good at this. Just give me a minute." She closed her eyes and took another deep breath. "Before I lived in Sunderland, Bristol was my home. I moved there to escape from my Dad. During my late teenage years he used to hit me, then he found out I was a lesbian and tried to rape me."

Jocelyn closed her eyes and past memories flooded into her brain. When she opened her eyes again, Alice was looking at her intently.

Alice spoke with understanding, "I know these memories are painful but would you like to continue?"

Jocelyn gave a small nod of her head, "I escaped from his clutches, and was in the process of throwing a paperweight at him when Mum came through the front door. All she saw was me attacking him. Of course she took his side, and wouldn't hear or believe anything I was saying. So I know, or think I know, that the nightmare of all those years ago had the basis of that night."

Alice asked, "How long did they last?"

"Nearly every night for about three months. I was a total wreck"

"Do you have any thoughts to why they stopped?"

Jocelyn thought for a minute then replied, "I got in contact with my Nan. I told her some of what happened. She knew that Dad was hitting me, but not the attempted rape. At the same time, I was given a job, just when my money was running out. I think I suddenly felt safe and not alone. The nightmares stopped."

Alice leaned over and touched Jocelyn arm, and said, "Thank you for sharing that with me."

"Thank you for listening, but what about the ones I'm having now?"

A bell quietly rang. Alice spoke, "I'm afraid our session is coming to a close.

"So soon?" Jocelyn was astonished. "Wow. That went by quickly."

"Normally when it is your first session it is a double one, as it usually takes that amount of time for some to speak." Alice paused, looked at Jocelyn, who gave a small smile, "And I am aware that we have barely touched the surface."

"I've only ever told three people what my Dad tried to do. My Nan knew he hit me and guessed something else had happened but I couldn't tell her. I didn't want her to know what sort of man her daughter had married."

"I think we need to talk again, sooner rather than later. In fact, tomorrow would be good." She walked over to her desk and had a quick glance at her diary. "Could you make it at the end of the afternoon? Say around half past five?"

Jocelyn pulled out her tablet and said, "Five Thirty is good for me. See you tomorrow. Thank you."

ঌ

Jocelyn's phone rang as she was opening her door. She scrambled to get it out of her bag and dropped it on the floor. As she bent to pick it up the phone cut off. She swore quietly under her breath. She looked at the caller ID and called back.

"Hi love. Sorry I didn't answer but I dropped my phone. Why are you phoning, I'll be around in about an hour?" she didn't allow time to answer and continued, "Did you have a good day?"

"Yes I have, but stop deflecting talk away from you. You know fully well, why I called. How did your session go?"

"It went well."

She paused.

"So are you going to tell me or am I going to have to drag it out of you."

Jocelyn laughed, "I'd prefer to tell you when I get up to you, but she seemed a very nice person. She did that not talking thing. You know, where you felt you had to talk to fill the silence."

Trina joined in the laughter, "I bet you hated that."

"You know me so well. Yes, she was good." She paused, "And you'll be pleased to know I'm going back to see her tomorrow."

"Good. I'll see you in about an hour."

"Love you."

"And you too."

ꟃ

Chapter Twenty One

Tuesday

"Jocelyn." Alice looked over to Joy, "Would you like to come through?"

Jocelyn followed Alice into her consultant room. Alice placed some water on the table whilst Jocelyn made herself comfortable.

"Please take a seat. It's going to be a double session to make up for yesterday. Is that okay?"

"Fine with me."

"How are you doing? I've listened to the tape of yesterday's meeting and taken down some notes. Is it alright to again tape today's meeting." She looked at Jocelyn, who nodded agreement, "Did you have the nightmare again last night?"

"I think I must have. I woke up and the sheets were all crumpled. The memory was fleeting, but it felt as though it was the same dream. I felt restless all morning. I really need to be dream free. What does it mean?"

"Before I tell you what your dreams could mean, you mentioned that you are launching your new company on Friday and you feel like you are pulled in too many directions. Perhaps we need to explore this avenue." Alice looked expectantly towards Jocelyn.

Slightly taken aback, Jocelyn started to think about what she had said and why she said that comment. She tapped her finger on her lips and replied, "I don't really think I am being pulled in too many directions, but perhaps my self-conscious thinks I am."

"Okay. So tell me what is going on in your life. You know work, relationships, family, friends, and those kind of things."

"I am seeing a lovely lady called Trina." A big smile crossed over Jocelyn's face. "Trina is an old school friend of mine. She was my bestie all through our school years. She was so supportive when I was bullied for being gay. She is a divorcee and we got together as a couple when I came back to Bristol for my Nan's funeral. We have been seeing each other for about seven months. However I have only finally moved back completely so it is like we are starting over again. She has two beautiful children, who I adore. Peter is eleven and Cathy is eight, and I love Trina to bits."

"How do they feel about your relationship with their mother?"

"It appears as if they are in favour. Cathy always wants me to read her bedtime story and Peter recently persuaded his Mum to allow me to stay overnight. Something I only ever did when they were staying at their fathers." She laughed, "The first time I stayed over Cathy wanted me to take her to school with her mum so she could introduce me to her teacher. Her words to her teacher was, 'This is Joy. She is going to be my other mummy. She is a lethbeen. When she moves in properly I'm going to call her mummy J'." Another laugh exploded from within. "Poor Trina. It looked as though she wanted to crawl under the nearest rock. The teacher gave a little wink and a knowing smile."

"What do you think about, umm, Cathy," she looked at Jocelyn for confirmation, "wanting for her to call you mummy J?"

Jocelyn paused, and happy thoughts played across her face. "I feel privileged and really content, the most content I have in years."

"Anything you would want to change?"

"We are still taking it fairly slowly. I would like us to be a proper family, but that would be a little further down the line. I can see us living together and getting married."

"Have you discussed this with Trina?"

"Good lordy no. The time has to be right for the both of us. She will always put the children first, no matter what. So I am going to have to be patient."

"Can you do that?"

"I will have to."

Alice looked at her notes. She asked, "Workwise. You mentioned that you would be launching your company on Friday. Would you like to fill me in on how you are feeling about that?"

Jocelyn took a deep breath and began, "Where do I start." She paused, "I have the whole gamut of emotions flowing through me. I'm happy, frightened, delighted, fearful, apprehensive, excited and everything between the two extremes. Trina has been so supportive, and so has my brother and sister-in-law. I have three good young workers on board who are keen as mustard. I know that it is a stepping stone for them, which they will go on to bigger and better things, but at this precise moment in time, things are moving as I would want them. I have a few firms on board which is tidying things over okay. I have a meeting on Thursday with a decent size company, which if they sign on the dotted line will keep the business afloat for the important first year. If that goes well then I can settle down to make this venture the success I dream it could be."

Jocelyn closed her eyes.

Alice thought for a moment and asked, "What would you do if the meeting doesn't go as you planned? Tell me your thoughts and worries."

"I would have to try to find another fairly big client. That would mean more work for me, and the team. I wouldn't be able to guarantee jobs into the next year and I wouldn't be able to grow the company."

"How does that make you feel?"

"As though I am a failure, again."

"Again? What makes you say that?"

"Well I failed in having a relationship with my parents and I failed at my first meaningful relationship."

Alice steepled her fingers together, "Let's put those thoughts on the back burner for a moment. What have you succeeded in? Earliest memory to more recent."

Jocelyn smiled, "Earliest memory of success, if you could call it that, was being able to break out and into my parent's house without being caught." She looked at Alice's passive face. "Alright, my early successes were getting into all the school sports teams I tried for, passing my exams, with grades I wanted. Then it was finding my first job on leaving school." Jocelyn stopped speaking for a few moments and then continued, "My next was selling a successful company I co-founded, which has left me comfortably well off, allowing me to pursue this dream back in my home town."

"That seemed a big gap between school and selling your business."

"As I told you, I had issues with my father which took me longer to come to terms with. If I ever have."

Alice smiled and nodded, then said, "Your failures you mentioned. Were either of them your fault?"

"I'm gay. So that didn't help with the relationship I had with my parents but the relationship I had with my dad had broken down years before I came out to them. As I said yesterday he used to physically abuse me."

"Was any of the abuse your fault?"

Jocelyn paused for a moment. Different memories and thoughts were flitting through her mind. "My first girlfriend I caught in a passionate embrace, so no. My parents are a different story. A couple of times I know I wound Dad up, but not enough for him to knock me about like he did."

"Did you try to tell anyone?"

A big sigh escaped from Jocelyn, "I did try to tell someone a couple of times. The first time I told someone about the physical abuse, I laughed about it. I still don't understand my reaction. You know, why I laughed." Jocelyn felt the pent up emotions bubbling under the surface. "I'd run out of excuses for why my body ached, and my PE teacher asked me why I was struggling to join in. I told the truth and as it all stumbled from my lips. I can remember chuckling as if it was the funniest thing to happen. I remember it clearly; I sounded like a laughing hyena."

Jocelyn shook her head, "Telling my teacher seemed such an absurd thing to do, to admit that I was being abused. From her reaction, I think she thought I was mucking about. How could someone like me allow themselves to be abused? So I kept quiet and didn't mention it to her again."

"And the other times you tried to tell someone?"

Jocelyn smiled, "The person who befriended me when I first moved away was concerned for me and asked what was wrong. I wouldn't tell them because I didn't think they would believe Dad abused me, because I never once filed a police report. Because I didn't usually fight back. At first, I knew I wasn't strong enough. But I'm not a shrinking violet; I'm a strong woman who can usually handle herself. Why would I allow someone to continue abusing me when I could do something about it? I thought they would think me crazy, to allow it to happen.

"Did you feel like a crazy person?"

"No. And yes you are correct; none of it was my fault."

Jocelyn breathed deeply and Alice studied her features.

"I tried to tell Mum when it first started, but I couldn't. I loved Dad, and could tell you plenty of nice things we did together. He only hit me when we were alone. It hurt like hell to feel so vulnerable. I couldn't do it. I couldn't tell her. If she did believe me, what would it done to our family life? I had to think about Duncan. I didn't think she would have believed me, in fact when it came to a head she didn't. At the time I was not strong enough for her call me a liar to my face. I needed her love. I wanted her love. It would have been awful," she breathed out heavily, "and when it happened, when she didn't believe me, it was awful. So awful I considered taking my life."

Alice didn't respond for a moment, and then said, "How many times have you considered taking your life?"

"Twice."

"And what stopped you?"

"The first time I felt so depressed. I had just been suspended from school, and both my Mum and Dad were telling me how worthless I was. I felt worthless. I didn't see the point in carrying on. I was going to take some tablets but there was only two in the bottle. I was on my way to the chemist when I bumped into Trina. She persuaded me to go for a drink with her and Mike. Her laughter and friendship stopped me from doing anything so daft. Talking to her and Mike about nothing and everything made me feel better about myself."

Jocelyn paused, as a small smile played on her lips, as she continued,

"You see Trina has always been there for me."

"And the second time?"

"The second time was that fateful day when everything went from complete joy to utter despair in the space of an hour." Anger flashed in her eyes. "I drove up to the suspension bridge and it was only the stupid comment someone had written about the nearest phone box that made me stop and think."

She looked at Alice and said, "All I think now is shame and guilt that I even contemplated taking my own life. I realise that there are many people who would have been affected by my selfish act."

"So you think it is a selfish act?"

"Yes. I do now."

Alice didn't respond.

Jocelyn spoke, "I'm aware of the time and I would really like to know what my nightmares could mean. Whether it is something I can work through myself. Or whether these deep lying emotions I have are having a bearing."

Alice studied Jocelyn and said, "I don't think it will be a quick fix, and I think you need to have a few more sessions. But to allow you something to think about, and to work through, I will give a precis on aspects of the dreams you are having. Is that okay?"

"Okay. Shoot."

"You have five main themes in your dreams. These are running, pain, suffocation, biting and attacking someone. Agreed?"

"Agreed."

"Don't forget that this isn't the definitive answer to your problems and fears. The explanations I am about to give you could, and only could, have these meanings. In fact, it might not have any basis at all. Do you want me to continue?"

"Yes."

"Okay. Firstly, let's look at what running might emphasise in dreams." She looked over to Jocelyn for permission, "If you are being chased, you are running from some confrontation. Is it something from your past you don't want to deal with? Or is it a confrontation you know you need to have. But you hope it will go away if you ignore it long enough? Alternatively, you may be running away from a primal urge or fear. Running in place means you're trying as hard as you can to move forward in life but something or someone is holding you back."

Again, Alice looked at Jocelyn, who nodded.

"To dream that you are in agony suggests that some decision or nagging problem from your waking life has crept into your dream. It will continue to torment you until it is resolved. The message of this dream is that you cannot run from this issue forever. The longer you ignore or avoid it, the more it will follow you."

Alice paused, "Pain often points to emotional pain. What part of the body is afflicted? Pain in the chest means hurt feelings. Pain in the head means hurt ego, pain in the feet means you're having a hard or painful experience getting where you want to go in life. Does everything so far make sense?"

"I think so."

Continuing, Alice said, "If you are suffocating someone in the dream, then you must ask yourself what is the situation in your life are you trying to extinguish right now?" She paused, "To dream that you are attacking someone represents pent-up frustration and anger. You feel you have been wronged. Your dream serves as an easy and safe way to express your anger."

Again, she gave a slight pause. "And finally, to dream that you are being bitten represents your vulnerability regarding some unresolved issues or emotions. To dream that you have a bruise represents stress and mounting pressure that you are dealing with in your waking life. It may also refer to a reawakening of old, family wounds that have not been properly addressed."

"Wow." Jocelyn shook her head. "That has given me plenty to think about."

"It seems to me that some of the trauma of your past hasn't caught up with you until now. You have tried to put it in some hidden part of your mind but it wouldn't go away completely. The fury you felt back then, sits deep inside you. You think that you should feel, or be held, accountable for other people's bad behaviour. You have plastered on your smile and gotten on with your life. But this fury has manifested itself and now the focus of the trauma shows up in your nightmares. You are not broken and you have faced the violence of your past. Something has triggered that past fury and is expressing itself in your present. I suggest you acknowledge your fury and not be afraid of the consequences."

"My brother wants me to go and see my Dad."

"And will you?"

"I despise him. So why should I go and see him. I know that he is dying and I should make my peace with him and Mum. But why should I, after all the pain and hurt he has caused me." Jocelyn gave a little laugh. "It's funny, even after all these years I don't really hate him. I think he is sick."

"It might be because, at the end of the day, he's your Dad."

"That's the thing. He isn't."

ஐ

Chapter Twenty Two

Thursday Morning

"Phone call about your meeting this afternoon." Lucy said, as she passed the phone to Jocelyn.

"Hi Mr. Riorden. How may I help you? I thought we were meeting this afternoon."

Jocelyn listened.

"Okay. Sorry you can't make the meeting this afternoon."

She nodded her head. "So I will be meeting one of your assistants instead. What is their name?"

She indicated to Lucy to bring her a pen and paper.

"Sam. And his surname?"

The colour drained from Jocelyn's face and Lucy silently asked what was wrong.

"Sorry Mr. Riorden, will you repeat. You did say Sam Morris. Yes. Okay. Same time but in the Mall. By the food hall."

She paused again.

"Thanks for letting me know. I'll look forward to seeing you tomorrow evening instead. Bye."

Jocelyn let out a big sigh and cradled her face in her hands. Lucy showed concern on her face as she asked, "Problems."

"Could be."

"So you are meeting with a bloke called Sam, who is one of the assistant managers. What is the problem with that?"

Jocelyn shook her head, "It's a woman called Sam Morris."

A light dawned, "You mean your ex, Sam?"

"I don't know. I hope not."

"Well, all you know at the moment is that you are meeting with a woman called Sam Morris. It could be a coincidence."

Jocelyn gave her a withering look, "I hope so. I don't want our paths to cross. I want my past, to be kept in the past. I don't want anyone or anything to rock the boat."

"Is that because you are afraid of what might happen?"

"Of course I'm bloody afraid." She snapped, "I'm scared I might not be able to resist."

"But you love Trina."

Jocelyn closed her eyes and slowly breathed in and out. She rubbed her hands over her face as if she wanted to erase all the thoughts that flashed through her brain, "I love Trina with all my heart and soul but do I trust myself to walk by if I pass Sam in the street? If I have to do business with her, I don't know if I could cope."

"I look at you and Trina and all I see is the love passing between you. Sam should not hold any fear for you now. She is the past; you and Trina are the future."

Jocelyn gave an unconvincing smile.

Lucy shook her head, "It could be hard but you will never be free in your head if you don't confront the demons of your past. She has no power over you anymore. You've moved on and so has she. You have laid the ghost to rest." After a slight pause she asked, "If it is your ex, are you going to tell Trina?"

"Yes. No. I don't know. I need to think what will be best."

"What? For you or for her."

"Don't start please.

Lucy held up her hands in submission. "I didn't mean to upset you."

"No, I'm sorry I snapped. You're correct as normal."

As Jocelyn was now to meet a different person, she felt the need to re-evaluate the proposal she had in mind and see how it could deviate from their normal practice. Deviate. She wanted to be new, be fresh, and be innovative. Deviate. The word kept going around in her brain. It kept on cropping up in conversation, as though her subconscious was telling her something. In a light bulb moment, she knew what her new company would be called. She spoke quietly to herself, "That's it. The name of the company can be 'DV8' and our tagline could be 'Different from the norm' or 'not your normal company'.'

"Did you say something?"

"Something just popped into my mind. What do you think DV8 as our company name?"

"I was wondering when you would come up with something."

"I was thinking along the lines of DV8. Deviate has been going through my brain a lot recently. Which tagline do you think fits best 'Different from the norm' or 'not your normal company'?"

"We could have both."

"What do you mean?"

"Before we give our pitch we use the research on the company to see which tagline would suit those best."

"It could work. Now I need to get our business cards sorted."

Lucy got out her phone.

"What are you doing?"

"I'm calling in a favour." She placed her finger on her lips, "Hi love. During your lunch break, instead of meeting me, could use your graphic skills to design a logo to go on our office paraphernalia." She paused, laughed, and then replied, "Capital D, Capital V and the number 8. Tagline 'Different from the norm' and 'not your normal company'. Two different ones. Yes. Different named business cards for the four of us and a blank one with only the work phone number." She looked across to Jocelyn for confirmation, who nodded.

Lucy paused again, turned to Jocelyn and asked, "What colour scheme do you want?"

Jocelyn shrugged, "Bright blue, yellow and grey?"

Lucy relayed the colours to Rose. She listened and laughed again, smiling she finished the call.

"Rose will email you some designs towards the end of her lunch break."

"You didn't ask her how much she wanted for her time."

"She owed me a favour. I'll make it up to her later." Lucy grinned. "Okay. Back to work."

ꙮ

Jocelyn sat with a cup of coffee in one of the outlets and waited for the person she was meeting to arrive. She hoped that it was all a coincidence that the names were the same. She impatiently drummed her fingers on the table and tried to calm her jangling nerves.

She saw her ex, Sam, making her way towards her table, and felt her heart plummet. She needed to keep focused on the task. She couldn't afford to turn away opportunities. But why her, why now?

Jocelyn rose from her seat and greeted Sam, giving her hand a precursory shake, "I didn't know you worked with John Riorden."

Sam laughed, "So you didn't keep my business card?"

Shaking her head, Jocelyn replied, "It's somewhere on my dressing table. I didn't look at it."

"I told you we would meet up again."

"No. You said I would phone you. And I don't think I did." Jocelyn sounded like a petulant child.

"Pedantic as ever."

"I'm sorry. Let's start again. Would you like a coffee? We have a business meeting to run."

"Latte please."

Jocelyn brought back the latte and fresh coffee for herself. She took a sip and found it difficult to concentrate. The nearness of the woman sat opposite her was causing too many distractions. She needed to engage Sam in a conversation about her proposal, without any connotations. Jocelyn wanted to know whether there needed to be any new approaches. This meeting had to be strictly a fact finding one. Jocelyn needed to figure out how the objectives of the company Sam worked for could be translated into a solid marketing plan.

She opened up the tablet and started the question and answer session. She started to input the data she received from Sam's responses into the survey, and so into the database. All the time Jocelyn was talking a small smirk played on Sam's lips. Jocelyn was going to give Sam an honest shot of getting the marketing plan. But would Sam do the same.

Sam stood up and said, "I would like to take you around the Mall. That's why I arranged to meet here. I want you to see how we market the company's products and services in this type of environment. On seeing that you might be better able to market them and give them a more advantageous approach."

On listening to Sam, Jocelyn realised that the meeting between them wasn't entirely about what she could bring to the company through her ideas. She kept getting the impression that Sam hoped more would go on as she flirted became more outrageous. Jocelyn felt a flutter in her stomach and tried to put away the thoughts that were invading her being. She tried to clear her mind; she had to concentrate on the work, and only work. She couldn't afford to deviate from her plan, and not look for more than that.

As they walked around the Mall, Sam kept touching her arm and directing her towards different displays. She explained what the company's products provided to people of all ages incomes

Sam's phone rang and she said, "It's the office. Would you excuse me for a moment? Continue having a look around our display. I'll meet you outside in five." She walked out of the shop they were in.

Jocelyn gave Sam a nod of approval. She hated people having loud conversations or conducting business inside public places. She let out a deep sigh and closed her eye. She muttered quietly, "Keep it together for a few more minutes. Don't deviate from the plan."

She slowly followed Sam. Seeing that Sam had finished the call, she sauntered over.

Sam stared into Jocelyn's eyes, and Joy recognised the longing she saw in Sam's face. Jocelyn tried to put an end to whatever crazy thought were going through her brain. She needed to behave as though she was merely a client, not as her once forever love.

"Whatever you are thinking, it's not going to happen."

"Please tell me what I am thinking, because I haven't a clue what you are on about."

"Stop playing the innocent." Jocelyn shook her head. Her lips pulled together in a tight line. "It has been really lovely to see you but I love Trina and am very content in our relationship.

Sam's mouth thinned into a tight smile, "She didn't seem too content when I saw her in the toilets on Friday night. I would say that she was a little upset. What about, I don't know, you'll have to ask her."

"You spoke to her on Friday?"

"I didn't need to. She knew who I was." Sam became business-like, and suddenly asked, "Can you have a proposal ready for Tuesday, ten o'clock?"

Jocelyn looked at the woman in front of her. She seemed to be able to change her persona on a whim, so she also decided to play it the same way.

"Sure. I'll courier a hard copy of the proposal over to your offices first thing in the morning. Would you like electronic copies as well?"

"Of course."

"They will be meeting to discuss all the pitches later that day and you will get your answer in a week or two after that."

"Thank you for meeting me and letting my company have the chance to pitch our ideas to you. Will you be accompanying Mr. Riorden to the launch tomorrow?"

Sam again gave Jocelyn that knowing smirk, "I'll be there."

"Until tomorrow then."

The two women shook hands, and nodded. Suddenly Sam leant in and gave Jocelyn a passionate kiss. They broke apart. A look of triumph was plastered on Sam's face. Whilst Jocelyn looked shocked.

Sam walked away and after a few metres she turned and said, “I’ll be expecting that phone call anytime soon.”

With that passing remark, she waved her hand in the air, and continued walking, leaving Jocelyn as a car crash in her wake.

ꟿ

Chapter Twenty Three

Thursday Afternoon

"How did the meeting go?" Lucy asked as soon as Jocelyn walked into the office. "Was it her?"

"Yes. It was her." Jocelyn answered flatly.

"Are you going to tell Trina?"

"Yes. No. I don't know."

"You are going to have to. Joy, it's not fair on Trina if you don't."

"I know. I know. Why did it have to be her?"

"Life throws you a curve ball at the least expected moment. So what are you going to do about it?"

"Nothing." She breathed deeply, "Let me tell you about the meeting."

"Well? How did it go? Have we got it?"

"Sam liked our ideas. She wanted to tweak a few things and to include some aspects we hadn't thought about. It seems as though our ideas marry with theirs. We have to have our proposal on their desk by Tuesday, ten o'clock. They are having a meeting late morning to go through the different ones they have received."

Lucy thought for a moment, "That doesn't give us much time to work on it. As you can see I picked the short straw and am holding the fort, both Sean and Charlie are out in the field sorting out a couple of things. I know that this one is your baby, but if you would rather we all work on it together, we will." She paused, "Seeing that your ex is now involved." Lucy didn't hear any rebuttals so continued, "If all goes to plan Sean should be back in about half an hour, and Charlie rang to say he was leaving the out of town shopping centre in about five minutes."

"Thank you Lucy. It might be a good idea if we all work on it, as I don't particularly want to meet up with my ex again. Even though it's only for work."

They moved towards the conference room and Jocelyn gave a more detailed outline of her ideas. Soon Lucy became engrossed in putting together the best proposal, However, Jocelyn found herself daydreaming. She couldn't settle down and concentrate on work. The meeting had released emotions in her that she thought had been firmly placed on the back burner. They were now at the forefront of her mind and kept invading her thoughts with uncertainty. Had her fragile mind been playing tricks on her all those years ago? The office felt hot and airless, and for the first time she felt uncomfortable with her surroundings.

She kept on asking herself how you stop emotions ballooning into something else. She was having a tough time to cope with these other feelings invading her thoughts. She loved Trina.

She tried not to think about Sam. She was acutely conscious of the disloyalty she was feeling towards Trina, so why did Sam's face invade her thoughts? Jocelyn knew they were so happy, there was no evidence of them limping along in the last throes of a relationship, so what was happening. Jocelyn tried hard to rationalise her thoughts. She knew she shouldn't even be speculating about it. Yet something, some invisible force, was directing her in a direction she didn't want to go. Or was it. Jocelyn's subconscious knew she still had unfinished business before she could be truly settled. Was Sam only a part of this unfinished business?

She turned to Lucy and said, "I've got to go out for an hour or two. Will you be all right working on this by yourself?"

"Sure." Lucy looked at Jocelyn enquiringly, "Are you okay? You look a little pale."

"I'm fine. I've remembered there is something else I need to do today."

"You've nothing in the diary."

"I know. It's a last minute appointment."

"Do you want me to contact you if anything urgent comes in?"

"I'm sure you can deal with it."

Jocelyn picked up her bag and walked into the street, leaving Lucy with a worried frown.

ꕥ

She let herself into her apartment and poured neat vodka and downed it with a slight grimace, and then poured a second. She knew she should have driven straight around to Trina's but she had allowed self-pity to invade her thoughts. She didn't know how the imagined scene would play out. She didn't want to live with any consequences. She was happy now, wasn't she?

She hadn't sought out the connection and it felt like a complete betrayal. She was settled in the relationship with Trina. How had she ever let this problem happen, she wanted to deny that it had ever happened. Yet she felt herself being carried along by it. A fleeting and inconsequential meeting between two ex-lovers.

She never expected that brief meeting with Sam would bring out such emotions, the feeling that had a hint of hope. The clamour in her blood told her she hadn't imagined it. Everything would get back on track, but would it?

Jocelyn took the photograph of her Nan and sat in her favourite chair. Rain suddenly splattered against the window as an eerie light filled the room. She watched the rivulets racing down the pane. The strained emotions, added to the rain and gathering gloominess brought on a feeling of melancholy. Gradually the rain faded to a quiet patter.

Jocelyn studied the loving face looking at her. She breathed in deeply trying to inhale the wisdom she knew her Nan would give her. She sat with her eyes closed. The melancholy lifted and she felt at comfort and in peace. She felt a certainty that nothing could harm her and everything would turn out all right.

She returned the photograph to its rightful place and made her way back to the office.

ꟹ

"How did your meeting go?" Trina asked, later that afternoon.

Jocelyn hesitated for a moment, and then replied, "It went well. And I've also come up with the name of the company."

"And that is?"

Jocelyn smiled, "It came to me in a flash bulb kind of moment. I was looking around thinking I wanted to be different to all the usual. That I wanted to deviate from the norm, be fresh, and be innovative. And so was born 'DV8, not your normal company'. What do you think?"

"I've a feeling it doesn't really matter what I think. However, when you look at yourself and your co-workers, you all are a little different."

"Exactly. Lucy got Rose to work on a design for the logo during her lunch break. She emailed me a few designs. I've chosen the one we will use and Sean is on his way to the printers to have business cards and flyers printed off. What do you think?" She pulled up a logo on her tablet and passed it to Trina.

"Looks good. I like the colour scheme." Trina smiled, "You were cutting it fine. Remind me again, when is the launch night?"

"I know. But it is all sorted now." She nodded feeling pleased with herself.

Suddenly, a flash of Sam found its way into Jocelyn's thoughts. She shook her head, trying to clear it and made herself think of the beautiful woman in front of her.

"You zoned out for a moment. Are you alright?" Trina spoke with a worried tone.

"Yes. Many thoughts going through my mind that is all."

Jocelyn studied Trina and smiled. Trina was content and made the best of any situation thrown her way. She was easy to get along with. She was a thoroughly decent person so why did Sam keep wheedling its way into Jocelyn brain. The smell of her perfume, the feel of her touch on her arm, the goodbye kiss that lingered longer than polite, all made their way to the surface.

Her thoughts flitted all over the place. All were vying to be the most important thought. Yet each were conflicting into a confusing whirlpool of emotions, and frustrations. The problems with the plumbing had delayed the necessary last minute work that needed to be done on the building. The only father she knew, who she detested with all her body and soul, was unlikely to last the month. Her emotions were all over the place. And to top it all she had to be ready for the launch tomorrow.

Work, family, love and life were pulling her in all directions. She let out the biggest sigh she could muster.

"That was a big sigh"

"The person I met was Sam. Sam Morris."

Trina face displayed the fear she was feeling.

"Did you know you were meeting her?"

"I had no idea at all."

Trina had an instinctive gift. She always knew the right words to say to make someone feel better but she had no words for herself.

"So you will be working with her again?"

"I don't think so. She was standing in for her co-worker who had family issues to deal with."

"So it was her I saw on Friday night?"

"Yes, she said she saw you."

"So what happens now?"

"What do you mean? What happens now?"

Trina gave Jocelyn a look, which said a thousand words. Jocelyn saw the hurt that lingered there, and said, "I need this contract Treen. I cannot turn away security for our future. We have worked hard to get this far and have to submit our proposal Tuesday morning."

"I know." Trina replied with resignation in her voice.

"If we secure the deal then I will make sure one of the others deals with it." She took Trina's hands in hers and was just about to speak again when both Cathy and Peter came flying into the house.

"Hi Mum, Hi Joy." They both shouted as they came to give their mum a kiss.

"How was after school club?" Trina scooped the two precious beings into her arms and gave them a kiss on their heads and a squeeze in return.

Peter extracted himself from her arms and said, "Us boys had a big game of cricket. Mum," he asked, "Can I play on my game until teatime."

Trina ruffled the boy's head, "Have you any homework?"

Peter rolled his eyes.

"Homework first and then you can play."

"Thanks Mum." He shouted over his shoulder as he ran out of the room.

"Me and Amy and Judy made a den but when we finished two of the older girls pushed us out. So we went and played with the water tank. Look Mummy. I'm all wet."

"I can feel you are. Go and get out of those wet clothes and change into your blue shorts and a T shirt."

Cathy turned to Jocelyn and asked, "Joy. Help me pick out a T shirt please."

Jocelyn noticed the slight shake of her Trina's head and said, "You're a big girl now. I'm sure you can pick out a nice top to wear."

A pout appeared on the girls face as she stomped up the stairs.

When quiet had descended over the room Trina confided, "I don't really want you to see her again."

"I know. I'm sorry. And I can see where Cathy gets that cute little pout."

ꕤ

Chapter Twenty Four

Friday Morning

Smiling, she studied Lucy, Charlie and Sean. She waved away the objections with a generous wave of the hand. "You've all earned it. We are a small company and because of that, you have taken on several different roles that were needed in the day to day running of the company. I would like to thank you for your flexibility on operating the phone etc. etc. You have worked above and beyond getting ready for this day."

She looked at the smiling faces across from her.

"Sorry chaps but its pep talk time."

Her tone was genial as she had learned the more congenial the request the more unlikely it could be denied. She hoped that they would realise that congeniality shouldn't be confused with mildness or lack of determination. She stopped to grip her coffee mug with both hands and peered into it.

She thought for a moment then spoke, "As you know, I get really annoyed with self-absorbed jerks. All I expect from you is good, hard, honest work." she paused. "So far I have been extremely impressed with everything you all have done. We are getting to the stage where we will be meeting more and more people. Everyone who works for me can dress as you want, can deviate from the usual business suits, be different from the usual. I want you to dress to the job you are going to be doing. If you are meeting people, I expect smart. If crawling around then casual."

"The other way to impress me is how you treat others. Some things are just part of a person, like the colour of your eyes or the colour of your skin. It should not define who you are, as it is always with you, nor should it be a barrier to what you can become. You have to take time to show consideration and warmth to others. To show them respect. It doesn't cost a penny but it could change a perception. I want all our clients to leave us with a good perception. I don't want you to speak technical to the uninitiated, make everything understandable. Make sure you understand all aspects of our business and be able to talk competently. To look it up on our website is a cop out for those too lazy to be bothered to provide a complete service.

Charlie spoke up, "You have an unlimited amount of faith in us, don't you?"

She held up her hands and tilted her head. "You said it. But I've had a good few years mulling over how I want to achieve things. I prefer to surround myself with positive people, not ambiguous and questionable people or impersonal vases or pictures. And I absolutely believe that women should make the same wages as men. I don't class myself as a feminist but I believe in equality."

"As you further your careers, either with me or elsewhere, don't be impressed by money, followers, degrees and titles. Be impressed by integrity, kindness, humility and generosity. When you start doubting yourself, think about how far you have come. Remember everything you have faced, all the battles you have won and all the fears you have overcome.

Sean asked, "Do we meet your standards?"

She smiled, cleared her throat and still with that forceful air, said "Of course. I have been more than pleased with you all." She laughed, "You would have soon heard if I wasn't impressed."

Jocelyn looked from face to face and they seemed absorbed in what she was saying. She continued, "I wanted, and needed, to surround myself with people I can trust and objects that mean something to me. And if these people can laugh at themselves now and then, that would be a bonus. I have been so lucky to have the three of you on board because you tick all the correct boxes. We need just one last push to get everything ready for tonight. Does everyone know what they have to do and finish off? Anyone need any clarifications?"

Lucy spoke as she rose, "I'm good. I'll get onto the caterers to check no last minute hitches. After that, I have a couple of hours to finish off the tweak you asked me to change. Then anything that you put my way."

"Sean?"

"I'm going to the printers and then will double check with the employment agency about staffing for tonight. I also have a meeting with Masons, which, hopefully, won't take too long."

"Charlie?"

"Moving some of the furniture to accommodate the hired tables and chairs which should arrive in," he looked at his watch, "just over an hour. I'll then be checking over the presentation and timings."

Lucy asked, "Are we picking up the glasses and drinks from the local or are they bringing them here?"

"I said we would pick them up mid-afternoon, after the lunchtime rush. So if we can all meet back here about two, pick up the bottles and glasses." She picked up her tablet, "I'm going to meet a couple of contacts. If anyone needs me, I will be at the end of the phone." She thought for a moment, "It might be better to text. I'll see you back here at two or before."

Soon they were all busy at their tasks.

"Anyone need anything on my trip to the printers?" asked Sean. "I'll do a mid-morning cake run on the way back"

"Danish please." answered Lucy.

Charlie thought for a moment, "I can't decide between a Belgian bun and apple turnover. Whatever looks more appetising. You decide."

"Righto. See you in an hour."

Sean walked into the bright sunlight and started to whistle the annoying tune to an advert, which was on the radio, whilst he was eating his breakfast this morning. He hoped it would soon leave his consciousness as it was driving him barmy. He smiled and tried to concentrate on other matters. He looked back at the office and felt blessed with the friendships he had made since moving to the city. He didn't feel so much of a geek. His mind replayed Jocelyn's pep talk. A grin came over his face. Whatever the future held he knew it would be good. He was pleased he made the decision to enrol at the college. As the annoying whistle passed his lips, he crossed the road and continued on his journey.

Charlie started humming to himself. He was looking forward to the launch that evening. They had all worked hard to get to this place. He felt at peace and was comfortable with life. He had grown up where casual racism was the accepted norm, and he was gratefully aware that none existed between the four of them. He liked the mix of gay and straight, black and white. Yes, there was banter, and the four of them each had something they could be teased about. But it was the gentle teasing that helped them bind together, to bring out the best in themselves, and each other.

"You're sounding happy." Lucy stated as she looked up from her screen.

"Very much so. I was thinking how well we all work together. Tonight is the culmination of all our hard work. It should be a good evening. I'm looking forward to it." He paused for a moment and asked, "Do you often think about what could have been if Jocelyn hadn't come into your life?"

"All of the time. Joy has been more of a mum to me in the past eight months than my real mother. And a lot of that time, she was still living away. I dread to think what would have happened to me."

"Was it tough? You never have really spoken about that time."

"I don't really want to speak about it now. Suffice to say, I would not wish that on my worst enemy. Living on the streets was a living hell. I saw no hope. I was so cold and lonely, existing hand to mouth. I could feel my dignity and humanity slowly eeking away. I started not to like the person I had become. I think I would have liked myself even less if I had stayed out there much longer." She gave a weak smile, "But that is all in the past."

Charlie walked over to her and gave her a loving bear hug.

"Stop that now or you'll make me all emotional."

"You know I love you."

"And I love you too, you big bear. Now get back to shifting that furniture. It won't shift itself and I have proper work to do."

ℌ

Chapter Twenty Five

Friday Evening

"And finally I'd like to thank you all for coming. I hope we all have a successful partnership, and to those of you not yet on board," she smiled at the crowd of people in front of her, "what's stopping you"

A murmur of laughter filled the room.

Jocelyn indicated for Sean, Lucy and Charlie to join her on the small, temporary platform.

"If you have any questions, please don't hesitate to speak to either myself or my wonderful team." Jocelyn waved her arm to indicate the three who were standing alongside her.

She changed the projection to show the company's new logo and tagline. A list of all their clients scrolled along the bottom, continuously.

"Thank you for what I hope will be many years of success between us. Please help yourself to the food and drink and enjoy the rest of the evening."

A ripple of applause filled the room.

Jocelyn turned to her co-workers, "Well done all. Now let's go mingle and work the room. We all know who to target before they disappear?"

Charlie, Sean and Lucy all nodded.

"Let's do this. Let's drum up some more orders."

They all started to move to different parts of the room. Jocelyn took in the bosses and managers of the different firms they had been dealing with and she felt a positive vibe around the room. Her eyes rested on Trina, who gave her the thumbs up, and mouthed 'well done'. A loving smile passed between them. She stepped off the platform and passed by Duncan and Sharon, who both gave her a quick squeeze.

Pride shone through his eyes as Duncan said, "Well done Dumps. A very impressive presentation. Where do I sign?"

Jocelyn laughed with him and felt light-headed at her brother's praise.

"Catch you later." she replied. "I have to network. There is an important client to whom I have to talk; this conversation could set us up for a very long time."

"Go and nail it big sis." Duncan replied, giving his sister a last hug.

Jocelyn laughed, replied, "Less of the big." and walked towards two men and a woman. Their glasses were in the process of being replenished. Jocelyn was pleased with the way the catering staff had gone about their jobs, quietly and efficiently. Everything appeared to be running smoothly and she hoped it would continue for the rest of the evening.

"Mr. Riorden. I'm glad you could make it."

"Ms. Harrold. Please call me John." he replied smiling.

Jocelyn gave him a warm smile, "Thank you John."

"You have met Samantha Morris."

Jocelyn nodded a greeting to Sam.

"This is Julien Grey. Our CEO."

"Mr. Grey. Pleased to meet you." She reached out and shook the proffered hand.

Julien replied, "A very impressive presentation Ms. Harrold."

"Thank you."

Julien continued, "I was extremely impressed with the content of the presentation and also in the articulate way you portrayed it. You have provided an excellent marketing approach. I enjoyed the touches of humour that flowed through, that didn't distract from the message. I liked how you incorporated old ideas and new innovations."

"Thank you."

"If your marketing proposal, and the detail involved, is as impressive as this evening, you will have exceeded all my expectations. I want our product to be reachable for all ages and incomes. So that no one is left out, that each of our targeted group had something for them. Please send all the necessary paperwork to my secretary Tuesday morning, which I will peruse at my leisure. Hopefully, if your proposal meets our criteria, and there are no unexpected hitches, I will free a date in my diary on Wednesday to sign the completed forms."

"Again Mr. Grey, thank you. My team and I will not let you down."

They shook hands. John and Julien walked away, leaving Sam and Jocelyn standing together. Sam leaned in, touched he arm and whispered something in Jocelyn's ear.

Trina watched the two men walk away and saw the way that Sam interacted with Jocelyn. There seemed to be a certain intimacy and the ease of their contact made them look as though they were more than just friends. Trina's stomach gave a lurch and sadness filled her being. She felt as another nail was being hammered into her coffin. This should have been one of the happiest days of their fledgling romance, instead she felt as though it was the beginning of the end. Just as she was deciding whether to intervene in the cosy tete a tete she was witnessing, she felt a hand on her arm.

"You're Trina aren't you?"

Trina looked at the man touching her arm with a puzzled frown, "Yes. And you are?"

The man reached into his pocket and pulled out a business card and a letter. "My name is Richard. Would you be so kind as to give Ms Harrold this letter?"

"Why not give it to her yourself. She is over there." Trina replied pointing.

"No. I have to go and I can see she is deep in discussion with a client."

Trina tried to cover up the involuntary snort that escaped with coughing, and replied, "Sure. I'll guarantee she gets it."

She took the letter but he held onto the business card before letting it go, saying, "If at any time you want to contact me, please do."

He wandered into the crowd with a wave of his hand. Trina watched him go. Her face revealed a pensive look, as she couldn't comprehend how he knew her name. She placed the letter in her back pocket and studied the card. The name seemed familiar, but she couldn't place where she had heard it before. She tapped the card against her lips and was deep in thought.

She felt a pair of strong arms wrap themselves around her waist. Trina looked over her shoulder as she took hold of the hands. A smile lit up Jocelyn's face and excitement poured out of her.

"I think we've nailed the big one."

"How can you be sure?"

"You know I've been pursuing that big order, the group that Sam works for."

Trina felt her hackles rise as Sam's name was mentioned. "Yes."

"Well I've just had a conversation with the CEO of the company. He hinted that if we get the bid in and it is as good as the presentation then it would be mine to lose. Sam said that he was making favourable comments all through the evening."

Trina tried hard to join in the excitement Jocelyn was feeling, but found it difficult to blank out her reaction to Sam. Rather lamely, she said, "Well done. You and the team thoroughly deserve it. You and the team have put so much effort into securing this deal."

Jocelyn leant in and gave Trina a quick peck on the cheek.

"I must get back to doing some more networking. Help yourself to more food and drink." Jocelyn started to turn away, hesitated and said, "I'm sorry I've been a bit of a grouch this past week."

"Nothing new there then."

"Cheeky. I must have been under more pressure than I realised."

"Now go and take care of business. I'll have a catch up with Sharon and that adorable brother of yours."

Jocelyn gave Trina another quick kiss and cuddle.

"Love you."

ॐ

Chapter Twenty Six

Sunday

Jocelyn shoved her chair back from the breakfast table to scrutinize Trina as she pushed her breakfast around her plate.

"What's wrong love?"

"I'm fine." Trina replied with a slight shake of her head.

"As long as you are." Jocelyn smiled, "Are you coming down with something? You look a bit peaky?"

Annoyance flitted across Trina's face as she replied, "I said I'm fine."

"I know you did love." She smiled as though attempting to add some lightness to the conversation.

Jocelyn started to stack the dirty dishes in the sink and filled the bowl with hot water.

Turning to Trina she asked, "Have you finished?"

Trina muttered under her breath, "I haven't started yet." Jocelyn frowned. In a louder voice, she replied, "Yes. You can take my plate."

"What do you fancy doing today? Shall we go for a walk? Perhaps to the seaside."

"I don't want to do anything." Jocelyn looked around from the sink and again asked, "Are you sure you are okay?"

"For goodness sake. I'm fine."

Jocelyn gave her an anxious, disbelieving look. "You don't look fine. What's wrong?"

"You really want me to tell you what's wrong."

"Yes. I do."

"You won't like it."

"You are worrying me now."

"I bet not as much as you worry me."

Jocelyn frowned, "What's that meant to mean."

"At this precise moment in time I don't really want to be in your company."

Shocked, Jocelyn asked, "Why?"

Trina shook her head but didn't reply.

Jocelyn picked up the tea towel and died her hands, and sat back down at the table. She tried to take hold of Trina's hand but her hand was batted away.

"Trina, you can't say you don't want to be in my company and not tell me what I've done. You were a bit distant all day yesterday. What's wrong? Please tell me the truth."

"You're asking for the truth. Are you sure the truth is what you want to hear."

A pained expression played on Jocelyn's face.

Continuing Trina said, "You have no idea have you?"

Jocelyn thought back over the past couple of days. Everything had gone well. She felt as though all she had worked for had come to fruition. She was feeling on top of the world and yet Trina was acting annoyed. Her whole demeanour was distant, as though something major had happened, but for the life of her, she didn't know what.

"Has something happened? Are the children all right with Mike? Is it you?"

Trina let out an exasperated sigh.

"No it's not any of those things."

"Well what is it?"

Trina stayed silent.

Realisation made its way into Jocelyn's understanding, as she asked, "You're annoyed with me, aren't you?"

Again Trina let out a big sigh, shaking her head she responded, ironically, "Hooray. Give that girl a peppermint."

A pained look came over Jocelyn's face as she replied, "Trina, I honestly don't know what I've done."

Trina continued to look displeased, "Just think about some of your actions, especially Friday night."

"Before or after the launch?"

"What about during?"

"During?" Jocelyn replied incredulously, "During the launch I gave my presentation and then I was networking. I all but secured the big deal, which you know I have spent yesterday working on. And will be spending all day tomorrow on it. I then made sure all our other clients stayed happy and their glasses and plates were replenished."

Trina shook her head, "Then why was it every time I looked over, or tried to come close to you, like any loving partner should, you were in a cosy chat with Sam. Touching her hand, her shoulder, her waist. It was as though she was your partner, not me."

Jocelyn's jaw dropped open. She shook her head in disbelief, "Now you're being silly."

"Am I? I know what I saw. Even your Duncan made a comment."

Jocelyn shook her head, "I was chatting to everyone."

"But not to me. You never once included me, introduced me, or even spoke to me. Apart from when you first came off the podium. I might as well have not been there."

"I did include you."

"When?" she asked accusingly, "When did you include me?"

Trina's accusing tone made Jocelyn's stomach clench. "That's ridiculous."

"See. You are trying to remember, but you can't, so instead you call me ridiculous."

"I didn't mean you are ridiculous. I meant the whole situation is ridiculous."

"So you weren't cosying up to Sam all night?"

"I talked to her with her boss and then a conversation with her." Jocelyn replied on the defensive.

Keeping a level voice, Trina recounted, "Which went on for a good twenty minutes."

"So you were timing me." Jocelyn accused.

"No. Your Duncan made the comment. And seeing that I was beginning to become a little annoyed he asked me not to make a scene as it was your special night."

Incredulously Jocelyn asked, shaking her head, "You really think there is something going on between Sam and myself?"

"You tell me."

Jocelyn let out a big sigh. "There is nothing going on between me and Sam."

"This is the second time that you and Sam have been a bit too familiar for my liking."

A puzzled look spread across Jocelyn's face as she replied, "Second time?"

"Yes. Second time. I saw you and her outside the pub. I saw the kiss."

"Did you also see me pull away?"

"Yes. But I also saw how you reacted when she gave you, what I can only presume, was her number. So I will ask again. Is there anything going on which I should be worried about?"

Jocelyn looked at Trina, and tried to hold her hand.

Trina moved her hand out of the way and questioned, "Well is there?"

Pushing her chair back, Jocelyn said, annoyed, "I don't need this."

Shaking her head Trina responded, "Neither do I."

They sat in silence, each with their own thoughts. Jocelyn reached out to touch Trina's hand. Trina pulled her hand away.

Until now, Trina had always been warm, loyal, funny and supportive. How could that change so suddenly? Trina had fought for Jocelyn when they were younger so why was she pushing Jocelyn away now.

"Do you want me to go?"

Trina shrugged.

"Right. I'll go then." Jocelyn spoke, waiting to hear Trina ask her to stay.

Instead, Trina said, "That's your prerogative. I have things to do anyway."

"I'm off."

"Okay."

Shocked, Jocelyn expected Trina to try to stop her. Jocelyn picked up her coat and bag and as she made her way out she shouted, "I'll see you sometime."

Trina shouted back, "Whenever."

The door closed with a resounding bang.

ꙮ

Chapter Twenty Seven

Tuesday Morning

Lucy bounded into the office.

"The bid was duly delivered on time. Here's a receipt saying they have received…" Lucy froze in midsentence, her grin fading, with concern and a frown replacing her bright disposition. "What's wrong?"

Dashing away a silent tear, Jocelyn jumped up and attempted to hide her melancholy. "Nothing, I'm fine. I…"

Jocelyn smoothed at her hair, a look of sadness was etched on her features.

Lucy reached for her hand. "Did I do something to upset you?" she began, willing to take whatever Jocelyn would say in order to get the ball rolling.

"Whatever makes you think that?"

"You seem so sad."

Lucy stared into Jocelyn's eyes, and noticed the smudged mascara. She pulled a tissue out a packet and held it out to her.

"Are you going to tell me what is wrong or am I going to think the worse. And don't tell me nothing is wrong because I can see that there is. All day yesterday, you were like a bear with a sore head. Also, when you say that you are fine then I know you are not. So spill."

Jocelyn let out a huge sigh. Her face showed the emotions of someone weighing up her options. She suddenly started talking, "Ever since the launch on Friday there has been an underlying tension between me and Trina. On Sunday, it blew up into a massive argument, and we never argue. In all the years I have known her we have only had cross words a few times."

"So what did you do to annoy her?"

Jocelyn frowned, "Why is it my fault."

Lucy tilted her head to the side, placed her hands on her hips, and gave her a look that implied 'really'. Jocelyn let a small smile play on her lips.

Shaking her head she said, "I honestly don't know why."

Jocelyn thought back over events of the weekend. Nothing stood out to her but she could sense something was slightly off kilter. She thought back to Sunday and replayed the events leading up to her storming off.

Jocelyn was brought back to the present as Lucy's voice cut through her thoughts.

"Are you listening to me? I said take her around a big bunch of flowers and a bottle of wine and tell her how sorry you are. That it was your entire fault, even if you don't think it was. Tell her how much you love her and grovel." She laughed, "And do it quickly as I can't stand walking on eggshells."

"You're correct. It is my entire fault. Trouble is, she got things going on with the kids and I wasn't going to be seeing her until Thursday."

"So get them delivered. Text her. Message her. Do something instead of sitting around here moping. Sometimes, for an intelligent woman, you are so daft."

"Well thanks for that vote of confidence." Jocelyn added sarcastically.

"You're welcome." Lucy walked away, then turned and said, "Get it sorted."

"Yes Mum." Jocelyn gave a small laugh.

Lucy moved the few paces back to Jocelyn and said, "Oh by the way Trina asked me to give you this."

Lucy retrieved an envelope from her back pocket. It looked a bit crumpled at the edges.

"When did she give you that?"

"Yesterday. After my appointment with Standon Brown I was picking up some bits and pieces and bumped into her in her local supermarket." She looked at Jocelyn's face and asked, "Are you alright."

Anxiously, with the thoughts of her altercation with Trina fresh in her memory, she replied, "I hope so."

She saw her name on the front and started to frown. Jocelyn didn't recognise the handwriting on the envelope and let out the breath she didn't know she was holding. For a moment, she had thought the worst.

Studying the envelope, she asked, "Do you know what it is and where Trina got it from?"

"Trina said that a bloke gave it to her at the launch and asked her to give it to you today. She said that as she wouldn't be seeing you so would I pass it on."

Jocelyn turned the envelope over in her hands, looking for clues.

"Are you going to look at the envelope all day or are you going to open it? The suspense is killing me. It seems a bit strange that he didn't want it opened until today."

Jocelyn tore open the envelope and pulled out a single sheet of paper and a business card. She read the greeting and the signature at the bottom. She quickly folded the paper back up and returned it, and the card, to the envelope.

Lucy noticed the faint gasp Jocelyn let out and asked, "Any problems."

"No problem. It's from an old acquaintance asking me to get in touch."

"And there was me thinking of all manner of cloak and dagger stuff." She walked towards the kitchen area. "I'm making a coffee before I take over manning the phones. Do you want one?"

"Yes. Please."

When Lucy left the office, Jocelyn took out the letter and read it in its entirety.

My dearest Jocelyn.

I hope that receiving this letter doesn't come as too much of a shock. I know that you have recently found out that the man you believed to be your father is not. I am also aware that you know me to be your biological father. And yet, we have never been formally introduced. I think you deserve an explanation.

Your Mother and I loved each other during my late teenage years. If circumstances had been different, we would have married. Unfortunately, my family frowned on our union, and whisked me back home. One day you will be able to hear the complete and sordid story. Your mother and I had a brief, illicit affair when I returned to Bristol a couple of years later.

I was again called back to Canada and our affair ended. But not before your Mother had conceived. It was years before I knew about you. Please do not hate me or be angry with your Mother. I am so sorry that I haven't been part of your life but your Dad forbade it. Your Nan found out that you were mine and she has kept me up to date as best she could.

I have watched over you from a distance, whenever possible, and have seen you grow from a gangly girl to a beautiful woman. I am really proud of the woman you have become and what you have achieved. You showed true courage coming back to face your family for your Nan's funeral and your tribute was very moving.

Congratulations on your launch evening. Your presentation was very good. Trina seems a lovely woman, and her children are adorable. You have made a good choice in your life partner.

When you read this letter I will be back home in Toronto. Please excuse my prior indiscretions. I am not ashamed to have fathered such a wonderful person, in fact I am full of pride. I know I am not part of your past but I would very much like to be a part of your future, even if it is from a distance.

My phone numbers and address are on the business card. I would love you to get in contact, but only if you so desire.

I will also understand if you want nothing to do with me.

Kindest regards

Richard

Jocelyn screwed up the piece of paper and threw it into the waste paper bin. After a couple of moments she retrieved, smoothed, and replaced it back in the envelope. She put it into her back pocket ready to read again at her leisure.

Lucy placed a cup of coffee on the desk as Jocelyn jumped.

"I didn't hear you come in."

Lucy smiled. "You were away with the fairies. The way you jumped you almost made me drop the cup. You okay? You look a little shaken."

Jocelyn gave a slight smile and nodded, "Just some mixed emotions going through my head."

"And as I told you earlier, have some flowers delivered. Text her. Message her."

Jocelyn picked up the phone and replied, "I'm on it now. Thanks for the coffee."

"No probs." Lucy responded as she left the office.

ꕥ

Chapter Twenty Eight

Thursday

Jocelyn rang the bell and waited sheepishly.

As Trina opened the door, Jocelyn spoke quickly, "I'm so sorry. You were right and I was wrong. I did spend too much time with Sam when I should have been spending it with you. Please forgive me."

Trina stepped aside and let her in. As she walked past the living room, she noticed the flowers that she had delivered. She smiled to herself. They looked gorgeous.

"I'm so glad I secured the deal. Now I can pass the reins over to Sean or Charlie. Shall I make us both a cuppa?" Jocelyn asked looking over her shoulder.

Trina gave a slight nod and sat at the kitchen table as Jocelyn busied herself making the tea. She placed a cup in front of Trina and sat down opposite.

Trina let out a big sigh and looked earnestly into Jocelyn's eyes, and said, "You will make that phone call. You will go and see her."

Jocelyn choked on her tea. She knew that her so-called involvement with Sam had upset Trina, but until now, she didn't realise by how much. "No. I am going to stay away."

"I know you and you won't be able to." Trina shook her head. "You don't have it in you to stay away."

Jocelyn wondered why Trina was unwilling to rethink what had, or in this case, not happened. Trina got up and walked towards the back door. Jocelyn could see her eyes close from across the room. Trina wanted to give Jocelyn the benefit of the doubt, but she knew what Sam had meant to her all those years ago. She stood like that for a while then opened them. "So what are you going to do?"

Jocelyn could tell from the hard expression on her face that she wasn't going to let it go. Panic swept through her, she sighed and shrugged, "I'll make sure I don't see her again. I'll get Charlie or Sean to deal with her."

Trina shook her head and gave her a look to say that it would never happen.

"You won't be able to stay away."

Ignoring the sarcasm Jocelyn offered a weary smile, and responded, "Maybe, maybe not, but I'm going to try. I don't want to turn back time. I love you."

Trina continued giving her the look, and spoke quietly, "Not like you loved her. Your first love is your forever love. You know that and I know that. Yes, it would hurt me. In fact, it would hurt like hell, but we will always be friends, we will always have a type of love between us. We both know that we were a temporary solution to both our problems. We both needed someone, we both needed comfort, but as I said months ago, you and Sam need to talk. Really talk."

Jocelyn clenched her jaw, her heart plummeting, but realised the truth of Trina's insistence. For years, she had been putting thoughts of Sam on the back burner, but one fleeting sight of her brought all the feelings of love, hurt, and betrayal to the surface. She looked at Trina and gave a tiny smile, which didn't quite reach her eyes, and shook her head.

Jocelyn saw Trina's brow crinkle as she put on a brave face. Trina said, in a voice that made it clear there was no room to argue. "I'm right and you know it. You had a deep love for her, and whether you think it has gone, it's still inside of you."

Her smile vanished and she felt suddenly angry. A moment ago, she had felt as though Trina understood, but she was wrong.

"I love you." Jocelyn said. Her voice had lowered to a whisper as if saying it aloud would completely break her heart.

Trina shook her head and saw Jocelyn flinch. Trina didn't think that her reaction was unjustified. She was worried and really pissed off with Jocelyn, but she had to prepare for the worse. Jocelyn barely shook her head. Her shoulders lifted as she took a fortifying breath and inwardly groaned.

Trina continued, "Love is an emotion that doesn't always have words. It isn't in the things people say. It's in their eyes, their look." She squeezed Jocelyn hand, and then pulled away, not wanting to show the vulnerability she too was feeling.

As Jocelyn didn't respond, Trina added, making the question sound like an accusation. "So what are you going to do?" She breathed a sigh that said more than a hundred words, tilting her head, studying Jocelyn in condemnation.

Silence stretched between them, carrying the worry Trina felt for their own relationship. Trina had so enjoyed the closeness that the two friends had enjoyed these past few months and she realised that it would soon end. She also knew that if she fought for Joy, she would win the fight, but would Jocelyn forever feel that she had settled for second best. A shadow of anxiety passed over her eyes.

"I love you." The three syllables were all Jocelyn could manage. Trina didn't answer knowing that silence is better than unnecessary drama.

Jocelyn hated the silence that spread between them and filled the void. "I want you, I need you. I don't want you to tell me what I should do with my life. Or who I should be. I know what I want and what I am. I want you and I am in love with you. I love you with all my heart and soul."

As she looked into Jocelyn's eyes, her glance lingered longer than necessary. She saw in her eyes all the familiar emotions she had grown used to. Trina's voice spoke with a timbre that she didn't know she had. It had the sound of quiet determination. "You do at the moment. But I saw how you looked at her. How you touched her."

Jocelyn gave a small sigh.

Trina continued, "You are allowed to be weak and make mistakes. You cannot be strong or correct all of the time. At the moment, you are mired with guilt, over your feelings for Sam, and worry, over your feelings for me. Your head is all over the place. I think that we should stop seeing each other until you know what you want."

Jocelyn knew from the look in Trina's eyes that she meant what she said, that she would brook no other deal. She began to feel sick just thinking about it, "No Trina. Please. I want you. My heart is here with you and that is all that counts. The only thing that matters is whether you feel the same."

Jocelyn hoped that these simple words would tip the scales in her favour. Jocelyn flinched as their eyes met. Trina's eyes are full of worry, of hostility. There is also a hint of compassion and something else. Something that was hard to define. Then it showed. There was a look of steel in her eyes. Jocelyn tried to hold her hand but Trina batted it away and gave her a look, eyebrows raised, eyes angry and narrow, and jaw clenched.

Jocelyn wondered whether her expression was as rigid with shock as the rest of her felt. She wanted Trina to stop looking at her as she was. It was as if in this moment time had slowed down. As if everything was being played out in front of them, that the next moment would change their destiny forever.

"Don't lie." She added nothing, and there was a pause, as each looked the other.

Jocelyn didn't know what was worse, the hint at anger or the defeat in Trina's voice. She pleaded, "You are the best thing that has ever happened to me. You must realise that. I don't want to compromise what we have together."

Trina quietly spoke, "Your head and heart says different things. I don't want your pity. I am giving you the chance to walk away whilst we are still fiends, until you know what you want. I'm giving you your freedom to do and achieve your ambitions."

Pain etched on Trina's face, and all Jocelyn wanted was to wipe it away with something clever and wise. Instead, she shook her head, defeated.

"I don't want to walk away." Jocelyn's voice had become more of a whine. "Are you saying it is a full stop, or may it be a comma at the end of this journey where I may knock on your door and be let in? Are you saying that it is over or may there be a chance for us in the future?"

Jocelyn stared at Trina, who stood unmoved.

Trina started to speak quietly, "We cannot move forward until we are completely honest with each other. Now, you are not being completely honest with yourself so how can you be honest with me. Once you start being honest and lay to rest the ghosts of your past then you will know whether it is a comma or full stop."

Jocelyn shook her head, "When? When can I see you again? How long is that going to be?"

"In your heart of hearts you will know. Don't even contemplate getting in touch until you do. Come and knock on my door after you have made your decision. Your decision will decide whether I let you in or not." Her voice gave a little break, "Now go. Sort out your true feelings. And know that you go with my blessing."

"Trina, please." Jocelyn beseeched, seeing Trina's resolve begin to waver.

"Go now," Trina shouted, "before I change my mind."

Trina gave Jocelyn a small shove towards the door. The sheer power of Trina's emotions hit Jocelyn with a force, as though a blast had gone off nearby. These emotions flooded Trina's eyes, her mouth, and her jaw. Jocelyn felt as if she had become caught up in the blast and it sent her hurtling through the air, with no knowledge of where she would land. Trina could feel tears burning the corner of her eyes, as she tried to push them back. She was stronger than her emotions were leading her to believe, and she was determined to save her tears for after Jocelyn had left.

Sadness permeated the whole of Jocelyn, through her facial expression to her physical demeanour. She moved towards the door, gave Trina a last look, and walked out into the crisp evening air. Her head knew there was no going back, her heart hoped not.

Trina watched Jocelyn walk out. She waited until she heard the gate close and for her to leave her line of sight and closed the door. Then let out a haunted, mournful cry as the tears flowed down her face. A deep wave of sadness washed over her, as she buckled under the weight of her sobs. The sound of her own sorrow filled with desolation, reverberated around the room, as she cried out into the emptiness. She wished desperately that

Jocelyn would come back, put her arms around her, and tell her everything was going to be all right. The impending emptiness of her home without her stretched ahead, and she didn't know if she could cope.

Slowly and steadily the agonised crying began to subside, she wiped her tears and tried to remember how to breathe. She was angry and furious, hurt and bewildered but it was something that had to be done. She looked at her watch and knew she needed to get into autopilot mode, as her adorable children would soon be home. She needed to be able to take care of them despite feeling that she had lost half of her being. That her heart had been ripped to shreds and she would never get back the happiness she had felt since Jocelyn had walked back into her life.

She attempted to tidy the house but everywhere she went there were little subtle reminders of Joy. She could see her face and hear her voice, teasing. Trina walked back into the living room and spied the framed picture of them both smiling happily at the camera. She placed the picture face down as another overwhelming sob racked through her body. She realised that she had to get a grip before too long or she would be a complete, uncontrollable mess.

She went to the bathroom and tried to wash away her emotions. She filled up the sink and continuously dunked her head into the cool, refreshing water. She looked in the mirror and her blotchy cheeks were beginning to return to their natural colour but her eyes still were red rimmed. She spied the Bristol Blue pendant hanging around her neck. The pendant was a present from Jocelyn when she had first came back home. She lifted it to her lips, kissed it, closed her eyes, and gave a silent prayer. She again doused her face with water. She was towelling it dry, when the front door opened and two bundles of energy ran inside.

Trina began to feel an overwhelming sense of loss and yet the two most important people in her life had just walked through the door. She walked down the stairs and gave them the best smile she could muster as Peter shouted, "Mum, we're back."

Trina moved towards them, gave them an extra big hug and a kiss.

"Hi Mummy, may I have some juice?" Cathy asked as she pulled herself out of the smothering hug.

"There's some on the kitchen table."

"Where's Joy? I want to show her something," asked Peter.

Trina took a deep gulp of air, "She's not here."

"Oh." he replied, sounding a little disappointed. "When will she be back?"

"I don't know."

Peter looked closely at his mother and asked, full of concern, "Mum. What's wrong? Where's Joy?"

"She, umm. She." Trina stuttered, finding it difficult to speak. She tried again, "She had to go somewhere and do something." Trina managed to get out, choking back the sob that tried to escape.

Peter looked at his mother's face and buried his face into her body, "You haven't broken up have you? Joy was nice."

"Oh Peter." Trina let out a quiet sob, "Joy is nice but I don't know, love. She has things she has to sort out."

"Oh, like she did when she had to go back up to Sunderland."

Closing her eyes and, keeping a close embrace with her eldest child, said, "Yes Peter something like that."

"That's alright then. She'll be back soon."

"I hope so." She sighed, "I'm hoping she will come back soon."

"I like Joy a lot, not like Dad's girlfriend. She's a cow."

"Peter, you can't go around saying things like that."

"But Mum, she so is. She makes Dad go back on his promises to us."

Trina held her son at arm's length, "Your Dad loves her, so you have to be a good lad."

"I try to be," he said. And then sounding older than his years Peter continued, "Did you have an argument? We are always arguing so it doesn't mean to say she won't be back." He gave his mum the biggest hug he could. "If she loves you, she'll be back. And I think she loves you very much." He pulled away from the hug and asked, "What's for tea? I'm starving."

Trina felt the start of a smile play on her lips. Thankful for the love of her children, she ruffled Peter's hair, "Let's go and see what we can rustle up."

ഇ

Chapter Twenty Nine

Thursday Evening

That evening Jocelyn had stared at the telly without taking in what she was seeing. Her mind was racing. What had happened to her over the past couple of days? How had she come to this? She had gone down the wrong route now. She saw that now. Why wasn't she more assertive? She knew that there were more questions than answers.

She should be trying to build bridges with Trina, but she couldn't stomach it. She couldn't face the reality of rejection again. She knew that she should have considered Trina's feeling before allowing Sam back into her life. Albeit, through work. Nothing irrevocable had happened yet between Jocelyn and Sam, and conceivably nothing would.

A strange feeling came over her. As though she could taste what she wanted, but what was it? She was on the road to somewhere, although she didn't know exactly where. She opened her laptop and saw various items that needed to be completed today, still pending. Was this a hint of her current indecision or did it mean something more. She shrugged and knew that these thoughts would continue to invade her mind, especially when she was least expecting it.

She realised that her concentration was wandering so she closed the lid and settled herself in the chair by the window.

Only a small section of moon appeared in the night sky, but it delivered enough light to reflect on the calm water of the floating harbour. The moonbeams worked together with the slight breeze to create dancing shadows. Her thoughts again turned to her Nan and she spoke aloud, "You were amazing Nan. You were like… like the water I'm watching, calm but with an indeterminate spirit that wants to break free."

Yet calm wasn't the word that best described how she was feeling, calm hadn't brought her peace of mind. Her whole core had been shaken, and she could feel her life tumbling down around her. She thought she knew what she wanted and where she was going. But there was a chance that the future she had mapped out had changed in an instant.

In Sunderland where she had previously lived, her life had been drab. She couldn't say directionless because she had been going in a direction she knew was not fulfilling. She was now at another crossroads in her life. She wanted, needed, yearned for something that she couldn't quite grasp.

Had she always been like this? Almost reaching happiness then pulling away from the brink. Was she afraid of taking things to the next level? Her relationship with Trina had still felt new and fresh. Jocelyn wondered whether it was over before it had really begun.

How could she have been so happy with Trina, she didn't do happy. It was true that she had fleeting glimpses of happiness, but usually life got in the way of these emotions. She wondered if she had a self-destruct button for when life was going well.

The phone rang suddenly pulling her out of her contemplations.

"Hi Lucy."

"Did Trina like the flowers?"

"I think so. She has them in a big vase in the living room."

"So why do you sound so down?"

"We've split up."

"What do you mean, you've split up?

Jocelyn stayed silent.

"You did grovel and ask for her forgiveness." Lucy asked accusingly.

"Yes. I did apologise and ask for her forgiveness but she wants me to sort out my feelings and who I really want." A slight sob escaped as Jocelyn continued soberly, "She doesn't want to see me until then."

"So you're going to let this situation develop?"

"At this precise moment in time I am."

"Give her a ring. Talk to her."

"She told me not to get in contact. To sort myself out."

"And are you going to do that?"

"If I want a future with her I am going to have to."

"Oh Joy. I'm so sorry. Do you want me and Rose to come over?"

"No. You're alright."

"We could be over in five minutes if you want some company."

"It's okay. I'll try to make a start on the pitch I've got to put together."

"If you're sure." Lucy sounded dubious.

"I'm sure."

"I'll see you at the office tomorrow." Lucy paused for a moment, "Again I'm sorry about you and Trina."

"So am I." Jocelyn replied, replacing the phone in her pocket.

Jocelyn continued to stare out of the window. She knew she loved Trina. She loved everything from her smile through to her idiosyncrasies. She loved that by saying a couple of words she could lift her spirits and take her from sinking into doubt. She loved the life they had been forging together and she loved her children. They mirrored the innate goodness of Trina, and both had developed some of Trina's endearing mannerisms.

Yet something kept nagging at Jocelyn's subconscious. She realised that Trina had put the wheels in motion and forced her hand. She knew she had to have the discussion with Sam, to clear the air so that she could move on with her life.

Jocelyn tugged her mobile back out of her pocket and pulled up Trina's number. Her beautiful face stared back at Jocelyn from the screen. She tapped the phone against her lips and tried to decide whether to phone or not. She plucked up the courage to press the green button but straight away cancelled the connection. She could feel her anger rising and threw the phone across the room. How had she let things get this far?

She closed her eyes and took some deep breaths. When she opened her eyes, she looked over to the photo of her Nan and began to feel an inner peace spread through her.

Talking to the photo she said, "Why do I always make such a pig's ear of my life. I could really do with some guidance this minute."

A cloud passed in front of the moon and silence answered in return.

She sighed and bid the moon goodnight. She wondered if the other two billion people that had shared its light that night, found life as perplexing. Taking a deep breath, she wandered to her computer, opened it up and attempted to work.

ꕥ

Chapter Thirty

Tuesday Afternoon

"I can honestly say it was one of the best feelings I could have had. Once someone else knew about the abuse it was as if a weight had been lifted from my shoulders, like a darkness that had left and a brighter light was rising over the horizon. I had carried this guilt and shame around with me for so long." Jocelyn paused for a moment and reached out towards Alice. "Thank you for making me realise that the guilt that belongs solely on the shoulders of my abuser. My so-called father. I have nothing to feel guilty of, and I shouldn't be ashamed of being gay."

Alice gave her a warm smile, "It was you who finally realised it. I only gave you a gentle push in the correct direction. You needed to forgive yourself so you can move forward. The idea that it was your fault is all too common. I still think you need to talk your feelings over. That way you will stop being a victim and be the one that is totally in control. When you are ready, share your story with others, people that you trust. Find people who are there to listen, cry, hug, and love. The more people know and speak of similar situations then the more likely abuse like that will end."

"My Nan's friend Meg was the first person I told. She was the one who set the ball rolling, so that I could finally admit that I needed help. And for that, I will always be truly grateful.

"I'm glad that she was there for you." Alice smiled. "Sometimes it's easier to talk with someone outside the big picture."

Jocelyn looked up at her and said, "You're easy to talk with."

"Yes. But this is what I have trained for years to do."

"I know."

"Remember no matter how down you get, you have to refuse to throw your life away, it may have been devalued, and yet, someone believed in you. We should be here for each other, in the good times, but especially in the tough times." Alice took a breath then continued, "Enjoy the refreshing sunlight warming your face as you spend your energy focusing on the things that really matter in life, things like love, friendship, and activities that nurture your soul. You have to believe that only the best of all the love, pain, suffering, and healing will stay with you. Understand those feelings, so from there, you'll have new solid blocks to build on."

"Your positivity gives me hope. The biggest thing I have to do is forgive the person that abused me. To prove I am better than him."

"But remember, you must give yourselves a break from trying to be strong. Otherwise, you could welcome disaster in and destroy everything you've worked so hard to maintain. You still have to stay strong, but find the correct balance."

"I know I need to be strong, as I have to move forward no matter what." again she paused, "But that's not always easy. Problems keep on getting in the way."

"Life is not always easy. Sometimes life comes and smacks you around the face, and throws a spanner in the works. Problems will always get in the way. It's how you deal with them that will set you apart."

"Tell me about it." Jocelyn replied, pensively.

Alice continued, "Your life is made up of a series of hills and valleys. Everyone experiences both."

"Some always seem to have highs."

"Do you really believe that?" Alice responded, incredulously.

A slight smile played on Jocelyn's face, as she shook her head, "Not really. I realise that some people are better at hiding their feelings."

"Everyone who has ever walked by your side, in front or behind of you, has also entered into your journey. It will be similar, but unique to them. Their own experiences will change the outcome for them. They might not perceive what you see as a difficulty more as a stepping stone to elsewhere."

"The worse problems are those that pinches your heart and tears you up inside."

"You have to squeeze that problem in between your hands. Take control over it so it has no power. Then throw it away."

"What if you don't want to throw it away?" Jocelyn asked.

Alice frowned and studied Jocelyn, whose face coloured as she looked away.

"Are we still talking about your father?"

Jocelyn shifted a little on the spot where she was stood. Alice's question had made her feel uncomfortable.

Alice prompted gently, "Well?"

"Trina has told me to spend some time away from her and the kids, and sort myself out. To find out whether I want to spend my life with her or someone else."

"I see." Alice sounded unsure.

"I don't think you do." Jocelyn paused for a moment, taking a deep breath, "Anyhow, during this meeting I have decided on a couple of things. Firstly, I will go with my brother Duncan to see my father. He asked to see me and I feel strong enough to be able to face him. Duncan told me he is getting worse and I need to square up to him whilst he is still able. I need to give him a chance at redemption. Secondly, I am going to get in contact with my biological father. I received a letter from him. It appears as though he has been keeping a watch on me from afar. I want to know what his motives are. Whether it is anything sinister or that he just wants to be in my life."

"Those are two major developments in your life to do at the same time. Do you think it is wise?"

"I am not going to let my past shape my future."

"Please be sensible."

"That will be difficult because of everything else going on."

"Why? What?"

Jocelyn took a big sigh, "Because the person who has been negotiating my company's biggest deal is none other than my first true love."

"I see."

"And Trina saw how we interacted together and didn't like what see saw."

"Do you still love her?" Alice asked, qualifying it with, "Your first love"

"I don't think so. It should be an easy decision, but she was my first love. Do I go and have a talk with her and bring up the past. But my fears and worries aren't about love. It is about promises and commitments, and all of the things I'd held sacred in my life. And all the ideals that she threw away on a whim. Yet she still seems to have this hold on me, the feelings that I had for Sam were real."

"What about your feelings for Trina? And the children?"

Jocelyn didn't respond straight away. It wasn't that she hadn't thought about all of this stuff herself. It was just that her emotions were in turmoil.

The bell rang gently, announcing that the time was up.

"I love Trina. Always have, always will."

"It's not me you have to convince. I suggest you book another appointment on your way out."

Jocelyn got up and shook the hand of Alice, and said, "Thank you."

ꟾ

Jocelyn walked out into the bright sunlight and as she walked to her car, she pulled out her phone, "Hi Punky Dunky."

"Hi Sis. To what do I owe this pleasure?"

"I have been thinking."

Duncan cut in, "I bet your brain is aching now."

"Har de har." Jocelyn giggled. "As I was saying before being rudely interrupted. Are you available sometime soon to go and see Dad with me?"

"That's an about turn."

Jocelyn sighed and tutted.

"Hold on let me look." After a short pause Duncan replied, "How does Friday sound to you? About six o'clock. I know Mum goes home around then."

She sat behind the wheel and opened her appointments, "Six thirty would be better for me."

"Six thirty it is. Shall I meet you outside?"

"Please."

Duncan quickly asked, "Before you ring off please tell me how you're doing. I want the truth. Sharon would have my guts for garters if she found out I hadn't asked."

"So you're asking for Sharon. You don't want to know for yourself," she teased.

"That's not what I meant."

Jocelyn softened, "Trina and I have argued."

"So do something about it."

Jocelyn ended the call. She bit her lip, as she was thinking through her options; all the while, she tapped the phone against her chin. She took out a business card from her purse and tapped in the number. The time it took to be connected seemed like an eternity. Finally, the call was answered.

"Grady Dynamics, Rosalind speaking. How may I help?"

"Good evening Rosalind." Jocelyn always made a point of using the other person's name and was pleased that she had said it clearly. "Will you put me through to Richard Hendon, please?"

Rosalind didn't answer for a moment then replied, "Did you say Richard Hendon?"

"I did."

"I'm sorry but there is no Richard Hendon working here."

Annoyance flashed across Jocelyn's features.

"Could you please check again as Mr Hendon gave me his business card and told me to ring."

"And the business card was for Grady Dynamics?"

"Yes."

"One moment. Will you hold the line?"

Jocelyn drummed her fingers on the steering wheel as she waited.

Rosalind came back on the line and said, "I'm sorry about the confusion and the delay. I will put you through."

Straight away a man's voice spoke, "Jocelyn. Is that you?"

Shocked, Jocelyn asked, "How do you know my name?"

"There are now only two people who would ask for Richard Hendon, you and your Mum."

"I don't understand."

"Richard Hendon is the name I use when in the UK."

"I still don't understand."

"May we have a video call in an hour's time so we can talk face to face? I have so much to tell you and explain to you. Would that be convenient?"

A myriad of emotions were flowing through her as she hesitated, after a moment of deliberation, she replied, "That will give me time to get back to the office. So yes. I'll wait for your call in one hour. Do you have my number?"

"Of course."

ℵ

Chapter Thirty One

Tuesday Evening

Jocelyn sat impatiently at her desk, nervously glancing at her screen every couple of seconds. She knew the call would be deeply emotional, she hoped she wasn't having fantasy expectations. After all, Richard was a stranger and there could be further estrangement. She didn't want to open her heart only to find it not reciprocated. Fear and trepidation flowed through her, as well as a little excitement.

Finally, exactly an hour after their previous conversation, Richard appeared on her screen. Jocelyn recognised the face staring back at her, but for the life of her, she couldn't remember when and where she had seen his face. A face that had a passing resemblance, especially around the eyes.

Richard spoke, "Hi Jocelyn, or may I call you Joy?"

"Whatever you feel comfortable with." Jocelyn answered.

"Joy, you obviously received my letter. You must have so many questions"

Jocelyn butted in, "Plenty. I'm going to treat you as a stranger, but a stranger I would like to know better. I will keep you at arm's length if that's all right to you"

"That's fair enough. To you I am a stranger. I have had most of your life to reach this point; you haven't had that luxury yet. To you it's first contact. A mutual connection takes time to forge and maintain. Let's take baby steps and hopefully, over time, that familial bond will strengthen naturally."

Jocelyn nodded, "I will open a door to you, but I need boundaries. I will want you to be respectful of the boundaries I set."

"That goes without saying. If you ever feel uncomfortable, please let me know. Feel free to stop the call at any time. Is that okay?"

"Yep."

"I want you to remember you are who you are, and no matter what happens with the two of us, you are still the same person inside. Give yourself the opportunity to be happy, to have someone else in your life who loves you." He paused for a moment, "As I said at the start you must have a myriad of questions so during the course of this call I will try to answer them."

Jocelyn shrugged, with indifference, "I have only recently found out about you. I wasn't much into finding you. It was somewhere way down on my things to do list. It would have been more out of curiosity than trying to form a long-term family attachment. I'm going to take my time and keep my expectations reasonable"

"That's understandable."

"So why did you abandon and disown me." Jocelyn accused, trying to keep her voice steady.

"I don't think I really abandoned you, as I had no idea, until years later, that you existed."

"Disowned me then."

A hint of irritation was heard, "I never disowned you."

Jocelyn began to interrupt.

"Please let me finish. Then you can have your say." He stopped and smiled a dazzling smile, one that would melt any heart. "I wanted to be a part of your life but your father forbade it. He said if I ever tried to get in touch he would kick you and your mum out and make her go through a messy divorce. You know how that would have played out. She would have struggled being a single Mom, if she didn't want to move over here. As well as the stigma of the truth coming out."

With a slight shake of her head, "So tell me your version of this sordid tale."

"There is nothing sordid about falling in love. That was what happened between your mother and me."

He sighed.

"We fell in love as teenagers when I was working for a subsidiary of the family firm. I was being groomed to take over the reins, so I was shipped over here to gain experience. They didn't want my co-workers to know my real name, that I was the owners' son. My parents didn't want me to have any preferential treatment, and that is why your family know me as Richard Hendon. Hendon is my mother's name.

My parents found out I was seeing your Mom and forbade me to continue seeing her, to break off our relationship. I promised I would do their wishes. But when they found out we were still together, they recalled me back home. I pleaded with them to let me stay but they said they would cut me off from my inheritance. So after a teary goodbye I returned home."

"So you gave up on her." Jocelyn replied, with a hint of accusation.

"Not then. I always planned to come back. My parents would not harbour any talk of my time in Bristol. They thought it was the biggest mistake of my life getting involved with your Mom, but I did love her."

A faraway look came into his eyes as though he was reliving the past.

"I knew it was only a couple of years until my trust fund kicked in when I was twenty one. So I came back, those years later, as we had planned. I arrived at your Nan's house. She was shocked to see me, but I could see from her face that something was wrong. She tried to let me down gently, because, by then, your mother was married. I drove away, but I needed to see her one last time so I turned around and came back.

I had to speak with her, to tell I was sorry, how much I missed her, loved her. She told me that she was unhappy and that she still loved me. I asked why she stopped writing. She told me she only stopped when I didn't reply. I never received all the letters she said she had written. I found out later that my parents had intercepted them. I know I should never have become involved again, but she begged me to take her away. And so we began our short life together."

"My Mum said you were a one night stand."

"It was more than a one night stand. We were together for four months."

"So what happened? Why did you break up?" Jocelyn asked intrigued.

Richard replied flatly, "My mother died. I went back for the funeral. Your Mom wouldn't come with me. She hated flying. My father was so overcome with grief that I ended up staying. I began to take over the reins of the family firm. I wrote to your Mom and asked her to come and live with me. That I would pay her passage on a cross Atlantic liner but she didn't reply."

Jocelyn shook her head, "You gave up on her."

Richard gave a short nod of her head, "Yes. I gave up on her. I became so caught up in work and keeping everything running smoothly. You know how it is, trying to run a business. Any additional aggravation would have been an unwelcome distraction. I couldn't manage a long distance relationship, and keep the business afloat, so after a few months I gave up and stopped pursuing the contact."

Jocelyn gave Richard an understanding nod.

After a moment of silence, where Jocelyn digested the tale she had been told, she asked, "Did you go on to marry anyone else? Do I have a step Mum, siblings?"

"No. I didn't want anyone else. I immersed myself in work and tried to forget about Heather. Now I fear I'm too old and set in my ways."

"You're never too old to fall in love and find your soul mate."

"Bless you." again that glorious smile shone through.

A far-away look flashed across his eyes. He took a deep breath and continued speaking, "Some years later, your Nan wrote to me."

Another sigh. "She thought I had a right to know, that I had fathered a child and enclosed a picture of you. She said that your Mom was completely sure it was yours. Your parents were back together and your Dad was bringing you up as his, and said you were premature, to cover any discrepancies. She said you were a happy family unit."

Jocelyn was sure Richard had more to say so she stayed quiet.

"So was it a content childhood?" he asked.

"Until my teens. Then things started to go wrong. There always seem to be inconsistency between the ways I was treated and how my Dad treated my brother. Then there were the major disagreements."

"You shouldn't read too much into that sort of disagreement. There is always going to be conflict between parent and child. A parent has this desire for safety, security and survival. Whereas you, the child, want to go off and explore."

Jocelyn shook her head, "I would normally agree with that but will explain why, in my case, you are so wrong. But that will be for later. Please continue with your story."

Intrigued, he replied, "I'll keep you to that. I know you have a story that I have not been privy to. Your Nan wouldn't tell me why you had moved away. She said it was your secret to tell."

Jocelyn shared his nod and replied, "I will tell you. But not now. Please continue telling your story."

"I felt as though I needed proof that you were mine. But back then, people couldn't take DNA tests. Your Nan, in her letter, told me your birth date and it fitted in with my time in Bristol. I read and reread the letter over and over again. During the next few weeks, the idea of having a gorgeous daughter began to grow on me."

Sadness took over his handsome features, "Believe it or not, I suddenly felt abandonment. I felt as though a part of me had been ripped away. I wanted and needed someone to talk to. My remaining family wouldn't understand. Luckily, I had the means to travel the thousands of miles across the globe so I came back to Bristol, and met with your Nan. I fell in love with you the first time I saw you. You were without doubt my little girl. It was like looking at a female version of me as a boy."

He took another deep breath, "I struggled with my conscience. Who was I to intervene in your, their, life again? Yet I had to see your Mum and know that you would be fine. That is when your father frightened me off and your mother appeared not to want anything to do with me.

I was not listed as your father on your birth certificate. Your father stated clearly, that I couldn't see you, talk to you, support you, or help raise you. I had to put you first. I had to do right by for you and myself. I simply did not think I was a good enough person to look after you. I didn't think I alone could give you what you needed. I felt unworthy of fatherhood. I convinced myself I would bring you more harm than good if I elected to fight for custody. And so I decided you would be better off without me. That is the reason why I never got in touch. It might not be a good reason, but it is a reason nonetheless.

Jocelyn felt as though she wanted to reach out and hug him. Instead she smiled and said, "Thank you for telling me and feeling you could trust me and be honest with me."

The sadness lifted slightly, as he said, "However, I asked your Nan to give me updates on your progress and send regular photos. And whenever I was in the country, I came and checked on you. I think I was wrong all those years ago. Perhaps I should have fought to be part of your life."

Philosophically, Jocelyn nodded, "Perhaps, but as you said it was years ago."

"Your Nan was a very special person. I was so sad when she passed. She had dignity and integrity. She loved you so much."

"I know." Jocelyn replied with a sad smile. She paused for a moment then continued, "You were at her funeral, weren't you?"

"Yes I snuck in the back and had a quick drink in the pub."

"That's where I remember seeing you. I think I was too sad for it to register."

Lifting the mood, Richard asked, "So how are you doing? I was very impressed with your presentation."

"You were there?"

"Of course. Do you honestly think I would miss one of the most important days of your life?"

In the background, a phone rang.

"I'm sorry. I'm going to have to take this. It's an important call. Can we continue this the same time tomorrow?"

"Certainly. Same time tomorrow."

"Until tomorrow, Joy. Bye."

"Bye."

Jocelyn tapped her fingers on her lips and a smile spread to her eyes, as she thought, "I was loved as a child."

She scrolled through her phone. She wanted to tell Trina but she knew she couldn't, "Hi Dunc. You'll never guess who I've been talking too."

ꙮ

Chapter Thirty Two

Wednesday

Joy sat at her desk staring at the screen. She had plenty of work to do but the conversation she had had with Richard the previous evening, kept on repeating. Unwanted thoughts pestered her brain and stopped her concentrating on her work. She knew that family had a way of disappointing, as few things can. Family doesn't usually match expectations, perceptions, and dreams. She knew that forming some sort of relationship with Richard, no matter how loosely, could hurt, and once preconceptions are broken, it could leave an empty feeling.

These endless variety of emotions flowed through her. Did she want another complication in her life? Did she need another one? Did Richard have a sense of entitlement or an alternative motive, even if he was unaware of his motives? She thought of Trina and realised that things couldn't have been much worse than they were right then.

She knew that Richard had agreed to take things slowly. He had said all the correct things. Could she trust him? Jocelyn realised that she was under no obligation to continue any contact, but she also knew it felt right. She closed her eyes, rested her head on her arms and let out a huge sigh.

She was suddenly aware of Lucy standing over her, clasping the works phone. "R and G Industries are on the line."

"Is it Riorden or Grey speaking?"

"Neither. She said her name was Morris. Are you okay? You look desperate. Is this that Sam speaking?"

Jocelyn knew she was doing a good impression of a goldfish, as panic spread across Jocelyn's features. Hurriedly, she replied, "I'm not in. Can you deal with it, please?"

Sounding unsure Lucy said, "Yes. Why?"

"I'll tell you later. I just can't speak to her at the moment."

Lucy nodded her head, pressed the mute button and said as she left, "I'm sorry Ms Morris, but Ms Harrold is having a conference call. May I be of assistance?"

As soon as Lucy walked off, Jocelyn closed the door went back to staring at the screen. She took a deep breath. She knew what Sam was like, and knew that she would hear again from her soon. Albeit under the guise of work.

Sam was like a whirlwind; she would come in, and totally turn Jocelyn's life upside down. Jocelyn wondered why did she let Sam get to her so much? Why was she thinking of letting her into her life again?

A while later Lucy walked back in with two cups of coffee. She placed both cups on the table and plonked herself down in one of the other chairs. She carefully scrutinised Jocelyn and asked, "Are you going to tell what is happening?"

"Oh Lucy. I don't know what I'm doing. I'm so torn."

"Would you like to elaborate?"

"I wish that my ex hadn't come back into my life. She has turned everything upside down. I knew what I wanted and where I was going." She paused, before continuing, "Now. I don't have a clue. Why am I hurting Trina? Because I know I am. But."

Jocelyn let the last word hang in the air.

Lucy waited to see if Jocelyn was going to add anything else. After a minute or two she said, "You can either have your life ruled by your head or your heart. So what does your head say?"

"That's it. I don't know. I need a resolution. Every time I see Sam, I am transported back to the worse day of my life. I really loved her, you know." She closed her eyes for a millisecond. "And yet she still has this draw over me," Jocelyn continued, with a shake of her head, "and she knows it." After a slight pause, she added, "And so does Trina."

Jocelyn took a deep breath, "I know that Trina would never do anything to deliberately hurt me but I'm not so sure about Sam. I know she has this ruthless streak about her. Trina is so easy going, she puts her children first, which is a given, and her heart is full of goodness. Sam has this magnetism. She knows what she wants and goes for it. She takes you along for the ride."

A huge sigh escaped and Jocelyn took a deep breath.

Lucy then asked, "And your heart?"

"Again I don't know. I do love Trina and I did love Sam." Jocelyn shrugged. "This uncertainty is eating me up."

"Do you want to know what I think?"

Jocelyn gave a slight laugh, "You might as well, cos I'm not doing a good job thinking for myself."

"You need to use both your head and your heart, as a bit of both is best. I think you need to take some time out. Has Sam said that she wants to get back together?"

"Not in so many words. But she has implied it."

"Don't you think you should meet up with her, ask her. Otherwise, you are working yourself up over nothing. Take some time, but not too long because that would be unfair on Trina."

"When did you become so wise?"

Lucy laughed, "Rose said the same to me last night. Anyhow it's time to get back to work."

Lucy picked up the mugs and as she was walking away, she turned and said, with a bigger laugh, "It's time for me to get back to work and for you to start."

Laughing, Lucy darted away before Jocelyn could think of a comeback.

ဢ

Chapter Thirty Three

Wednesday Evening

"Hello Joy. Everything okay your end?"

"Hi." Jocelyn was unsure how to address her biological father. "I think so."

"Of course. This must all have come as a bit of a shock."

"A little. I found out your name and that you were my father just after Nan's funeral. So when I received your business card I was surprised but not shocked." She gave a little laugh, "To tell you the truth I screwed up your letter and threw it away. But almost straight away I retrieved it."

"I see." Richard replied with an understanding nod.

"My stubborn self, told me I didn't need another person in my life. My amenable and inquisitive self, won out. I'm glad, I think." she added with a nervous laugh.

"You've had time to mull over the conversation we had yesterday, is there anything you'd like to ask?"

Jocelyn nodded, "Just a couple of things. You've had a few chances to introduce yourself to me. Why haven't you? You could have spoken to me at my presentation?"

"You were too busy. I wanted you to concentrate fully on your evening. I didn't want to be an added distraction. I had a good chat with Duncan and Sharon. They seem a nice couple."

"Yes they are. Did you tell them who you are?"

"No. I wanted you to be the first to know."

"You were taking a bit of a gamble turning up. Weren't you worried that my Mum and Dad were going to be there?"

"I thought I had read the situation between you and them correctly, and that I would be safe."

Satisfied with the answer, Jocelyn reflected, "I'm so glad that Duncan and Sharon are back in my life. Their twin boys are cheeky little monkeys. They wind the other up. They get away with so much with the winning smiles."

"I'll have to meet them sometime."

"When are you next back in Bristol I will introduce you."

"I'll look forward to that."

Silence prevailed for a few seconds and Richard let Jocelyn decide about what they were going to talk about next.

"When I moved to Sunderland, did you follow my life?" she asked.

"I must admit I didn't as much as I had been when you were growing up. Your Nan had always kept me informed. She mentioned that you and your Dad hadn't been getting on and you had been through a rough time. Suddenly you were in Sunderland, and were making something of your life. She would occasionally give me an update but these weren't as frequent as before."

Continuing he said, "I still have no idea why you left and your Nan became secretive about the reason. She said she didn't know and you wouldn't say. We haven't any ties with the north east, so having the time to go there was difficult. I know you and another started quite a successful small company, and you allowed your business partner to buy you out. I know that you also bought your Nan her flat. So it was all a bit of a mystery." He paused for a second before asking, "Why did you move there?"

"It's a long story." Jocelyn took her time to weigh up her next words, "My father was never interested in me. Thinking back now, it must have been eating him up inside, that I wasn't his child. It didn't help that he was in the first stages of the growth on his brain. I didn't understand, at the time, why he hated me so much."

"A tumour? Is it cancer?"

"No. Duncan, my brother, said that it has affected his thought processes and his balance, as well as his personality."

"I'm so sorry. Mind you, his personality needed changing." Richard realised that he was talking about Jocelyn's Dad and continued quickly, "Apologies that wasn't kind of me."

"But it was truthful. My father was a horrible man. He was mean, spiteful and good with his fists."

"I'm so sorry that you have been through all that. In a way I'm glad your relationship with him broke down. The bond between a parent and child shouldn't drag you down. It should lift you up. If it doesn't, then not having the connection is better than being abused or disrespected. It takes strength to walk away from a poisonous relationship, whether it is a parent, friend or lover. Don't let anyone tell you that it was your fault that you were abused. Don't devalue yourself, know your worth."

"Thank you. Your family house is meant to be a place of warmth and love. Your safe haven. And yet, it was cold and unforgiving. It gave me my greatest heartache. Mum always took Dad's side against me. And Duncan could do no wrong. It was fine when both or either of them were in the house. When it was only him and me, I didn't feel safe, and therefore it was not a home. It was a just place to lay my head at night."

"But the other end of the country. Surely, there was somewhere close by you could have gone? Your Grandparents, friend, lover?"

Jocelyn stared at the screen, different thought processes played across her features, "I wasn't going to tell you like this, but if we are to have any sort of relationship I will have to."

"I would like to have a father/daughter relationship. You are obviously troubled by something, but only tell me if you are sure. It can wait if you are not ready to talk."

She hesitated for a moment, as though she had reached a decision, "Please listen and not interrupt as I still find it difficult relieving that one night. Is that a promise?"

Richard frowned and nodded. Jocelyn spoke in monotones and relived that fateful night.

"And that is why I ended up in Sunderland. As the saying goes 'You can choose your friends but you sure can't choose your family'"

Shocked, Richard could only mutter, "Oh my. No wonder you wanted to move away. How are you now?"

Jocelyn thought for a moment and replied, "The trauma of any abuse doesn't disappear overnight. Sometimes just thinking about it is enough to hurt you all over again. But it is getting better, easier.

"Did someone help you back then and is someone helping you now?" Richard asked in a concerned voice.

"Not then. I tried to put it all behind me. I didn't want to relive that night. Gradually over the years, it faded. But coming home has made the memories resurface."

"And now? Are you seeing anyone now?"

Jocelyn gave a small laugh, "Yeah, I've been talking to a counsellor."

"You don't always have to be strong. Some of the strongest people I know break down in tears sometimes."

"Are you speaking from experience?"

Richard shrugged his shoulders, and gave a small grin, "I might be. Remember, don't be somewhere or someone you're not because the world says you're supposed to act in a certain way. Be who you are, what you are, and be that to the best of your ability."

"It's taking time for me to feel strong." She smiled, "But I'm getting there. Sometimes it feels for every one step forward I take two steps back."

"You'll get there with love and support. I have every confidence in you. Your girlfriend Trina seems extremely supportive."

Jocelyn groaned, "She is."

Richard looked curious, "I detect a but in there."

Again Jocelyn groaned.

"What is it, love?"

"We've separated."

"Whatever for?"

"Oh Pops I think I have made the biggest mistake of my life."

"Whatever it is I'm sure you can work things through. You both looked so happy. You could tell she is madly in love with you."

An anguished sob escaped from her lips.

"Do you want to tell me what's happened?"

Jocelyn relayed what had happened between her and Sam, and how Trina had told her to leave, to sort out what she wanted.

Jocelyn then asked, "Am I unworthy of love? Am I destined to grow old and die all alone? Still something inside makes me thinks it all was my entire fault."

"Do you need to meet this Sam?"

"I feel as though I want closure on everything. I'm going with Duncan on Friday to see Dad. I want to be released from the power he had over me. I also think that Sam comes into that category. She has magnetism about her. I need to see if all my hopes and fears should stay where they are in the past."

"So you are willing to forsake the love of Trina for a person you don't really know anymore?"

Jocelyn shrugged. She knew he was just looking out for her and warning her to be cautious, but didn't he realise how monumental this was?

As Jocelyn hadn't spoken, Richard continued, "Give yourself permission to be happy. But remember, the grass is not always greener on the other side. People change over the years. You've changed. So, I expect, has this Sam. Don't do anything that you do not feel comfortable with."

Jocelyn gave him a weak smile.

"I know you will do the correct thing." He paused, then a smile spread across his features, lighting up his whole face. "Did you realise you called me Pops earlier."

"Did I?" Jocelyn sounded shocked.

"I liked it. Feel free to call me Pops anytime."

ꟿ

Chapter Thirty Four

Thursday

As she finished making the bed, Trina felt a sudden rush of sadness. She wasn't sure if it was an emotional response or simply exhaustion. So she sat wearily on the bed. Tears threatened, and it occurred to her that she had not fully considered the impact of Jocelyn moving on. The pale morning sky held an emptiness she felt to her bones.

"Just stay busy," she thought, "stay so busy there'll be no time to think."

She could take things as they came. Trina's thoughts were scattered, she was mostly trying to focus on getting through the day. She had decisions to make. She needed time to meditate on what she was going to do with her life now. The shattering of her life had happened so suddenly. One day she was in what she thought was a happy and stable relationship, the next she was again by herself looking after her two wonderful children. She tried to rein in her thoughts so she could get through the day, to look after the children. She needed to get through one day at a time.

She needed all the compassion, empathy and humility she could muster to meet all the challenged that she now faced. She had done it once and knew that she would do it again. She was a survivor.

She realised it was going to be hard for her to have Jocelyn gone but she didn't have any choice. She knew that Jocelyn needed to do this. She needed to put her past behind her and if at the end of it Jocelyn came back to her then so be it. She also knew that she would be waiting. It seemed as if she had been waiting for Jocelyn for all of her life. She knew she would have to have a little more patience and hoped that the wait would be worth it.

She thought for a little while and started to believe that there was going to be a happy future for them, whether together or apart. She hoped it would be the former. Trina was a fatalist and all she knew was that Jocelyn came back into her life for a reason. What will be will be? Her son's words found their way into her consciousness when he pointed out, 'if she loves you she will be back'.

She knew she would have to let some time pass before she made any decision she would later regret. She would have to give Jocelyn the time, and the space, to the conclusion what would be best for her, and ultimately for them. Trina hoped with all her heart that she would feature in Jocelyn's plans.

She couldn't break down. She couldn't go there. It would not help anyone, least of all herself. She had two lovely children who needed her. She sat on the edge of the chair, too emotional to cry anymore, too empty to care. But she did care. She cared too much. Images of their time together flashed through her mind. She tried to put the images away into the compartment labelled 'here, now, future'. These images kept on jumping to the compartment labelled 'over, gone, finished, and lost forever'. Racking sobs came again.

She looked at the clock and realised it was time to take the children to school, even though Peter walked on ahead. She went into the bathroom and splashed cold water on her face. She looked in the mirror. The reflection told her that she might get away without any comments. She again splashed cold water and dabbed her face dry. She sparingly applied some make-up and at once felt loads better.

She shouted out, "Have you both finished breakfast and brushed your teeth?"

Peter shouted back from the kitchen, "I'm ready. And Cathy is putting on her shoes. We'd better hurry otherwise we're gonna be late."

Cathy went flying up the stairs and said, "I've forgotten Pingo."

Confused Trina called out, "You can't take your hamster to school?"

Cathy cried. "I have to Mummy. I asked you yesterday. We have to bring something in and talk about it. I asked you if I could take Pingo and you said yes."

Trina couldn't remember having this conversation, but she had forgotten a lot recently.

"Cathy, why don't you take Mr Snake?"

"But Mummy, I want to take Pingo."

"And I told you no."

Cathy defiantly continued over to Pingo's cage.

"No Cathy. Please take Mr Snake. Then you could tell everyone where you got it from."

Cathy started to cry. "I wanted to take Pingo."

"Cathy, love, I sorry but I don't want you to take your hamster."

"It's not fair mummy. You promised." Cathy wailed as she grabbed Mr

Snake. She ran out of the bedroom shouting, "I hate you."

Trina recoiled and a sob caught in her throat. At that moment, Peter put his arm around his Mum's waist.

"She doesn't mean it Mum. She misses Joy."

"I know. I think we all do."

"I'll talk to her and look after her."

Pulling Peter into a hug Trina replied, "You're a good boy, and you know I love you. What would I do without you?"

"I love you too Mum."

Finally, Cathy stopped crying as Peter and Trina did their best to console the disconsolate child. They left the house and quickly made their way to the school gates. Trina stood slightly away from the other Mums as she waved them into the school.

"I love you both," she shouted after them

Simon's Mum, Lorna, came up to her and gently led her further away from listening ears. Softly she said, in a voice full of concern, "Simon told me that you and your partner had split up."

A gulp escaped her throat. She was terrified of letting anyone know she was coming apart inside, or that she wasn't as strong as everyone thought she was.

"Don't worry. They were talking about it yesterday evening. No one else knows. Simon asked him why he was quiet this past week. Peter told him that you had split up and he was missing Joy."

Trina held her hand to her mouth and closed her eyes.

Lorna touched Trina's arm. "I know you are being so strong for your children and don't want to upset them but who is looking after you."

Trina couldn't speak; she blinked back the tears by scrunching up her eyes. When she re-opened them, she saw Lorna studying her with sympathy.

"Is there anything I can do?"

Trina shook her head, still not trusting her voice.

"Why don't you come to ours for a coffee? You can fall apart there, if you want. I can see you are close to the edge. You can just be you. I'm not here to judge or to make comment, not unless you want me to. I will listen and be a shoulder to cry on. If that's what you want, if that's what you need."

Tears filled her eyes. No one, who was not a close friend, had ever said anything like that to her before, had noticed, had been kind.

Lorna handed Trina a tissue. She gave Lorna a nod and a grimace.

"Dry your eyes and follow me." She was guided to a house around the corner from the school.

Lorna led Trina into the front room and invited Trina to sit.

"I'll make us a coffee. White? "

Trina nodded.

Lorna placed the coffee on the table and sat in the chair. She could tell by the way Trina held her head, looking towards her feet, that Trina was hurting. Lorna didn't know what to say so she waited, quietly, patiently.

Finally Trina said, "I love her so much but I asked her to leave. I miss her terribly."

A giant sob escaped and Trina desperately tried to hold in the tears. Seeing Trina inconsolable, Lorna went over and wrapped her arms around her.

Between sobs, "I saw how she was whenever she met her ex. I think she still wants to be with her. Even though her ex helped to break her heart."

Trina closed her eyes and took a deep breath

"I had to let her go. She has to come back to me because I'm the one she wants not because she feels she has to."

"That's true but I know people like you. People who do what they think is right, even though it breaks their heart. I'm not going to judge you and I don't presume to know what is best for you. All I know is that you are hurting. And perhaps by talking you can let out the pent up emotion that is deep inside you. Perhaps, and I mean perhaps, it would help to sort what you want. I feel that at the moment you are only just managing."

"I can't stand the thought of being second best. Either she will want to be with me, or she won't. If I bully her into staying, or plead with her, I know she would stay with me. But how many years down the line will she start to resent me, when she had the opportunity to make things right with Sam. I am not that person and cannot be the person. I want her to love me like I thought she did."

Another deep breath through the sobs

"I cannot put my children through this again. Peter is trying not to show how much he misses Joy. He tells me he is fine, but I can see he is struggling."

"Children have more resilience than we give them credit for."

"It's not that simple. This morning Cathy told me she hates me."

"She doesn't hate you. It's her way of telling you she's unhappy and that she misses Joy."

"I know. But it doesn't stop it hurting."

"Do you love Joy?" Lorna asked, as she picked up the mug and sipped the coffee.

"Yes"

"Would you take her back if she came back this minute?"

Trina didn't hesitate for a second, "Yes. But I know there is a variety of ways someone can love you. I don't want her to come back if it is conditional love."

Lorna frowned, "What do you mean conditional love."

"Where love is based on conditions. You do this for me; I do that for you. It's based on fear. You are afraid of any issues you have, or indeed, they have. You have a fear of getting hurt, a fear of being alone. When a relationship is built on fear, you are on uneven ground. You're building on sand; the house won't stand when the tide turns, or when the storm comes." She paused for a moment "When love is based on the condition that you must love me back the way I need, or want you to. Then warning signs will raise their head. You are sort of saying if you don't love me the way I insist you do, I'm justified in replacing you, or at very least no longer being in love with you."

"I think I understand."

"Unconditional love is very different. It loves for no reason. It wants what is best for the one you love. You will be willing to sacrifice your happiness for them." The frown she had been wearing lifted from Trina's features.

"I have a feeling that is what you are doing now. And in the past you have also been in a conditional love relationship."

"Oh you've met my ex-husband" Trina butted in and managed a small smile

"And I'm betting at the first sign of trouble, he didn't stick around very long to try to work things out."

"You've definitely met my ex." She sighed, "I think I'm destined to have the people I love leave me. What have I done to deserve this? All I did was fall in love. I feel undervalued and emotionally weak."

"Sometimes the strongest people are those who are willing to admit they can't do everything. That's not weak. It's real."

"So you love Joy unconditionally."

"I think so, yes. That is why I let her go. She needs to sort her own feelings out." Trina glanced at her watch. "Is that the time. I have to get to work." She started to stand up. "Thanks for the coffee and listening."

"You're welcome. What are you doing Saturday? Why don't you and the kids join us for tea? Simon asked Peter to come over but he declined. I don't think he wants to leave you."

"Thanks. If that's alright with Sal as well, we would love to."

"She's the one who suggested it."

Chapter Thirty Five

Friday

"Hi big sis. I thought you might chicken out on me."

"I did think about it. Are you sure Mum is not going to be there."

"No. Mum will not be there."

"How can you be so sure?"

Duncan smiled, "Because I have just seen her leave."

"Did you talk to her?"

"Should I have?"

"No."

"I can understand why you are so against a Dad but why Mum, apart from the obvious."

He searched her face, waiting for her to explain.

A whole gamut of emotions flashed over her face, "I can never understand why Mum took Dads side. I know that living with Dad's illness, has been hard for her. But back then, the symptoms didn't appear to be that bad. And her not believing me, felt as though she had died to me. Several emotions flashed her face, ranging from anger, sorrow, through to contriteness. Her throat was suddenly dry and she tried to swallow. Now she acts as if I'm the devil in disguise, as though everything that has happened has been my fault."

He waited for her to continue, but the lump in her throat was choking her. "And?" he offered.

"Growing up and all through school her mantra to me was you're failing to live up to your full potential."

"Then the time Nan said I could stay with her cos she could see I was unhappy she changed to saying if you and stay with her, You'll eventually come crawling back here devastated and broke, and I'll have to pick you up once again and put you back together,"

Following a deep breath she continued, "In my final year at school it was 'You know you are nothing without my guidance and direction. You've proven that point often enough, failure after failure." Jocelyn shook her head, "What failure? I nearly always earned top grades; I left school with glowing reports and had myself an extremely good job."

She pursed her lips, "I lost her love for me all those years ago, and at the time it was devastating and frightening. So until she changes her opinion of me and shows me some love and respect, or even just acceptance, then I'll struggle to like her."

Her voice broke, hot tears burned at the back of her eyes and a lump collected in her throat. Jocelyn felt emotion rising through her whole body and Duncan noticed the change. He took hold of Jocelyn hand but she pulled his hand away and shook her head in an attempt to convince him she was fine, but the harsh words her mother had said rang in the back of her mind.

Even though she tried to blink away the tears, they gathered at the corners of her eyes. She dabbed at them with her knuckle.

She sniffed and shrugged one shoulder. "That Sunday around your house was the straw that broke the camel's back, I guess. She's never going to be proud of me. Not even a little. She's never going to believe me. Never."

An old familiar pain crashed through her heart, and she sniffed, the breath felt as though it had been knocked out of her chest. She felt as though a panic attack was close.

He wrapped her in his arms saying, "I'm proud of you and I believe you. Do you feel strong enough to see Dad? We can always go another time."

She fluttered her hands in front of her face, dismissing his worries. As she attempted to dry the tears that had escaped, she continued, "If I don't do it now I never will."

"There's something else you should know."

Jocelyn looked at her brother expectantly.

"His recent operation." Duncan paused.

"What about his recent operation. All you told me was that it removed some of the pressure on the brain. And I will be able to tolerate the man he is now."

"It has. But it is like a tap gets turned on and off. One minute he is back to the Dad of our childhood, the next he becomes upset and confused. He is the man that you will not like."

"So you got me here under false pretences."

"No. But it might be a good idea if you wait outside his room until I see what type of mood he is in. Okay?"

Reluctantly Jocelyn agreed.

ઈ

"Hi Dad. How are you feeling?"

"I'm good son. Your Mother has just left."

"I know. I saw her leaving. Joy is outside. Do you want to see her? You know, to apologize?"

His Dad took hold of his arm.

"I do. Did you have to force her to come?"

Duncan didn't answer straight away.

"I honestly didn't know if she would come." he paused, "Or even if she is still outside."

"Go get her."

Duncan walked back in with Jocelyn. She stood at the bottom of the bed, and scrutinized her father.

"I want to apologize and say I'm sorry, Joy."

"Is that it? You're sorry."

Her father looked at her confused.

Jocelyn sighed, "When you say I'm sorry, is it an acknowledgement that I won't let you forget that night, when you tried to rape me? Or sorry that you caused me pain and injury? Or sorry that you didn't get to do the deed."

He looked contrite. "Two of them. Sorry that I caused you pain. Sorry that I attacked you. I'm glad you stopped me."

Jocelyn shrugged, "You still can't say it, can you?" Her voice rose, as she said slowly, "You tried to rape me."

Duncan put his arm around his sister and gave her a squeeze.

"I think your apology lacks the understanding of what you tried to do to me. How it has affected how I look on life. My relationships. My wellbeing. By saying sorry doesn't make everything all right." She pursed her lips. "I don't think I can accept that apology."

"That's okay, I don't know if I can forgive myself either."

"That's it though. You haven't asked to be forgiven. All you have said is sorry. Sorry covers a magnitude of sins. Asking for forgiveness means that you have thought about what you did to me, and how those actions had an effect on me."

He looked directly in to Jocelyn's face. "I accept responsibility for what I tried to do and the amount of pain I have caused you."

"By acting that way towards you, whilst you were growing up, I probably made you feel unloved."

"That's an understatement."

"My doctor has told me that the tumour had altered my perceptions. That is not an excuse but it is a fact. I was angry with your Mother."

"I know about Richard."

Her Dad sucked in his breath in shock.

Jocelyn continued, "I've spoken to him and heard his side of the story. But I'm not here to talk about him."

Her dad looked at the notes he had in front of him. He continued, "Then to find out you were a lesbian. I just couldn't control my anger."

"So that makes it all right."

"Of course not. None of that was your fault, and it was wrong for me to take all my insecurities out on you. Please forgive me."

"I am not going to say I forgive you as that may be seen as excusing your actions."

"I do not expect to be forgiven easily. I have prepared for the worst but I hoped for the best."

"I am still angry with you. I will always remember what happened, but I am no longer going be bound by it. I cannot forget the incident ever happened. I don't want to include you in my life."

"I understand. I just hope that time can bring us closer together again."

Jocelyn stood, arms crossed. "Why now? Why after all these years?"

"I think my illness..." her dad closed his eyes. When he opened them he looked confused. "Where am I? Why am I here? Who are you?"

Duncan moved to by his Dad's head. He took hold of his hand and said, "Hi Dad. It's me. Duncan. Joy is with me as well."

"What's she doing here?"

"You asked to see her."

"Why ever would I do that?"

Duncan turned to Jocelyn. "Wait outside. I'll be out in a minute."

ഈ

"Are you okay?" Duncan asked as he put his arms around Jocelyn, and pulled her into a bear hug.

"He actually apologized. I never thought he would say those words."

"So how are you feeling?"

"I honestly don't know. I have spent half my life waiting for that to happen and now it has I feel empty. I clung to my anger because it felt justified. He expressed regret, so perhaps now I can heal."

"I hope so, Dumps. I really do. Now go and give Trina and the kids a big kiss. I'm going to spend some more time with Dad."

Jocelyn smiled a sad smile. Now was not the time to tell him that they had split up. Instead she said, "Give Sharon and the boys my love."

"Will do. Love you Sis."

ഈ

Chapter Thirty Six

Saturday

Jocelyn held the card between her finger and thumb. She looked at the name and phone number written on the embossed card. She tore it in half and then held the two pieces together. She could almost remember the number by heart.

Fighting back the feelings of betrayal towards Trina, she picked up her phone. The curiosity and need to see Sam again, speak with her again pushed aside the longing she thought she had overcome. Did she have it wrong all those years ago? Were the conflicting reports she had heard correct? What did she want with her now?

Visions of Sam and the promise of lust and love flashed through her mind. Lush curves, piercing blue eyes and lovely flowing long golden blond hair greeted her. Her large frame and generous hips and bosom set her apart. Jocelyn remembered the intoxicating scent of Sam's perfume, and had to choke back a sigh. She knew that smelling great didn't make the consequences safe. In fact, she knew that she was heading into dangerous territory where there was no turning back.

But did she want to turn back? Because going meant facing her. Because going meant sensing every feeling that Sam dredged up in her. She didn't want these feelings anymore. Or did she? Could she cope with the emotions she didn't want to admit she could even still have.

And yet she wanted the feel of those strong arms around her. She needed the warmth and anticipation. She realised that she still craved her with all her heart. Her soul had met its match and no walls could divide them. There could be no shields or barriers. Her stomach took a nosedive as her heart leapt and sang. She forced herself to take deep breaths to try to calm the hammering in her heart.

"Hi Sam. It's Joy."

༄

She should have been more cautious when agreeing to meet. Yet she could feel a sense of excitement growing, knowing that she would be soon in her company. She felt as though she was walking towards a precipice. A huge sigh escaped. Would she walk over the edge so that the life as she knew it would end up shattered on the ground, or would she stay in the here and now, savouring her present life to the fullest.

Jocelyn felt as anxious as she had ever felt in her life; her nerves were jingling as she moved quickly into the pub. She saw Sam sitting in a quiet corner at the back of the room. There were only a couple of other punters sitting at the bar. Sam got up and waved across to her.

They stared at each other for a moment and then Sam sat down opposite her. Jocelyn felt uneasy. Sam made her feel nervous. Sam cocked her brow and watched Jocelyn turn beetroot.

"I've got you a whiskey." Sam said as she pushed it across the table "Your choice. Or you could have a lager." She took a sip of her drink. Jocelyn sighed and took it as a cue to take a sip of hers. She lifted the glass, breathing in its aroma.

Sam smoothed the front of her shirt down a little self-consciously, assessing Jocelyn. Then as if liking what she saw she nodded and smiled a knowing smile.

She looked at Sam and found it annoying that a hundred butterflies took flight in her stomach. She saw the self-assured woman opposite her and wondered how many times Sam had done the happy dance since she had been gone.

Putting those thoughts away, she jumped as Sam lightly held Jocelyn's hand. She fought not to let herself feel it as Sam's thumb rubbed across and over hers, but not feeling it was all but impossible. It ricocheted through her, stealing her thoughts and her sanity. She swallowed hard but the swallow didn't help, neither did the breath she never really managed to take.

Jocelyn pushed Sam's hand away as she spoke, "We need to talk, really talk. We never fought and never had an argument about anything important so I could never understand why you betrayed me." She paused for several seconds and appeared to be gathering her thoughts. It was difficult to know how to judge the situation.

Sam gave another smile, "Now you're being over-dramatic. You saw me in another woman's arms. That didn't mean you would want to kill yourself. I have also told you that she pounced on me and I came looking for you.

You do know that truth is completely unaffected by whether you accept it or not."

"No, that alone wouldn't. Oh never mind the rest of the story can wait for another time." Jocelyn stopped talking and flexed her jaw. To relive every moment was hard when every moment seemed like a lifetime. She sighed, "I have no desire for drama, conflict or rage. I may be slightly broken, perhaps more than a little broken. I was a little bruised, but those bruises soon faded. I also think I am permanently scarred from that night, but I refuse to be beaten. I came back stronger after all the setbacks thrust upon me."

They sat in silence, each looking at the other, weighing up their thoughts and feelings. Jocelyn felt as though the first step to the resolution she wanted and needed had been put into place. Sam felt smug, she realised Jocelyn still wanted her.

With a different sense of liberation, Sam and Jocelyn talked about their lives and stayed on at the pub for another round, then another. They looked at each other for a long moment.

The sexy woman in front of Jocelyn frightened her to pieces. She had planned to walk away after the talk and the drink, to get closure from that part of her life. She knew she would need time to rebuild her relationship with Trina before it was too late. Yet every instant spent in the company of Sam was another moment she wanted to wrap her arms around her and kiss her, until both were left breathless. Until their touches made them feel inebriated, and their perfumes made them faint. Jocelyn snapped back to the present.

"I'm sorry," Jocelyn said once she had regained a semblance of control, "I thought I could handle it. I thought these emotions had long since gone."

Jocelyn wanted distance between them. She sought perception on the feelings that were churning away at her insides. She needed to feel grounded.

"Why don't you come back to mine? I only live around the corner. Then we can, as you so succinctly put it earlier, really talk. I don't think the pub is the best place to clear the air."

Sam smiled at the uncertainty on Jocelyn's face and continued, "If you wait for the perfect time then it will never happen. And I can see it in your eyes that you want it to happen."

Jocelyn frowned, and it was accompanied by a slightly puzzled look.

"Want what to happen."

Sam gave a self-depreciating smile, "Us. It is written all over your face." Laughing she downed the rest of her drink and handed Jocelyn her glass and waited for her to down it. She stood up and said, "Come on let's go."

ꙮ

Chapter Thirty Seven

Saturday

Whilst she waited for Sam to come back from the kitchen, she glanced around the room taking in all the objects lying around. She expected it to feel homely and yet it felt sterile. Jocelyn usually found an emotional connection between the place the person lived and themselves. The room would give her a hug, but today the connection was lacking.

Before she could think of it further, Sam came back carrying the drinks and the bottle. Sam poured a good glug into each glass.

"Do you want some ice?"

Jocelyn nodded.

Sam took the glass back out into the kitchen and returned with the ice clinking in the glass. She passed the glass back to Jocelyn and, on picking up her glass, said "Cheers."

Sam placed her glass down on the coffee table, "So what happened that night?"

Jocelyn realised that this would be harder to say. She didn't want to revisit that night ever again. She felt grateful for the copious amounts of alcohol she had imbibed. Yet she felt she owed Sam an explanation. She closed her eyes and the memory was etched there. She wondered whether to skirt around the issue. She swallowed the frog that had caught in her throat. Instead, she blurted out, "That night my father tried to rape me."

Sam downed her drink and sat next to Jocelyn. She put her arm around Jocelyn and leaned in for a kiss, tentative at first. Jocelyn felt defenceless; the slow, cautious and amazing kiss shook her to her core. All thoughts of here and now vanished. Sam's mouth and tongue explored with a deep desire. Sam, in Jocelyn's arms, felt so right but at the same time, felt so wrong. At that moment in time, Jocelyn felt at peace. The demons that had once taken control of her life raised their head for a moment. As Sam stroked her hair, the door slammed on the demons and slowly their protestations dimmed.

They pulled apart. Jocelyn gave a fragile smile. Jocelyn knew she had played with fire and had been powerless to douse the flames. She had tried to keep all the feelings of need and desire locked away in a place where she had no access. But the key to the door had been found, and the door was swinging open.

Jocelyn's mind reeled at the fact that Sam was standing in front of her. She had a need in her that had to be released. That had been building up since the first time she had seen her again after all those years. Could she escape her past? She knew the good times and the bad had defined the person she is today.

"I didn't know." Sam stated flatly. "I knew he was a bully."

"Why should you"

Sam spoke to her. "Let's have another drink. Let me get you another whiskey. I think you need it."

Sam took the glass.

Jocelyn shook her head, "I don't think I want another."

Her brain and her heart were in a battle. Her heart reeled at the fact that she was there with Sam and was telling her to make new memories, to step, again, into the unknown. Her brain was telling her not to betray Trina, to stop looking for the impossible dream and to be content being surrounded by love.

Sam pushed, "Go on. One more drink won't do any harm."

Her brain kicked into gear and although the alcohol flowing through her veins, caused her head to buzz. Jocelyn spoke, and her voice cracked as her heart thumped. "I need the loo, will finish my drink and I'd best be getting home."

"Why don't you stay?"

"No. Sorry. Not a good idea. It was good catching up and for you to explain things from your side, all those years ago. But we have both moved on. Is it at the top of the stairs?"

Sam nodded.

Jocelyn came back, and sat on the arm of the chair. Sam closed the distance between them. She looked at Jocelyn, smiled, and laid a hand on her arm. Sam leant in placed a kiss on her forehead. Jocelyn then found her mouth had connected with Sam's and all the stories of their time together were told in those few minutes. Jocelyn could taste whiskey breath. Jocelyn could taste Sam, her being, her soul. Sam eased Jocelyn's mouth open and Jocelyn became lost in a delirious long lost feeling, a distant memory. Their tongues apologised and mourned for what was and what could have been.

Jocelyn let out a contented sigh. Happiness welled within her and emerged as a cheek-to-cheek grin. But did she want more than a grope, a kiss, an exploration of lust.

Sam's hands started to explore but Jocelyn's hands were unsure, fearful of the consequences. Tentatively Jocelyn rubbed her hands down Sam's arms and could feel the taut muscles, could feel her take control. One of Sam's hands reached up into the hair at the back of Jocelyn's neck and gripped it, holding Jocelyn in place.

Emotions she'd fought hard to supress emerged in a torrent and she felt her whole body being slammed by waves. The consequences soon disappeared as a moan of pleasure escaped Jocelyn's lips, and she is transported back to the past, to when they had a future. She looked at the woman next to her.

"I suppose that little tart you've been seeing, knew about your Dad?"

An emotion washed over Sam's face that Jocelyn couldn't quite make out; a smirk, a sneer, self-assurance.

Jocelyn stared at Sam, and couldn't believe what she had just heard. She felt as if a stake had been driven through her heart. How dare she call Trina a tart?

"What did you just say?" Jocelyn asked in astonishment.

"I said I bet Trina knew about your Dad. She always seemed to know everything about your family. Does she know about you and me?"

"There is no you and me."

Jocelyn began to feel ill at ease; there was something about the smirk that passed across Sam's face.

Jocelyn shook her head. "I'm sorry. I have to go."

She tossed her drink down her neck, picked up her bag and stood up. Then suddenly Jocelyn's felt strange. Her vision began to blur, she felt confused and found it difficult to raise her arms, to move. She was helped to stand and felt Sam guide her out of the room.

ꕤ

Chapter Thirty Eight

Sunday

Jocelyn woke up suddenly with a jolt. She noticed bruises that were beginning to show on her wrists. Her head was fuzzy and she had little recollection of what had gone on. She felt battered, bruised and sore. She groaned as she moved.

Sam stirred beside her and then woke up with a start, and said dismissively, "Oh. You're still here. I thought you'd be gone by now."

Jocelyn was taken aback.

"What happened? Where am I?"

"Where do you think you are?"

"I'm at yours?" she asked incredulously, "I was leaving?"

"Then you suddenly jumped on me."

Confusion spread over her features. She couldn't understand, she couldn't remember. She shook her head and tried to remove the fog that surrounded her, but the movement made her head swim.

"Surely you remember how you pleaded with me to play with you?" Sam smirked, "I didn't know you were like that." Her voice changed, "But now I want you gone. My lover is due back soon."

Hurt and perplexed, she had no recollection of the previous night. She could remember standing up to leave and then no more, she didn't want to appear weak, yet she was baffled by her lack of recall. Even when she was completely blathered she usually remembered the events, but she could remember nothing.

She gave her head a slight shake, and said in a quiet voice, "I don't understand. How did I get these bruises?"

"I knew you were drunk but you wanted to be tied up. So against my better nature I complied."

Jocelyn frowned, shaking her head. How could she forget that? She wouldn't do that. She hadn't, ever.

"Now go. I don't want to see you again."

"Didn't I mean anything to you?"

Sam smirked, "You stopped meaning anything when you didn't come back all those years ago. Just wanted to see if I could still have you, and found out that I can."

Anger and humiliation coursed through Jocelyn's veins. She felt anger towards herself and towards Sam. Speaking slowly she said, "You are one self-centred person. You have little regard for anyone else or anyone's feelings. You run rough shod over everything and anyone. How have you become this person?"

Sam laughed; a laugh full of mocking, "I learned from the best it seems."

All the different emotions again flashed across Jocelyn's face, but mainly humiliation. She had allowed this woman back into her life, even though she knew it could destroy the existence she now had, and everything else she held dear. The weakness she was feeling was pushed to the back of her heart, and in their place came a hard, steely resolve, as she spat out, "You've changed."

Sam shrugged; her sharp tongue cut Jocelyn down to size, "You left me. I had to change."

"Will you answer me one thing?"

Sam shrugged.

"Did we, you know, sleep together?"

"Well," she smirked, "you woke up in my bed. Now if you don't mind I have to get ready for my lover. She's due home any time now. Close the door behind you on your way out."

And with that Sam walked away to take a shower.

The room tilted when she sat up as nausea threatened to overwhelm her. She steadied herself by swinging her legs onto the floor. She then started quietly cursing. Trina's loving face invaded her thoughts. She squeezed her eyelids closed; felt tears of frustration and mortification prickle the corner of her eyes and wondered how she could have let this happen. The shame of the past few minutes allowed a headache to form behind her already fuzzy eyes.

Jocelyn dressed as quickly as she dared. She grabbed up all her belongings. She stumbled over to the dressing table mirror and looked at her eyes. Her face looked older, wiser and was close to the edge. She had been used and abused, and felt dirty. She picked up the business card, let out a hysterical laugh and it sounded brittle.

The bedroom door opened and in walked Marie. Her old school friend looked at her with disgust.

"What are you doing in my house?"

"Your house?" Jocelyn said in amazement.

"I came back here with Sam."

"So you are muscling in on my girlfriend as well."

"It wasn't like that."

"So what was it like? Look at the state of you. You look just like the slapper you always were, and obviously still are."

Another bout of shock trembled through her body.

"Get out." Marie screamed. "Get out." As she took hold of Jocelyn's arm and pushed her towards the door.

Jocelyn shrugged herself out of Marie's grasp, "Don't worry I'm going."

"Stay the hell out of our lives."

"As long as you both stay out of mine."

Marie smirked, "Don't worry. Everything has been achieved that needed to be achieved."

Jocelyn was desperate to preserve what little dignity she had left. Tearing the business card in half she stormed out of the house. As the door slammed behind her, she heard laughter.

Jocelyn felt foolish, frustrated and controlled. This wasn't how she wanted it to be, wanted it to turn out. She wanted to walk away as friends, or that's what she thought she wanted. What had happened last night? Why did she feel so used and abused? Had she thrown away everything she held dear and for what?

A quick fumble under the sheets, with a woman she no longer knew. But had she? She should have realised that Sam would be a different person than the young naïve thing she knew all those years ago. Jocelyn knew that she was.

Oh why did she let it happen, yes she had drunk but not that much. A few whiskeys shouldn't have made her so drunk that she couldn't remember what had happened. All she knew was her body felt battered and bruised, as though she had been abused against her will, but had she.

Jocelyn wracked her brain for memories of last night, but no memories came after saying she was going to leave. Why couldn't she remember? Her thoughts relayed the memories of the night, but no matter how hard she tried, they always stopped in the same place.

She had gone there of her own accord, she had accepted the drinks. She shook her head and tried to remove the fog. Could she remember following Sam into the bedroom? Everything what happened next was a blur. Why was it a blur?

She began to feel as if she was no longer in control of her emotions. They were disobedient and fazed, had she reacted to Sam in ways Jocelyn didn't understand, much less have control over.

The hard, steely resolve, dissipated, and an overriding nervous nausea hovered below the surface. It felt as if she was on the most frightening rides in the local theme park. She was waiting to go over the edge where she would not have any jurisdiction over what would happen. She started to feel a bit light-headed. The ground felt like it was rising to meet her. She had to steady herself. Using the wall as a support. Her breath came in short gasps as she waited for the inevitable endplay.

Although frustration with her was common, anger was rare. She took a deep breath and started to run. She didn't usually run but the adrenalin kicked in along with the anger.

She wanted to shout abuse at everyone she met, but realised she would be viewed as a crazy woman. And in a way, she was. One to be shunned, pitied, talked about. She reached the main road and leant against the bark of a tree, panting. She closed her eyes and tried the deep breathing that had worked for her in the past.

Gradually her breath returned to normal.

All the time her breathing calmed, her mind was whirling with all that had happened, but why couldn't she remember it clearly. She was trying to process memories that weren't there. Why weren't they there?

She tried to tell herself that this hadn't happened. That it was just a dream, no, it was a terrible nightmare. That at some time she would wake up and it would be yesterday morning and be in her own bed, deciding whether to phone.

The weight of large tears started to build behind her eyes, and threatened to escape. The shock of what had happened started to register. She needed to pull herself together. She couldn't turn back time, she could only move forward. But move forward to what?

It was a quiet Sunday morning and the traffic had yet to wake up. After a wait that seemed a lifetime, she managed to flag down a taxi and gave her address. She sank back into the upholstery and closed her eyes.

She felt the prickle of tears begin to form again. She blinked rapidly and willed the tears to stay put. Luckily, the driver didn't try to engage her in inane conversation. She noticed the glances he gave her. She must look a state. What had happened was bad enough but to endure the humiliation from an unknown taxi driver, made her more uncomfortable. She wanted to scream at him. Hadn't he done something he instantly regretted?

Miserably, she watched the quiet streets pass by. She tried not to think, she didn't want to remember. She wanted to deaden the emotions she was feeling. She wanted love and laughter back in her life.

She soon reached her apartment without a further breakdown and paid the driver. She took three attempts to key in the number and stumbled blindly up the stairs. She composed herself long enough to open the door, and run into her bedroom.

She flung herself on the bed and tried to compose herself. The more she tried, the harder it became. Soon the floodgates opened and all the pent up emotion that she had been holding in burst open. Like the approaching tide crashing through a dam made of sand, nothing was going to stop them until her emotions had run its course.

Her heart felt as though it was being held in two hands, and twisted. Twisted until all life was gone. The wracking sobs gradually turned to silent tears then to self-pity and loathing.

ꕤ

Chapter Thirty Nine

Monday Morning

She tossed and turned watching the hours tick by. Gradually snippets of the Saturday night worked her way into her consciousness. She played over and over the events in her head. None of it made any sense. She wracked her brain trying to understand what had gone on. She felt a knot build in the pit of her stomach, as her body broke out in a cold sweat. She just made it to the bathroom on time.

She woke up cuddling the toilet bowl as if it was a long lost friend. Her mouth felt as if she had eaten sandpaper and her throat still held the effect of the bile. She pushed herself up and leant on the sink.

She looked in the mirror, and was greeted by her face. A face that had aged twenty years. Her gaze slid up to her eyes, her exhaustion and frustration was clear.

She stumbled to her bed, grabbed a pillow and hugged it to her chest. An animal type wail escaped from her mouth. She hadn't stopped to think about what would happen if she and Trina broke up. Until now, she hadn't envisioned the consequences. She hadn't stopped to think about the fact that she'd grown up with her as both her best friend and her girlfriend and now that things had ended, she had lost both.

How did she let it come to this? She held her Nan's picture to her breast and tears of desperation and remorse ran down her cheek. Go to sleep she scolded herself. She struggled to think of nothing, but was overcome by every thought and worry.

Drowsiness started to come but visions of Trina loving face smiled down on her. Self-pity flowed through her as she cried herself to sleep. By the morning, she was drained both emotionally and physically.

Jocelyn caught a glimpse of herself in the mirror, and it was not a good look. Her eyes were puffy and her tear-stained cheeks were red and blotchy. Her nose began to run and drip, as she searched for a dry tissue. She knew she looked frightful. Mostly she felt contempt and anger. Contempt at the thought of being seen as weak, and anger for her selfishness at the pain she had caused. She felt she had lost completely, the respect others had of her. She felt as though she had thrown away her values and for what? The pain of her betrayal felt like red-hot pokers stabbing at her heart.

She knew she should eat but even though her fridge was well stocked, she couldn't bring herself to make anything. She tried to force a biscuit down, all the while, gagging, but it stuck in her throat.

She looked at the vodka bottle and empty glass and was tempted to take another drink. Temptation won so she swallowed a large vodka, shivering as the fiery liquid hit the back of her throat.

She flung herself back down onto the crumpled sheets as grief again overwhelmed her. She was vaguely aware that somewhere in the background her phone kept ringing.

ꟸ

Charlie asked, as he walked into the staff area and put the kettle on to boil, "Has she answered yet?"

"No it keeps going to voice mail and I'm getting a little worried."

"Do you want a refill?" asked Charlie as he pointed to her empty mug.

"No thanks. I've only recently finished this one."

Charlie took a sip of his hot coffee and said, "Joy might have gone on a bender and is sleeping it off."

Lucy shook her head, "Do you really believe that?"

Charlie shrugged, "There's a first time for everything."

Lucy replied, "I've never seen Joy drunk. A tad tipsy, but never drunk."

Charlie nodded. "She has been acting strange of late. I know she and Trina have split up but that's all I'm privy to. She always seems preoccupied, especially when R and G Industries are mentioned." He paused and spoke almost conspiringly, "She even sent me off to go over an aspect with them. It was almost as if she didn't want their account. Yet it's the one that is bringing in the most money. Have you any clue about what's going on?"

Shaking her head, Lucy said, "Not really and I don't think it's something we should be gossiping about."

"But if it affects us then we have every right to question." Charlie responded.

Lucy nodded agreement but added, "Trust in Joy to do the right thing. I do." She paused, "I think I'm going to ring Trina."

"No don't do that." He answered shaking his head, "They might have got back together and doing everything else that goes with making up."

"What like sharing a tub of ice cream?"

Charlie gave a small smile, "You know exactly what I mean."

"Nah Trina works on a Monday."

Charlie turned serious as he said, "So should Joy, but she's not here."

"If she doesn't answer by the end of the day then I'm going around there. It's a good job she hasn't any appointments today. I looked in the diary and she has something pencilled in with Hawkins tomorrow. That's one you helped work on isn't it?"

"You're getting me worried now."

"Don't be. I'm just thinking ahead. If Joy needs our help over the next few days then I think we owe it to her to do all we can. Look at everything she has done for us."

Charlie nodded his head, "If she's not in tomorrow and we can't contact her then I'll take over that one. Any others?"

Lucy flipped over the page in the diary, "Sean was going with her to see Bryant's. I'll email him so he can have a heads up. The other two I've done some work for them, so I'll take over the reins for them."

Charlie frowned, "Don't you think we are being a bit cautious. I can see Joy breezing in tomorrow having a good laugh at our expense."

Lucy put a hand on Charlies arm and gave a small laugh "I'd rather she laughs at me than we lose the contract. Any way you can say it was all my idea. That I had become a mother hen, and was beginning to flap."

"Fair enough." Charlie agreed, "I'll blame it all on you. I'll read the file tonight."

As the end of the working day approached, Lucy still couldn't get hold of Joy, she shouted to Charlie, saying, "I'm knocking off a little early and going around to Joy's apartment. To set my mind at rest. Are you all right staying on here until Sean gets back? I know it's my turn for the late shift but Sean said he'd do it. He said he had some paperwork to catch up on."

"No problem. Text me."

"Will do. Catch you later."

Lucy walked along the path of the floating harbour towards Joy's apartment. A group of youngsters were being taught how to sail on one side of the harbour whilst a group of six canoes were rafted together on the other side. One of the yellow and blue ferries was transporting passengers towards the Cumberland basin floated by. A running commentary of the sights could be heard over their speaker system.

Lucy quickly arrived at the entrance and bounded up the stairs. She let herself in and called out Joy's name.

Lucy was greeted with silence. She opened the bedroom door a tad and saw Jocelyn crashed out on the bed.

Jocelyn stirred and mumbled something, but was soon breathing the rhythmic breathing of a deep sleep. Lucy quietly closed the door and made her way out into the bright sunlit evening.

She texted Charlie. 'She's at home. Sleeping like a baby. Didn't disturb her. Fancy going for a drink? I'm meeting Rose in the Newfoundland in an hour.'

8๑

Chapter Forty

Tuesday

Jocelyn woke up from the troubled night. Why had she chosen a dream over the love of her life? Now the dream had become a nightmare.

She felt as though she was clinging on to the last vestiges of her dignity, as though she was hanging over a parapet and gripping on by her fingertips for dear life. That if she looked down all hope was gone. She had a sudden urge and felt as though she had had enough.

A deep depression had taken hold of her. That she wanted gravity to take over. She wanted to fall and leave all her cares behind. She couldn't care less what happened to her, whether she'd lived or died.

She wanted to feel numb because numb was safe. Numb didn't force her to meet her demons, to make decisions. Numb allowed her to ignore the world. Instead, she cocooned herself with another one of the bottles of vodka she kept in her cupboard for emergencies.

Jocelyn poured herself a large measure and downed it in one, making her shudder as she always did when the fiery liquid flowed down her throat. So many thoughts flashed through her mind. She had spent her life trying to be accepted, to be loved. She started to resign herself that perhaps now she never would. That the one good person may never want to be with her again. How had she come to this? A person wallowing in self-pity and doubt.

She knew that for years after that night, the anger she felt towards her parents and the disappointment she had felt with Sam, had blighted all of her subsequent attempts at relationships.

She had avoided any kind of commitment from the beginning. She was always convinced that there was no future in it and it became a self-professing. In the later years, she had felt so alone, so isolated. And these feelings magnified themselves year on year. Until six months ago.

She knew Trina before that event and she didn't have to explain herself, or her deficiencies. She could give and receive the love that had been missing in her life. So why had she thrown all that was good away. And for what? A night she couldn't remember. A night of not knowing what she took part in?

She let out a mournful cry as she looked at the bruises on her wrists and the shame made her pour herself another drink. Over time, the two drinks became a dozen. And one bottle turned into two. Somehow, the hours all joined together, and the cycle of drinking and passing out became the norm.

Alcoholic fumes escaped through her pores and the stench of stale breath and unwashed clothes permeated the apartment.

Jocelyn knew she was using alcohol as a crutch to escape reality for a while, like binge eating, drugs or other extremes, and all the while, a phone rang persistently in the background.

ꕤ

Around lunchtime, Lucy had again walked to Joy's. The smell of alcohol greeted her as Lucy cautiously entered the apartment. She cast her eyes around and took in the state of the place. She noticed empty glasses and bottles strewn across the usually immaculate room. She hoped whatever was troubling Jocelyn would pass quickly. And the Joy she knew and had come to love, both as a friend and as a surrogate mother, would return.

Lucy shuddered, and her mind was cast back to the many days she came home from school. During her years growing up she was often greeted by this mess and smell. She hated it with a feeling so profound she almost walked away, and yet she couldn't.

She tentatively peeked into the bedroom, and the sight greeting her made her worry. Seeing the vomit just about made her discharge the contents of her own stomach. Taking huge gulps of air, she managed to keep it down.

She rushed over and was relieved to find Jocelyn's breathing was shallow but steady. Lucy knew she couldn't leave Joy lying on her back. Placing her hands carefully, to avoid the worse of the mess, she struggled to turn Jocelyn on her side into the recovery position. She placed her head towards the edge of the bed, hoping that she wouldn't pick that time to vomit again.

After washing her hands, she brought the washing up bowl from the kitchen and placed it on the floor by Jocelyn's head. Moving to the bedside cabinet, she took away the almost empty vodka bottle and tumbler to the kitchen area.

She took a last look into the room and said aloud, "Oh Joy, whatever happened to get you to this state."

And that's when she knew what she was going to do.

After the phone call, she opened every window in the apartment and allowed the breeze to blow away the fumes. As she waited, she cleaned and tidied up the living room as best she could. Just as she finished putting the last item away the doorbell buzzed.

As Lucy opened the door, she was given a quick hug.

"Sorry for phoning. I didn't know who else to call. She's in there. I've tidied up as best I could, and tried to let as much air in as possible, but I don't do vomit."

They both made their way into the bedroom as Lucy said, "I've got to go as I've a client to meet in half an hour. Are you okay by yourself?"

"Yes. Go. I'll give you a call later."

Another quick hug followed then Lucy walked away.

ꟿ

Trina took in the state of the room. She gingerly pulled the duvet cover off and put it into a black bin bag. This was quickly followed by one of the pillowcases. She rolled the sheet into the middle and then cajoled the semi-comatose Jocelyn to sit up.

"Trina? Is that you?" Jocelyn asked, her eyes half open and unfocused. "I love you."

"I know."

Trina managed to remove the sheet and remaining pillowcase with a modicum of difficulty, placing them with the others. Holding Jocelyn where she would inflict the least damage.

"I was coming home." Jocelyn murmured.

"Uh huh." Trina replied, as she took off her own shoes, trousers and top.

Jocelyn giggled, slurring, "I'm in no fit state."

"Uh huh." Trina again replied.

"I can't remember." Jocelyn mumbled

Trina pulled Jocelyn to her feet and they both stumbled into the wet room. Trina let the water wash over them. She held Jocelyn against the wall

"I was coming home." Jocelyn slurred.

"Uh huh." Trina replied, "Arms up."

Jocelyn lifted her arms and Trina pulled the top over her head, and threw it on the floor.

"I didn't want to sleep with her." Jocelyn slurred as she began to slip down the wall. "I wanted you. Only you."

Trina tried to pull Jocelyn's joggers down as she tried to steady Jocelyn, but she had gone past the point of no return.

As Jocelyn sat on the floor, Trina ordered left leg up, the proceeded to remove all remaining vestiges of clothing.

Jocelyn toppled over and curled herself into the foetal position. Her eyes closed.

"No you don't. Sit up."

Mumbling Jocelyn slowly sat up. Trina was glad that Jocelyn's hair was short. She shampooed Jocelyn hair and rubbed her back.

Jocelyn let out a mournful wail. There was nothing Trina could do to ease the pain, except hold Jocelyn and tell her that she loved her. They held each other while Jocelyn sobbed, cruel, silent sobs.

"Eyes." Jocelyn moaned, as she tried to push Trina away.

Thrusting a flannel over Jocelyn's eyes she continued to wash her hair and as much of her body as she could.

"I love you."

"Uh huh."

Trina sat down behind Jocelyn, pulled her into a tight embrace and let the water wash over them. She felt Jocelyn relax into her body and an involuntary sigh escaped.

After a while, she manoeuvred Jocelyn against the wall and turned off the water. She dried herself and made sure that Jocelyn was safe. Trina moved into the bedroom, redressed herself and remade the bed.

She walked back into the wet room and noticed that Jocelyn had slumped a little. She picked up the pile of wet clothes and dumped them into another bin bag. She took both bags to the rubbish shoot out in the corridor.

She walked back to Jocelyn as she stirred.

"I'm cold." Jocelyn shivered.

Trina managed to get Jocelyn to her feet on the third attempt. She successfully manoeuvred her into bed and got in the other side.

Trina pulled Jocelyn into a gentle embrace.

"I'm so sorry."

Gradually the constant shivering turned into an occasional tremor. In her heart, she wanted to take Jocelyn in her arms and hold her all night. To tell her it would be all right, to whisper gentle words and forceful assurances. But would it? Trina's head was telling her to keep her distance. Trina looked deeply into Jocelyn's eyes and couldn't speak.

Jocelyn felt sorry for herself, and kept on repeating, "I'm such a failure. A drunk and a failure."

Tears began to fall before Jocelyn could stop them and before she knew it she was full-on crying. Trina pulled Jocelyn's head onto her shoulder. Quietly she whispered positive words, things that Jocelyn needed to hear, telling her that she was not a failure. Slowly the tears subsided. Trina shook her head and knew that until someone was ready, words would be wasted. The time had to be right. And sometimes the message had to be spoken several times.

Trina had never thought of Jocelyn as fragile and flaky but she soon realised that old wounds sometimes never heal properly. And Jocelyn had some very deep old wounds.

"You are so good to me, Trina," Jocelyn managed to say in her stupor. "You take such good care of me."

"I will always take care of you," she whispered as Jocelyn fell into a dark abyss. Continuing to herself, she said quietly, "As long as you will let me. I love you, you daft bat."

As she lay there, holding onto the woman she loved but hated at the same time, she wondered whether there was any going back from this precipice. She knew there were hundreds of reasons for her to stay, but one main why she should go.

Joy had to make the decision all by herself.

She slowly extricated herself from Jocelyn's arms and gave her a last check over.

She picked up her phone and texted Lucy. 'Thanks for everything you have done and for getting rid of the remaining alcohol. I have to pick the children up from Lorna and Sal's. Could you check on her tomorrow?'

She left the bedroom and apartment, and walked out of Jocelyn's life, back to an unknown future.

ꟿ

Chapter Forty One

Wednesday

Jocelyn woke with a start; her heart was racing. She tried to open her eyes but the lids felt as though they were glued shut. She managed to peel them open a slit and peered through the darkness.

Her mood sank when she realised that she wasn't in the garden of her dreams, with the woman she loved, but was instead in her own bedroom. She tried to recall the dream before it vanished entirely. But all she could hear was laughter.

Jocelyn took a deep breath. She cautiously turned her head to the other pillow; it felt as though her brain was rattling around in her skull. She could have sworn that someone had been cuddling her.

The darkness enveloped her and she slunk back into a troubled sleep. When she woke up again she allowed the grief back in. She felt tears spring into her eyes. Her heart physically ached for Trina, with a pain so deep; it felt like the weight of the world was compressed against it.

She tried to swallow but her throat felt sore as though she had been eating a rasp. Her mouth felt full of cotton wool. Daylight streamed through the open window and the curtains rustled in the wind, whispering to her, mocking her.

Jocelyn reached over, looked at her phone, and tried to focus on the screen. The time showed eleven o'clock. The light affronted her senses so she closed her eyes and sank back into the pillows.

A while later she again picked up her phone. Holding the phone closer than normal, she saw that she had two missed calls and a text message all from Lucy. The text told her she was coming to see her at noon. She tried to sit up but her head felt as though it would split in two and her stomach felt nauseous. All she wanted to do was fall back into an untroubled sleep.

She texted back, with fingers that wouldn't work, 'I'll call you later.'

Her phone pinged. 'I'm on my way. Get your backside out of bed and have a coffee ready. I don't care if you have the hangover from hell. I will be there at twelve xx L'

She angrily spoke to the phone, "Damn you all. I want to be left alone?"

She made her eyes focus on the clock and she realised she only had fifteen minutes to get up and ready. She wondered how Lucy knew that she was still in bed, and that she had the hangover from hell.

Gingerly, she swung her legs out of the bed then realised she was naked. She couldn't remember being undressed. She almost stepped into the bowl on the floor by the bed.

Jocelyn studied her room. She clocked that the window was open. She never slept with the window open. There was no evidence of her clothes.

She usually left them on the chair by the window.

She looked at the duvet cover. She shook her head slightly, making the hammers begin their pounding. She wondered how a new cover had been put on her bed.

She wobbled to the wet room and stepped under the shower and a vague memory lightly brushed her thoughts. She sensed that items had been moved and someone else had been with her.

She stood under the water for about five minutes and began to feel better. She turned off the tap and took two towels from the shelf. Wrapped herself in the large towel and made a turban from a smaller one.

Her teeth and tongue felt furry, as if a small animal had crawled into her mouth. She brushed her teeth and tried to scrub her tongue, but a tickling, tingling sensation caused her to quiver. She reached for the mouthwash instead.

Jocelyn looked in the mirror and her reflection taunted her. Her eyes were bloodshot and dark circles surrounded them. Lines had appeared around her mouth and her cheeks had lost their colour. If she was asked to describe how she looked, gaunt was the word that sprung to mind.

Jocelyn wondered how she had come to this, but of course, she knew. She had tried unsuccessfully to put her humiliation behind her and extinguish what had happened by pouring vodka down her throat. All she succeeded in doing was this massive headache.

She walked into the kitchen and switched on the kettle just as she heard the door opening.

"Look at the state of you!" Lucy said, as she entered the apartment.

Jocelyn thought, 'And this is post-shower. I'm glad she hadn't seen me half an hour ago.'

"Well? How are you feeling?"

"Like I've the seven gnomes in my head, mining away."

"Serves you right. You were in such a state."

"Tell me about it. Thanks for taking care of me."

"Why are you thanking me? It wasn't me."

Jocelyn looked at her quizzically.

"I came to find you as you didn't turn up for work and you weren't answering your phone. You had drunk yourself stupid and I didn't know what to do. There you were passed out lying in your own puke.

Jocelyn gasped, "Sorry."

"Not me you should be apologising to."

"Then who?"

"Who do you think came around and looked after you? Cleaned you up, stayed with you until late, and made sure you didn't choke on your own vomit. I'll tell you now it wasn't me. I've seen it all before with my own mother. I couldn't go through all that again."

"So who did?"

"There is only one person I know who would."

"Trina?"

"Of course, Trina"

"How did she know?"

"I called her. Because believe it or not, she loves you. After that episode I don't know why."

"Was I in that bad a state?"

"Yes."

"And she dropped everything and came here."

"Yes."

"Why would she do that?"

"Because she loves you." She shook her head, "Being in love is never easy. It's fragile but it is worth fighting for. Trina loves you. You can smell it, and taste it in the air, you feel it in the way she touches you, see it in how she looks at you, and hear it in how she speaks about you. Are you just going to give up?"

Jocelyn closed her eyes, took a deep breath and gave a slight shake of her head.

"What about the kids? They didn't see me yesterday."

"No. Lorna and Sal looked after them. So you really have a lot of apologising to do." She paused. "Do you want to talk about it?"

"I don't do the damsel in distress thing very well. I figure I got myself into this mess, I should get myself out of it."

"I've been really worried about you. That's why I'm asking. If you'd rather not discuss it, that's fine by me."

"Both my real Dad and therapist say I should talk more about my feelings, and I trust you that this conversation won't go further than these four walls."

"I hope you know you can trust me. But hold on a minute, real Dad?"

"Yes. Remember that note Trina gave you to give to me?"

"Uh huh."

"That was from my real Dad, Richard. He was at my presentation. I've spoken with him a few times since."

"Wow. What's he like?"

"He seems a nice, genuine guy. Let me take some paracetamol. My head is pounding."

Jocelyn walked over to the sink and downed a couple of pills. She sat down next to Lucy.

"I've been so stupid, so wrapped up in myself." She paused.

Lucy frowned, her dark eyes troubled. Her friend and boss rarely mentioned personal stuff. She knocked off anything that came close, with the wave of a hand. She knew she had been seeing a therapist and her ex-girlfriend had somehow had something to do with her split with Trina.

Lucy wanted to help her but wasn't sure how, and so she waited.

"How's everything going at the office? I'm sorry to have landed you, Charlie and Sean with everything."

Lucy realised that she would have to be honest. "We've held the fort. People think you have had a bout of the flu. But we're not you."

"What day is it?"

"It's Wednesday."

"Wednesday?"

Lucy looked deeply into Jocelyn's eyes, and said, "You need to get you act together and get back in there. That's if you don't want everything to go tits up."

"That's not the way to speak to your boss." Jocelyn said with a hint of a smile.

"Well someone has to. You are moping around full of remorse and self-pity. Getting so pissed that you passed out. For goodness sake, you should have seen the number of empty vodka bottles I threw away. And I'll tell you now, you won't find anymore lying around so don't go looking." She took a deep breath and continued "But it is not you I feel sorrow for. You have brought this all on yourself."

Jocelyn owned up, "I think I slept with Sam."

"What do you mean; you think you slept with Sam? Either you did or you didn't."

"That's the thing, I was getting up to leave and the next thing I remember is waking up in her bed. I can't remember how I got there. I think I must have ingested some sort of drug."

"So you're saying that Sam gave you something."

"I don't know what I'm saying. All I remember is getting ready to leave and finishing off my drink. When I woke up, she told me to go. Just as I hurriedly put on my clothes, her girlfriend came into the bedroom. Her girlfriend is my old school friend you thought was hot."

"I remember her."

"She chucked me out and then I heard the two of them laughing. It felt it was at my expense."

"You allowed someone to take advantage of you, to use you, and then throw you away as though you were a piece of rubbish."

Humiliated, Jocelyn nodded.

"Have you told the police that you think you were drugged?"

"No and I'm not going to."

"But."

"No buts. I am not going to report it. There will be no evidence."

"They might do it to someone else."

"I think they were both getting their own back. I don't think they will do it to anyone else."

"So instead of reporting, it you drank yourself stupid."

"That about sums it up."

"Are you alright now?"

"I think so."

"Are you coming back to work anytime soon? We have everything covered up until tomorrow evening. After that, we could struggle. We need you. The company needs you."

"I'll work from home tomorrow. Could you email me any I should know and do?"

"Will do." Lucy studied Jocelyn. "Just promise me you are not going to go on another bender."

Jocelyn knew Lucy had a point about work. She needed to concentrate on her fledgling business. There was only so long she could get away with being absent. Charlie, Sean and Lucy seemed to be doing a sterling job, holding the fort admirably, but she was being unfair.

"I promise. I'm sorry Luce."

"Both you know and I know it is Trina that needs to hear your grovelling apology. Perhaps then, we can get back to our normal selves without having to pussyfoot around you."

"Is that what you've been doing?"

Lucy gave her a look that implied she couldn't believe what Jocelyn had just asked. Instead, she replied, "I cannot for the life of me understand why you broke up with Trina. Meeting Sam outside of work was a mistake and it could be the biggest mistake of your life. However, what she did to you was unthinkable. I still cannot understand why you are going to let her off?"

Jocelyn shrugged.

"But your mistake and her actions should not define who you are. It didn't in the past and it shouldn't in the future. You have already proven that you can make a success of whatever you want to do. We can and we will hold the fort for you, whilst you sort yourself out, but we need your leadership. For goodness sake go and make it up with Trina."

"I can't."

"I know you don't want to hear this but stop acting as if you are the only victim in all this mess. You're the one who actively sought out your ex. You're the one who went on a bender. And yet Trina was the one who came to you aid."

Lucy could see Jocelyn becoming annoyed so she got up and moved towards the door. As she opened it, she turned and said, "For someone so intelligent you are sometimes so stupid."

"How dare you talk to me like that? Piss off"

"Deep down I know you will do the correct thing. She loves you."

And with that, she walked out the door.

ഊ

Chapter Forty Two

Thursday

Jocelyn had been so badly hurt before, and it had taken her a while to let her walls down to let in Trina. So why did she have to spoil it all.

She thought through the sequence of events that had led her to this place. Was there anything she should have done differently? Plenty. But would she? Maybe. Cause and effect. She might not be able to change the cause but she could change the effect.

Jocelyn had felt betrayal all around her as she was growing up, and felt her life was being dragged down to that level again. This time her Nan wasn't there to give her some sage advice.

Yet one of her favourite sayings came to mind 'Lack of purpose becomes an enemy for peace of mind.' She questioned herself. Was she lacking in purpose? Perhaps at this precise moment she was. Could she change that? Easily, by getting stuck back into her business.

The amount she had drunk had frightened her. She did not intend to go through that again. She wanted to put the days of self-doubt, humiliation and abuse behind her. And she knew she had to build bridges and fast, before everything she had worked for had gone, and everyone she had feelings for had left.

She picked up the phone.

"I bet you're wondering why I called you?"

"To check to see whether I have pissed off?"

"To apologise. Lucy I am so sorry. Hearing the truth is hard sometimes. I'm not good at it. But I'm learning. I was hurt and upset about what you said."

"I only told you the truth."

"I know. It seems to me that I'm going to have to apologise a lot to many people."

"Humph. You won't catch me disagreeing."

"Thanks for the emails."

"No problem."

"Anything I need to do."

"You received tomorrow's meeting notes?"

"I'm about to read them now." She paused before asking, "Will you and Rose like to come around for a meal tonight? Nothing fancy, just a lasagne and salad. Please say yes."

"Rose is out of town for a couple of days, so yes I will. I want to hear your grovelling apology."

Lucy could hear a small laugh from Jocelyn as she put the phone down."

ꕥ

Lucy slid onto her chair with a small sigh, meeting Jocelyn's eyes only for a moment. The easy amicability had returned and although Lucy thought Jocelyn had been disloyal, and that she should be doing everything in her power to get back together with Trina. To grovel if need be. She decided to hold her own counsel until the right moment. She didn't seem to realise that Jocelyn felt even worse.

"I do love Trina. You know that." Jocelyn said, as she was dishing out the lasagne. But she wasn't sure if she was convincing Lucy or herself. Jocelyn looked at Lucy's eyes where she saw genuine concern.

Lucy was unsure about what she should say, so blurted out, "You hurt her pride. I was going to keep my own counsel but I can't help myself."

"Go ahead. You obviously want to continue letting me know what you think. I can't believe it will be any worse than what I'm thinking and feeling."

"Okay. I will tell you exactly what I think. You allowed the situation to develop. Jocelyn, as I said yesterday, sometimes for all your intelligence, you are so stupid."

"You're right. I have been stupid but I'd rather think of it as naive. I have to try to regain some of her trust."

"Why should she trust her heart to you if you've already got one foot out the door?"

Jocelyn finally sunk in that Trina might not allow her back. "That door has truly been slammed shut. I agree I have made mistakes. I was caught up in a dream that became a nightmare. I have to make sure Trina doesn't slam hers."

Unable to hold back Lucy said, "If you love Trina as you say you do then I think you have one of two choices. You either decide that you're not up for the challenge of getting Trina back, or you decide you are."

"If it comes to Trina then I'm definitely up for the challenge."

"Well, most of us think of love as something we like fall into, like it's this easy, amazing thing. And it is, most of the time."

"To me love is fraught with obstacles." The second it was out of her mouth, she looked over to Lucy.

"Finally, you're opening up."

"Yeah, as I said yesterday, I've been told not to bottle things up. To be as honest as possible, without deliberately hurting anyone."

Lucy weighed up her words, "Sometimes love is fraught with difficulties. But it's also about making the decision to love that person no matter what is thrown at you and no matter how scary it gets. No matter what happens. Good or bad."

Jocelyn nodded.

"Do you agree that true love doesn't put on a show?"

"Yes."

"Do you agree with these statements? Love is patient. Love is kind. Love is loyal. Love is forever. Love is friendship. Love is dependable. Love is soul searching."

"On the whole yes."

"So do some soul searching and answer these questions. Trina is patient. Jocelyn is patient."

"Hey that's not fair. Don't include me."

"Who said it was going to be fair."

"Okay. Definitely Trina."

"Trina is kind. Jocelyn is kind."

Jocelyn smiled. "Trina is the kindest person I know."

"Trina is loyal. Jocelyn is loyal."

"Okay I get the picture."

"I could go on using all the statements."

Jocelyn gave a small smile.

"If you are going to make the commitment to Trina, you'll have to stick it out. She has two children that are also in the equation."

"When did you become so knowledgeable?"

Lucy smiled, and said, "I think you owe Trina more than you'll ever realise. She put you over her children on Tuesday. She didn't have to. That is how much you mean to her. Now it's up to you."

"I'll do anything to regain her trust."

"You can send the flowers, make the phone calls, plan the romantic dates, but it has to be what the other person needs. Not what you think they need or want. Don't have some image of who you think you want her to be."

"I do get it."

"I know. Tell me what you love about Trina."

"I love that at times those amazing green eyes are filled with questions and a thirst for knowledge, and at other times seem in possession of all the secrets of the world. I love how she loves unconditionally. She is fiercely loyal. She is strong, dependable, and trustworthy. There are too many adjectives to describe her."

"So why did you throw it away?"

Sadness engulfed Jocelyn, "I have no idea. She gives me a love that makes me want to be the best me I can be. A love that allows me to be me. A love that isn't false. A love that will allow us both a safe place to fall." Jocelyn sighed, "And boy, have I fallen."

Lucy nodded.

"I want a love that's strong, that's based on really knowing her and loving her for who she is."

Unable to hold back the tears any longer, Jocelyn cracked. Hiccupping sobs wracked her body and she covered her face with her hands, horrified that Lucy was seeing her fall to pieces.

Rising from her chair, Lucy circled the table and hugged Jocelyn from behind.

"I'm okay."

She gave Jocelyn's heart a little push. "I know you are. Now go listening to your heart and let it tell you what's right for you."

ꕤ

Chapter Forty Three

Saturday

After Simon and Peter were ensconced, playing football manager on the play station and Cathy was settled with her paper and crayons, the adults went and sat in the kitchen.

Sal poured them all another glass of wine. She handed Trina her glass and asked, "How's it going? I know you're putting on a brave face for the kids."

Trina took a sip of her wine. The other two women studied her intently. Trina closed her eyes and took a deep breath.

"If I tell you, I might start crying. Will that make you uncomfortable?"

Both Lorna and Sal shook their heads, Sal replied, "A good cry can ease the pain even though it never fully goes away."

The simple kind words made tears well in Trina's eyes. Angry with herself for losing control, she resisted with every ounce of energy she had. She started her silent mantra. 'I'm not going to cry. I'm not going to cry.' She lost the battle and a few drops trickled down her cheeks. She immediately cursed herself for being a wimp.

"I'm sorry." Trina spoke quietly, almost a whisper as though she thought that saying it quietly would lessen the pain. She used her knuckle to brush away the rogue tears that escaped.

"I'm so angry with her. Yes, I know she wouldn't have gone if I asked her to stay, but at that moment in time, her heart wasn't completely in it. I knew she felt as though she had unfinished business, both with her Dad and with Sam." Trina let out a shiver. "But she didn't really fight to stay."

Another couple of tears escaped and she deftly brushed them aside.

"I miss her so much. The children miss her. I never believed I would miss her this much."

Handing Trina a tissue, Lorna said, "That's because you truly love her."

"I want her back in my life. In our lives."

The women nodded but stayed silent. Both realising Trina needed to verbalise her thought.

"If we got back together, would she always be loyal to me? Or, would it give her permission to have another affair one, two, three years from now?"

Sal put a hand on her arm, "We can never predict the future, but you must make her realise the pain and hurt you have been through."

"I know if she does ask to come back to us and I take a chance on her and let her back into our lives I will tell her. On the other hand, if I don't take a chance on her I can't imagine my life without her. I have to be able to trust her. I don't like this feeling. It unsettles me and makes me feel insecure." She stopped, and then asked, "Does she even want to be with me anymore?"

Another bout of sobs coursed through her body.

"So tell me what you love about her?" Lorna asked.

Trina lifted her eyes and a slight smile played at the corners of her mouth.

"That familiar smile that would always make me melts into her arms, no matter how hard I tried to be mad at her. All she had to do was flash me that smile and I was hers, I think I've always been hers."

Lorna looked over at Sal and their own look of love passed between them. "So you love her smile. What else?"

Trina continued, "I love the way she puts people at their ease. She has a wonderful way with Peter and Cathy. They love her to bits."

Lorna replied, "I got that impression from Peter. He talks about you and her all the time."

"Does he? I didn't know that."

"You're his mum. He isn't going to tell you everything."

"Did he say anything that you can tell me, without breaking any confidences?"

"Only that he hopes that Jocelyn will come back soon. He gets upset seeing you so upset"

"He is a very sensitive child."

"A child who loves you a lot."

Trina took a deep breath, "I know. I missed her desperately when I told her to leave. I felt so consumed with jealousy. It felt as though I was being torn apart. I needed to do what was right for my kids. I knew if she stayed, we would start to resent each other for different reasons."

"Are you going to give her a time limit, an ultimatum?"

"I honestly don't know, but I'm struggling at the moment."

"You have to give her an ultimatum."

Lorna gave Sal a nudge under the table, urging her to back off.

"But I told her to take her time. To make up her mind and to come back if, and when, she is ready."

"If she walked in now would you take her back?"

"Yes. No. I don't know. You know I was asked to go to her apartment by her friend and work colleague on Tuesday. Thanks for looking after the children by the way. She was completely wasted. Goodness knows how much she had to drink. In her drunken stupor, she told me nothing happened. She mentioned drugs but Joy has never done drugs, not that I know of anyway. She also said she couldn't remember. So I'm still no clearer. I hate her for doing this to me."

"Do you think she will come back?"

Tears began to flow.

"Let the tears come." Sal passed her the box of tissues.

The sobs followed as Trina dropped her head onto her arms. Sal gently rubbed her back and waited. Gradually the tears subsided.

"I'm so sorry."

"Nothing to apologise for. We're glad that you feel comfortable enough in our company."

"Thank you." Trina looked at each woman. "To answer your question. I have no idea if she wants to come back."

"Didn't you ask her on Tuesday?"

"No. She was in no fit state to have any kind of conversation."

"The first thing you have to do is calm down and look at the bigger picture here. If you want her back, you are going to have to give her the benefit of the doubt. If she says nothing untoward happened and you love her, then you have to trust her."

Trina knew that if they were to have any chance of a happy relationship, then she needed to trust Jocelyn, but it was going to be so hard.

She forced a smile on her face for their sake.

Sal wrapped her arms around Trina, who said, "I know," letting her head fall wearily against her shoulder.

Cathy burst into the kitchen. "Mummy. Look what I drawed."

Trina took the piece of paper from her daughters' hand.

"That's lovely. You've done that so well."

"Mummy? Are you sad?" Cathy asked as she looked at Trina's troubled face.

"Yes baby. Mummy is sad."

"Mummy I miss Joy. Is she coming home soon?"

"I hope so, baby. I hope so."

ƐO

Chapter Forty Four

Monday

Jocelyn's phone pinged and a message from Richard appeared on the screen.

"Hi Joy. I'm free to talk now if you are available."

Jocelyn saved the work she was doing and contacted her father.

Richard looked at the gaunt face peering back at him and asked, "Are you all right Joy? You're looking a little peaky."

"There's a few things on my mind that I'm mulling over."

"Anything I can help you with?"

"I went to see Dad in hospital last Friday."

"And?"

"It has left me angry, frustrated and confused."

"I can understand why, after the history between you."

"Duncan thinks I should forgive him."

"And you? What do you think?"

"That the problem. I don't know what to think."

"When someone hurt us, it's normal to hold onto feelings of anger and resentment and to want revenge. Small transgressions may be forgiven easily, but some wounds need time to heal. Anger, bitterness and hate weigh heavily. When these emotions have no release, they can cause anxiety. But remember we can't hold on to anger and frustration, or it eats away at us. The longer we hold on, the deeper poison goes."

Jocelyn nodded her head, "It is still eating me up inside, and the poison is touching my heart."

"So free your body and your mind. Jocelyn, you need to heal. And the process itself is vital. If you can't bury the hatchet then you may not be able to heal. If forgiveness is to be part of your healing process, then you might have to take the first step."

"He has already made the first step. He said he was sorry and later asked for forgiveness."

"Forgiveness has to be earned."

"I know." She sighed.

"And when it has been earned you have to have faith as to its depth and durability."

Jocelyn didn't respond so Richard asked, "Do you want to forgive him?"

Jocelyn looked away embarrassed as she said, "I honestly don't know. What he tried to do to me has shaped my life. Believe it or not it is like a security blanket. I can hide behind his actions, and blame him if things don't go to plan."

Richard gave a small frown, as though he was deeply thinking about her words. Jocelyn noticed this was a common trait of his which she found endearing.

Finally he spoke, "Forgiveness isn't something you do for the person who wronged you; it's something you do for you. Forgiveness often gives the forgiver their power back. It puts them in control of the boundaries and expectations they have for the relationship going forward." He gave a small smile, "Or, perhaps, in control of the shield they have placed around themselves."

"So if forgiveness is something you do for yourself and if it can help you heal, why is it so hard?"

"Forgiveness requires that you are willing to forgive. Do not attempt to forgive before you have released your anger and pain. It will also put the final seal on what happened that hurt you. So the question is: - Have you worked through your feelings? Are you ready to forgive him?"

"I need to think over everything you've said. Thank you Pops."

"You are welcome. Remember you deserve to be happy."

Jocelyn let out a sob, "Oh Pops. I have been so stupid."

"What is it, love?"

"The last few weeks are like a bad memory I'd rather forget. I went to see Sam to talk and have closure. I was leaving but somehow I woke up the next morning in her bed." She shook her head. "I have no recollection of how that happened. Going to see Sam has been the worst decision I have made. And now I think I've ruined everything."

Richard kept his counsel and waited for Jocelyn to continue.

"I've let myself down badly and could have ruined everything I have worked hard to achieve."

"Want to talk about it."

Jocelyn closed her eyes and relived moments from the recent few days.

"I think I have lost Trina." Jocelyn sighed,

"If you really love her and you think the two of you have something worth fighting for, you should try again."

"I know she told me to go and find out my feelings for Sam or whether we, that's Trina and me, were meant to be. I've done some stupid things recently. Things I'm not proud of."

Jocelyn was getting used to Richards ways, as he again held his counsel.

"I drank so much I passed out. Lucy called Trina and she came and looked after me. Not that I have any memory of it happening."

Richard took a deep breath. "It sounds as though Trina still has feelings for you. And if you're lucky, she will realize why you did those things, and you will work through them. Together."

"She must hate me," Jocelyn said, a lump forming in her throat as she tried to talk. "I have really hurt her. All I know is that I didn't want this. I want to still be Trina, but it was only now that it was starting to hit me that she could be gone for good. I may have to face up to the fact she might not allow me back, no matter how much I wish she did, or how many rom-coms I watch."

Tears glistened in Jocelyn's eyes as Richard said, "Maybe this is how it is meant to be. For you to have this time to sort out your feelings."

Jocelyn rubbed her knuckle across her eyes, "I know that she doubted my commitment to her because of what she knew of other people. She did what she thought I'd want, or what she thought would be best for me, and I can hardly blame her for doing what she felt was right. I get that now. She did it because I think she loves me."

"Perhaps all that stuff had to happen for you to get over Sam," her father said in a calming, stoic voice. It didn't fail to help her put her relationships in perspective. "The right partner will help you blossom. The wrong one will watch you wilt. Who do you think will be the correct partner for you?"

"Without a doubt Trina is the right person for me. Do you think I stand a chance to get back in her good books?"

"Maybe," her father said, "maybe not. You know what goes a long way in patching things up?"

"What?" Jocelyn asked.

"A heartfelt, groveling apology," her father said. "Just don't rely on flowers or some other gift as a stand-in for a sincere confession. Asking for absolution is way different and way deeper than saying "I'm sorry". When you ask for forgiveness, not only do you acknowledge that you've caused hurt, but you also work to understand the pain it caused your partner. Recognise how it may have affected and have a grasp of what that experience was like for them. You will have to ask for her forgiveness, just like your father has asked for yours."

Something broke inside of her and she found herself choking back tears. By sheer force of will, she swallowed them down and got herself together.

"Jocelyn, it is okay to cry. It is best to let your emotions out. And if I could, I would wrap my arms around you. Go and try to patch things up with Trina and come up with guidelines and understandings that create a safety net around the two of you. So you both can talk through your emotions without doing harm. Listen to the words you will hear, the impressions you will feel, and act on what you know will be correct."

"Pops. Thank you for listening and being here for me." The words caught in her throat.

"I'll be here anytime you need me. I love you. I always have."

"Thanks Pops."

ည

When she went home that evening, she flopped down on the sofa and exhaled heavily. She thought about what her real Dad had said to her, about giving herself permission to be happy.

Jocelyn knew that Trina was the love of her life. Deep down Jocelyn knew that as soon as she walked out of her door. Was it only twenty days ago? So why hadn't she phoned or tried to get back in touch. Was it because Trina told her that she would know when? Or was she afraid of rejection? She smiled and acknowledged it was a fear of rejection.

Jocelyn took out her phone and looked at her screensaver. Trina's smiling face greeted her.

"Trina. I'm so sorry."

Jocelyn had so many things she wanted to talk about and had so much to say to her.

She realised that Trina added something to her life, something she had missed without recognition. She felt the dull aching in her heart, the loneliness that had been beating against her. All of it meant more than she would ever be able to tell her. Knowing that Trina was such a good friend, and lover, and was always there to support her, was what kept her going.

She knew that she had been blinded by infatuation, and had made mistakes. Grave mistakes. Jocelyn wished she could turn back to three weeks ago.

She knew what she had to do.

ည

Chapter Forty Five

Tuesday

As Jocelyn got out of the car, she noticed woman walking towards her. Lorna realised that it was Jocelyn getting out of the car at the same time and stood in front of her, arms folded. She scrutinised Jocelyn and said, "I take it you are about to see Trina."

"I am."

Lorna didn't say anything for a few seconds, continued to appraise Jocelyn. "Trina seems like she turned a corner last week, so I hope you don't plan on ruining her life again."

Jocelyn blanched. "It was never my intention to ruin her life. I love her."

"Humph. You have a very strange way of showing love. Are you trying to get back into her good books, wheedle your way back into hers and the children's lives?"

"I love Trina but getting back together...." She sighed, a deep and mournful sigh. "That depends on her, and how she feels about me. The new me, the real me, the old me. Our relationship is out of my control. I am totally at her mercy."

"Humph."

There was no denying the thick, uncomfortable air between them.

Eventually Jocelyn said, "If even a fragment of what Lucy had said held a grain of truth then I know that I owe Trina my sanity, my life."

"You won't find me disagreeing with you. But mark my words if you hurt her again you will have me to deal with. And I do not have the same forgiving nature as Trina. I don't want to pick up the pieces again."

"There's something about us when we're together. It's as if we're soulmates. We have Chemistry between us, beyond anything I've felt for anyone else."

"But you still walked away."

"I know. And that decision will forever follow me."

ꟹ

Trina was woken from her afternoon nap by a knock on the door. She opened her door to Jocelyn. Immediately tears crowded behind her eyes but she blinked them away. She would not let Jocelyn see how upset she was. She needed to keep the foundations of the wall that she had built around her solid. She checked and made sure that the mask she had been wearing was firmly in place. Jocelyn's emotional reaction to Sam had been too intense to dismiss. She had been drawn back to the distance days, and it still seemed to matter.

Jocelyn hoped against hope that Trina hadn't built a solid brick wall around herself, going into self-protection mode. She needed to be able to penetrate any veneer and appeal to her better judgement. She needed to regain that trust.

Jocelyn noticed that Trina normally immaculate make-up was smudged. Trina was wearing an old and comfortable top and a baggy pair of joggers. Jocelyn felt her breath hitch and so did her heart, and wondered how Trina would react, bracing for the rebuff.

Trina didn't make an effort to hug her, shake her hand or kiss her. Jocelyn was relieved not to reveal that her palms were exploding with moisture and a river had formed between her shoulder blades. Trina instead, gave one of her shrugs and waited.

The look on Trina's face almost made Jocelyn heartbreak. She thought that Trina was either going to break down in tears, or she was going to close the door in her face. She knew Trina had every right to hate her, Jocelyn started to panic at the swamp of emotion she was experiencing.

Only days earlier she had been forced to confront her past and had found herself and everything wanting. Her body was wracked with guilt. What was happening to them? There was only a threshold between them but today it felt like so much more.

Jocelyn gazed into Trina's eyes, trying to read them, trying to find what she was keeping close to her chest. Trina glanced back at Jocelyn and the look they shared was raw and honest. But Trina didn't want raw. She wanted to go back to wearing the mask. The mask most of us wear some of the time. The mask that says I'm good, I'm fine, I don't need you, I can cope on my own. When in fact there is this little voice pleading for understanding, and want, and need. The mask that Trina had held so secure in place had started to slip and she was finding it difficult replace it again. In that moment, Jocelyn saw the pain that was hidden behind her eyes.

Trina took a deep breath and folded her arms across her chest, forming a barrier between them.

"Is it over?" The question Trina asked didn't sound as hopeless as she felt. "Have you found what you are looking for?"

Jocelyn bowed her head and nodded. "I'm sorry."

Trina knew that feeling. She knew that move. It is the move a person does when they want to cut off the other person's emotions. They cut them off because the emotions trigger their own emotions and Trina didn't want to feel those emotions right now. She wanted to be behind closed doors when she went into meltdown.

Trina nodded back, "Thank you for coming to tell me in person." Trina began to close the door.

Jocelyn held out her hand and kept it open, looking Trina in the eyes, "No Trina. It's not that sort of sorry. I'm truly sorry for the hurt I've caused you and the kids. Please let me in. We need to talk."

"I don't know." she stumbled, knowing how dangerous this could be to her heart. It had been chipped, cracked, and broken before, and she wasn't at all sure she could endure that again.

"I am sorry Trina."

Trina continued to stand there with her arms folded. Finally she said, "The last few weeks have been horrendous –you broke my heart."

Jocelyn held her head in shame.

"I was walking away. I couldn't do it. I couldn't stay the night. I realised I loved you too much. I don't know what happened."

"What do you want from me? Forgiveness?"

"I expect you will never truly forgive me, but you must believe me when I say I love you."

Trina continued to fold her arms, but her stance implied that Jocelyn should continue.

"Lucy told me you dropped everything and looked after me when I... when I..."

"You can say it. When you drank so much you could have died. I stayed with you until it felt safe to leave, you know."

"I know, Lucy told me." Jocelyn hung her head in shame.

"I was ashamed of what happened with Sam."

"I don't want to know what happened. But I can imagine."

"I want to be candid; to this day I still have no recollection. It's you that I want. Now and forever. I could ask for absolution, but I know that would be wrong. Instead, I ask for clemency. I know I found out the hard way what I wanted, what I needed, but I found out."

Jocelyn saw that Lorna was still standing close by. "I'm sorry. Please let me in. So we can talk freely."

Trina noticed Lorna and gave a slight nod. Her next reaction was not with words. Her eyes widened, her lips pressed together and she took in a deep breath. She slowly let it out and nodded; she stepped aside and let her in.

ꕥ

Chapter Forty Six

Tuesday

Jocelyn too let out the breath that she had subconsciously been holding. The beating of Jocelyn's heart slowed and her chest loosened. She felt like a weight had been lifted off her shoulders. Trina touched Jocelyn's elbow and gently guided her into the front room. Jocelyn watched Trina's face carefully. The room started to close in around her as Jocelyn again held her breath and waited for an onslaught. But none was forth coming. The room was quiet apart from the steady ticking of the clock on the wall.

Breaking the silence, she whispered, "Is there hope for us?"

"It's not going to be easy." Trina's voice cracked.

Trina hated how she felt. She hated the weakness that she was feeling.

She let out a choking sound that sounded like a sob but it was ten times worse. Like an electric current going from her feet to her head, forcing out all the pain in one sound.

Jocelyn recognised the hurt in Trina's eyes. She was ashamed and full of remorse. She wanted to say sorry, but knew that the words by themselves would be inadequate. Tears knifed into the backs of her eyes, and she sniffed and tried to hold back the emotions they brought with them. Jocelyn diverted her eyes from Trina's hurt.

Coming out as barely a whisper, she continued, "Nothing is ever easy, especially if it is something worthwhile."

"So are we worthwhile?" asked Trina.

"I think so. No. I know so. We have too much love and history to throw it away. I'm so sorry to put you through all this hurt and sorrow."

Trina heard the words, felt the emotion and felt a tear escape. Jocelyn lifted a hand to stroke her cheek, to dry the stray tear with the back of her hand. She then brushed Trina's bottom lip with her thumb as gently as possible. Trina took a step back and folded her arms across her chest, still trying hard to maintain the mask she had been wearing.

Jocelyn pleaded, "Will you ever forgive me? I was completely in the wrong." She smiled, but it didn't reach her eyes. Her voice started to quiver, evident that she too, was holding back the tears. The words rushed out before she could assemble them correctly, she continued to stumble through her apology, throwing herself to Trina's mercy.

"None of it had anything to do with you. You didn't create my situation, or even aggravate it. Instead, you were an incredible partner—always supportive." Jocelyn finally lost her composure, the tears streaming down her face. She didn't turn away or break eye contact though. "You have always been there when I needed you, loving me. Can you forgive me?" Jocelyn rasped.

Trina needed some space, so she stood, walked a few steps toward the kitchen, changed her mind, then turned and said, "I feel so vulnerable. If I let you back, and I'm not saying I will, I'm going to be letting you inside here again." Trina patted her heart, her mind spun through the possibilities of what she would say next. Her eyes darted back and forth and she cleared her throat, looking for the best place to start. Her mouth opened, but nothing came out, so she closed it.

Jocelyn gave a small smile. Trina gave a slight shake of her head and thought, 'There she goes with that familiar smile. She's trying to make me melt into her arms. But I'm not to give her the satisfaction, no matter how hard she tries, but did she really think that it would work here?' In the back of Trina's mind, the fear of betrayal could happen again, and that gave her a hard edge that had been missing in the past.

"I am so sorry. I was weak, but as you said, I had to face my ghosts. I have faced my past and do not like what I saw."

Trina continued quietly, "I knew that you had to lay the last ghost to rest, to have the chance to live our lives together."

Jocelyn could not look into Trina's eyes whilst she spoke those words. Relief flowed through her, as well as anxiety, as she didn't know how Trina would react. Would she still want her? Could they go back to before? Would Trina ever trust her again?

Following a deep breath, Jocelyn said, "I must explain about Sam."

"And I told you I don't want to know."

"I was coming home. One minute I picked up my things to leave the next I woke up the next morning in her bed. Jocelyn shook her head, as if she was trying to remove a fog."

"So you were drunk?

"I did have a drink but I wasn't drunk. I think I may have been drugged."

"That's a little far-fetched."

"But I cannot think of any other explanation. Can you?"

Trina gave a shrug.

Jocelyn continued, "Sam was and will always be my first infatuation. That will never change. You said that your first love is your forever love. I didn't believe it then, but I believe it now. You are my first true love.

Trina smiled a small smile. Jocelyn squeezed her eyes shut, too embarrassed to smile back. She was finding it difficult to both look at Trina and to keep her composure. She tried to speak but shook her head.

"Please look at me, Joy."

Jocelyn shook her head. Trina lifted it gently so that she was forced to look into her eyes. All Jocelyn could see in that moment was a look so filled with love that it broke her heart. How could she ever doubt that this was the woman for her? A woman that was so loving and caring. A woman who always put others first before her own well-being.

Gently, Trina spoke, "All that matters is that you a here, now."

"But I betrayed you, betrayed our love."

Trina gave a slight nod then said, "But you had to go and find out for yourself."

Trina continued to study Jocelyn, who shifted her weight from side to side. Jocelyn realized that all she had ever wanted was standing in front of her. Jocelyn was overcome with desire, and want, and need and love, for the strong woman standing before her. She broke down into gulping sobs.

Trina pulled her in close and calmed her down with gentle reassuring words. "Hush my love."

Gradually the wracking sobs coming from Jocelyn subsided as she stood within Trina's close embrace. Jocelyn was reluctant to meet Trina's gaze; she was terrified what she might find. She tentatively looked into Trina's eyes and hoped. Jocelyn tried again to smile at Trina, drinking in all the wisdom that Trina's face held, but it came out more of a grimace.

After Jocelyn's sobs had abated Trina spoke quietly, "We still have a long way to go but as long as we are together, it will be worth the journey. Remember this, I have always wanted you, never wanted to lose you."

Jocelyn could hardly believe what she had heard. Was it possible that the two of them could restart their relationship? Jocelyn looked at Trina with renewed hope. She was the kindest, gentlest of woman she had ever met. And if she hadn't been in love with her before, she definitely was now.

"You know we can take it as slowly as you need. I'm not going anywhere again and I'm not going to break your heart." She gave her hand a reassuring squeeze.

"I hope not." She said, nervously biting down on her bottom lip.

"You make me so happy, you know that don't you, Trina?" she said suddenly. "I'm so sorry. I regretted it almost as soon as it was possible."

Trina grabbed hold of Jocelyn's hands and fiercely said, in a taut voice, "Never regret anything that has happened in your life. It cannot be changed, forgotten or undone. So keep it as a lesson learned and move on."

Jocelyn bowed her head and nodded. Her bottom lip quivered, on the verge of more tears.

"I'll make us a coffee and we'll talk some more. Okay?"

Jocelyn nodded her head and a weak smile flitted across her face as two tears escaped and made their way down her cheeks. She brusquely wiped them away and breathed in deeply. She held her breath and tried to remain as composed as she could.

ꕤ

Chapter Forty Seven

Tuesday

A while later Trina came back with two steaming cups, and placed them on the table. Trina reached across and squeezed Jocelyn's hand. Jocelyn didn't look up. Instead, her eyes were on the cup of coffee in front of her. They sat like that for a few minutes, each engrossed in their own thoughts.

Jocelyn suddenly glanced up and gave Trina a look full of need.

Trina spoke softly, "It would be a lie if I said it didn't matter because it hurt like hell."

Jocelyn rose from the chair; she was trying so hard to hold back the tears.

Trina put a restraining hand on her leg.

Jocelyn pulled her hand away, and went and stood by the window. Trina's words, softly spoken only accentuated Jocelyn's disappointment in herself. She wondered how she could have hurt this beautiful woman and asked herself how had she so badly mucked up what they had together? How and what could she do to make it better between them. She realized that she could have lost everything. She found it difficult to look at Trina.

"I'm so sorry, Treen. I have hurt you so much. Will you find it in your heart to forgive me?"

"There is nothing for me to forgive but I might struggle to forget the pain you caused. Yet I know it was something you had to do. Something you had to find out yourself. As I told you before, we cannot move forward until we are completely honest with each other. Perhaps now you are being honest with yourself." She paused, "So have you sorted out your true feelings?"

Jocelyn nodded, "I've sorted out my feelings. I know I have been stupid."

"You can't just stop loving someone when they do something stupid," she pointed out. "If you could, then you'd walk away from most people most of the time."

"What I did wasn't just stupid, it was extremely cruel."

"Yes, it was," she agreed. Then in a voice barely above a whisper, she continued, "But I still want you."

"Pardon?"

Trina shook her head.

"Did you just say you wanted me?" asked Jocelyn

Trina shrugged.

"Why?"

"Why what? Why did I say it, or why do I still want you?"

"Why do you still want me?"

"I don't know," she shrugged. "I just do."

"I'm glad," Jocelyn admitted to her. "You are all I have."

Jocelyn struggled to hear the words, she held her breath so no noise would interrupt, for Trina spoke so quietly, "I felt that I had lost you and I don't know whether I can go through that again."

Trina's face showed a mixture of rage and hurt, of longing and arousal. As if she was either going to strangle her or kiss her. She could either push Jocelyn away or embrace her close. She wondered then if he had ever really been in love before because it had never felt anything like this. Perilous. Challenging. Incredible. Amazing.

"You make me so happy, you know that don't you, Trina?" she said. "You make me whole. Without you, I'm not the person I want to be. I'm self-centred, unsure and weak. And I don't want to be any of those things.

She crinkled her eyes against the summer brightness, as the sun tried to poke its head through the light cloud cover that had shrouded the day.

Jocelyn whispered, "I'm so sorry. Please forgive me. I finally had to decide what the most important thing to me was, and I guess I realized that the most important 'thing' wasn't a thing at all. It was you and the kids."

"Why?"

"Because I couldn't stand the thought of a world that didn't have you in it, I couldn't stand the thought of waking up every morning knowing that I would never be able to see you again, no matter how hard I looked."

Trina pulled back and held Jocelyn at arm's length. "Now all we have to do is work out what happens next."

Jocelyn gave a weak smile, "You know we can take things slowly. I will woo you, romance you, wine and dine you, and prove to you that I am worthy of your love. I know it will take time for you to trust me fully but I promise you this; I'm not going anywhere and I'm not going to break your heart."

For a second they stood just looking at each other because Trina was caught in her eyes, and she didn't look away. The soft, wary trust in her eyes was enough to astound Jocelyn. As it was, the breath hardly made it into her lungs.

"Do we have a future?" Jocelyn asked tentatively. "I think you're amazing and beautiful. I love that you have such a warm and tender heart and you're not afraid to expose it in a world that can be less than accepting. I love that you are as beautiful on the inside as you are on the outside. I love you more than anything. You know that don't you. Please can we try again?"

Trina's reassuring presence joined her as she leant her head on the windowpane. Trina pressed her hands against Jocelyn's shoulders but she didn't move in for a hug, but she did stand close enough to feel her warmth, her companionship. They looked at each other; Trina put her hands on Jocelyn's shoulders.

Trina shook her head. "I can't –"

හ

Chapter Forty Eight

Tuesday

Jocelyn nodded in resignation, "I understand." All her hopes came crashing down around her again with a thud. "It's okay," Jocelyn said, in a voice that was barely audible.

"If you let me finish, I was going to say, I can't be without you. You mean the world to me, the kids love you."

"I love you." Jocelyn said with heartfelt emotion.

Trina gave her hand a reassuring squeeze. "I hope so," she said, nervously biting down on her bottom lip.

Jocelyn let out a deep sigh, looked up and was greeted by their two reflected heads. Trina's face showed a tortured smile. She stole a glance deep into Trina's eyes, and saw naked desire looking back. Trina placed her arms around Jocelyn waist as Joy leant her head back against her. Jocelyn watched Trina narrow her eyes, making them appear as though she was boring through her, into her soul, pinning her in place.

Jocelyn again smiled and it fully reached her eyes in deep contentment. A feeling of peace swathed them both. Their eyes continued to search each other as a bolt of lust flowed between them. Jocelyn's whole being sang and she knew that it was all going to be all right. She was home. The sun burst through the cloud and enveloped them with light, as though it was giving them its blessing, urging their love to blossom.

Jocelyn looked at her, and in that moment, she had the sensation of floating away, into a world that didn't seem real, that she hadn't known could exist.

She leaned in and kissed Trina. She kissed her as she had never kissed her before. Jocelyn wanted to show how much she loved and wanted Trina.

As Jocelyn pulled away, she buried her face in Trina's shoulder. "Please forgive me. I love you so much."

Jocelyn again turned and pressed her lips to Trina's then took her in another needful kiss. Her body shuddered with emotion as her heart thudded in her chest. Trina leant into the embrace and soon their hearts were beating as one. Jocelyn enveloped her and returned the hug.

"So are you staying?" Trina asked, breathlessly.

Tentatively Jocelyn responded, "If you'll have me."

Trina gave a small nod. Jocelyn felt the weight of the world lift from her shoulders and the butterflies in her stomach were released in a flurry of movement.

"Does this mean that you don't want me to leave?" Jocelyn asked her.

"I think that it does." Trina continued, "I hated not being able to be with you. When you left, I don't know, I thought I could handle it, but I woke up the next morning and I just … I just couldn't. It was too much, and I needed you."

It was strange how right the two of them felt together. Trina was beautiful, amazing, enthralling, and she took Jocelyn's breath away. A gentle, soft smile dusted Trina's lips as she stilled her with her gaze. Jocelyn's eyes fell closed, and her lips ached for the touch of Trina's, knowing, hoping, wanting. She opened her eyes and looked into the hope she found there. In the next breath, with a single brush of her lips, warmth spread through her entire being, whisking away what little was left of her sanity and strength.

Jocelyn grinned at her mostly because she couldn't help herself. The grin Trina gave her back felt better than anything she had ever felt before. She had gone through so many things. She had survived all the hurt, and now she was on the precipice of a dream she thought had slipped from her fingers by her stupidity.

Slowly, tenderly, she held Trina's hand in hers, spinning her fingers around it.

"Don't try to seduce me into forgiving you."

"As if I would be able to do that." Jocelyn teased. "But this feels right. This feels real, like it's something to build a life on."

Jocelyn leant down and lifted Trina up.

Smiling Trina said, "Put me down. You'll do yourself an injury."

"Don't make me laugh or I will drop you." Jocelyn replied

She carried her to the settee and, as gently as possible, laid Trina down.

Protesting, Trina said worriedly, "The children will be home soon."

Trina sounded reflective rather than reproachful, and Jocelyn knew she wasn't off the hook yet. Jocelyn was wary of pushing too hard, but despite her resolve she heard herself saying, "No they won't I've organised it that Lucy and Rose will look after them. They are picking them up from school, and taking them to the cinema, followed by a burger. I said I'd give them a ring when they can be sent back."

Shaking her head Trina replied, "So Missy, you had this planned all along?"

Jocelyn looked sheepish. "I wanted this to be the outcome. I wished it with all my heart. But I was unsure; I asked them more in hope than certainty. I could phone them now before they are due to be picked up."

Trina didn't say anything. Annoyance flashed across Trina's face.

"Treen. I'm sorry if I was too presumptuous. I only thought we might need more time to be alone to talk. Please let me show you how much I love you; want to be with you, in the best way I know. In the only way I know how."

Jocelyn looked down at Trina with so much love and tenderness. Jocelyn wanted to be the woman who made Trina smile, who made her insides quiver, and her legs turn to trembling jelly. She wanted to be her heart and soul, so that every kiss, every touch, every caress would blow her away. She wanted to make Trina continually think of lying with her, next to her, feeling their hands touch their bodies in ways that made them purr, that made them come alive. To know that just one kiss would turn her entire body to melted butter.

Trina saw so much love going from Jocelyn to herself. The words went beyond love. They felt ethereal. Trina felt as though the emotion that flowed from her would explode into a cacophony of senses. She hoped that she would soon be able to hear, see, smell, touch and taste her. Trina nodded, and knew she couldn't push her away and quietly said, "I know."

Reconciliation comes in many forms and Trina felt a deep sense of relief, a relief that Jocelyn was here, and wanted her. Jocelyn then silenced any other words with a deep and meaningful kiss. Trina pulled herself apart and noticed Jocelyn's skin was flushed with desire. Trina held her breath as

Jocelyn gazed into her eyes. All Trina could see was Jocelyn's gorgeous, beautiful, seductive eyes drenched with love. Trina tried to say something but emotion made her lose the ability to speak. Jocelyn's eyes wrinkled with love for the woman looking at her.

Their lips touched lightly, then hungrily as desire overrode any lingering doubts. Their kiss became a dance and they lost all their senses. Searing desires became an irresistible current. They had lain together many times before, but this time it was different. They were at a new beginning, the start of a new chapter.

"I really, genuinely love you." Jocelyn confessed, as she felt the need to become anchored. The words had come easily and truthfully from the heart. Jocelyn looked deeply into the eyes before her and saw so much love in them that it caused her to tear up again.

Jocelyn tried to blink away the tears that had threatened to escape, "I love you. You are beautiful. You are strong. Your true beauty comes from your strength."

She gulped in a lungful of air, and Jocelyn continued, "I don't think that I can remember when I didn't love you, I just didn't know it at the time. I can't imagine you not being in my life, not being beside me when important decisions need to be made. I want to be part of your life. I want to be part of your children's life. I want to share all the good times and not so good times. I want to love you, as you have never been loved before. I want to spent the rest of my life showing how much you mean to me, how you have always saved me from myself and others."

The word love, hung in the air between them. Trina wiped away the tears that had escaped and was falling down Jocelyn's cheeks. She gazed into Jocelyn's eyes and all she saw was sincerity, honesty and love, and these emotions tore at her heart. Trina smiled back a smile full of longing. She loved Jocelyn so much she didn't know how to say what she felt. She realised that the end was still unknown. That they had some way to go, but that was for the future. What she wanted was the here and now. Could she say the words 'I love you'? She was unsure but she had the rest of her life to try to say it again.

Trina quivered in anticipation. Jocelyn's words had poured into Trina and transcended everything else. Instead, Trina replied simply, "I need you and want you."

Jocelyn felt privileged that Trina had let her back into her life. She made a silent vow that nothing would come between them again. She could not stand to think of the consequences if Trina were to remove her from her life again. Jocelyn again silenced any more words with another deep and meaningful kiss. When they broke apart, she gazed longingly into the face of the woman she loved.

Trina smiled and spoke, "And here's my gift to you."

She leaned in, and kissed Jocelyn deeply and breathlessly.

Their lips slowly parted and as Jocelyn had started to recover from the deep emotional effect that kiss had on her; she said softly, "I like that gift. You can give that same gift anytime you want."

Trina smiled.

Nothing was between them now but respect, hope and mutual desire. Jocelyn asked, "I know I hurt you but I love you and want to marry you."

"I know that you love me, and this time I truly believe you."

"So will you be my wife?"

For a moment, the air was still. It was just them, nothing more, nothing else, no one more, and no one else. Trina smiled a smile full of love.

"One step at a time, my love, one step at a time." She murmured and walked away, leaving Jocelyn longing for more.

Concern flashed across Jocelyn's face, "Have I pushed too far too quickly?"

Trina raised her eyebrows, with mystery dancing behind her eyes, a slight smile played on her lips. Jocelyn's heart was brushed softly by the glint in Trina's eyes and a tiny laugh slipped from her. Trina looked over her shoulder as she walked out of the room, "Well?"

"What now?"

Trina gave Jocelyn a seductive smile, "Why don't you follow me to see for yourself?"

ꟿ

Thank you for reading *Back For Good (Book 2 in the Coming home series).* I hope you enjoyed following the continuing adventures of Jocelyn, Trina and Lucy. If you did then please help other people find it and to enjoy it too.

Recommend it: I would appreciate it if you would recommend this book to friends and reader's groups.

Review it: Please review this book by telling people why you liked it.

Reviews and recommendations are the lifeblood of any Indie writer.

I love hearing from my readers. You can contact me on my Facebook page at https://www.facebook.com/tapurkis.author/

Visit https://teresapurkis.weebly.com/

or https://www.amazon.com/author/teresapurkis

Other books by Teresa Purkis

Fiction Coming Home (Book 1 in the Coming Home series)

Coming home is a heart-warming novel about family and relationships. It interweaves humour and loss in a poignant, amusing story, laced with love. It will make you laugh, cry and appreciate life.

The last place Jocelyn Harrold wanted to be was back in the city where she was born. After moving away for a fresh start, she was home to attend the funeral of her beloved Nan who had recently passed. She was dreading spending the time with her family and all the unwelcome memories that would bring.

During her visit, love and life begins to blossom again. When greeted with a new bombshell can she risk her sanity and find the strength for a second chance at family life and love.

Fiction <u>Deliverance</u>

Earth 2495. A terrible catastrophe has forced the privileged administration to rule with an iron fist. Archaic rules forbids women an education and all unseemly behaviour is severely punished. The people of Earth have settled on other planets and all the satellite planets were under Earth control.

All, that is, except one.

This lesbian science fiction tells the story of a group of pioneers who disappeared from Earth during the catastrophe and colonised the planet Sythia.

They struggle to build a world safe for both women and men, to live their lives as and how they wish. This book explores what happens when their idyll is disturbed.

Non-fiction My Bristol: The History and The Culture

The Romans that passed through the area and the Saxon founders of the Place of the Bridge would not recognise the City and County, Bristol has grown into.

The prosperity that came with its industry, trade and maritime exploits, made Bristol into one of the wealthiest cities in the UK. The varying terrain and geology gave rise to flora and architecture unique to the city. It has given features such as the Avon Gorge, which splits the City between Gloucestershire to the north and Somersetshire to the south, the nearby Cotswold and Mendip escarpments, and the gentle rolling scenery.

The motto of the city is "Virtute et industria." meaning valour and industry, and this can be seen today by being a large cosmopolitan, diverse city; bustling with industry, arts, culture, music, adventure, sports and festivals. Many firsts have occurred here, from the first commercially successful brassmills, the first iron ship and the first supersonic aeroplane, through to the first president of a human rights organisation, the first paperback book press, the first British chocolatier and many, many more.

Packed with photographs and diagrams, this book will be a revelation to locals and visitors alike, an ideal reminder of this interesting and beautiful City.

ABOUT THE AUTHOR

Teresa spent her working career as a Teacher of Mathematics and Physical Education.

She was born in Bristol, England and has lived with her Civil Partner for over thirty years.

Teresa is thoroughly enjoying her retirement as it gives her time to gain different experiences and learn new skills and crafts. She enjoys discovering exciting places to visit, mainly through cruising holidays.

As well as writing, Teresa likes playing bowls and darts, in addition to watching her local football team Bristol Rovers.

Teresa has an interest in photography and has spent many an hour taking in the sights and sounds of the City she loves.

Printed in Poland
by Amazon Fulfillment
Poland Sp. z o.o., Wrocław

49296446R00195